# FLOCK

# FLOCK

WENDY DELSOL

CANDLEWICK PRESS

First edition 2012

Library of Congress Cataloging-in-Publication Data

Delsol, Wendy.
Flock / Wendy Delsol. — 1st ed.
p.   cm.
Sequel to: Frost.
Summary: Katla's hopes of dodging unfinished business during her senior year are dashed by the arrival of two "Icelandic exchange students," Marik and Jinky, who have come to collect Katla's frail baby sister and take her to the water queen.
ISBN 978-0-7636-6010-9
[1. Supernatural — Fiction. 2. Interpersonal relations — Fiction. 3. Students, Foreign — Fiction. 4. High schools — Fiction. 5. Schools — Fiction.]   I. Title.
PZ7.D3875Flo 2012
[Fic] — dc23      2011048371

12 13 14 15 16 17 BVG 10 9 8 7 6 5 4 3 2 1

Printed in Berryville, VA, U.S.A.

This book was typeset in Granjon.

Candlewick Press
99 Dover Street
Somerville, Massachusetts 02144

visit us at www.candlewick.com

*For my sons, Ross and Mac,*
*with love always.*

# CHAPTER ONE

Spending the morning ball-and-chained to a new kid was *not* my idea of a good kickoff to our senior year.

"Can't you find someone else?" I asked, hoofing it up the front steps to Norse Falls High.

"There's no time," Penny said. "I didn't expect two of them, and they have different schedules, so we need two welcome guides." I could hear the *slap-slap* of her clogs as she struggled to keep up.

As much as I admired everything about Penny — including her sis-boom-bah school spirit — I didn't think I was the right gal for the job. For starters, I still felt new to the place myself. Moreover, I was hardly ambassador material.

"I'm not feeling very welcome-ish." Reluctant to enter, I paused. It was crazy to think that one year ago I was the new arrival. Twelve short months later and I not only had a best friend but had also inherited a magical ability as a deliverer of souls, a human Stork. Oh, and I had a special someone, too. Standing there on the stone landing, I was already wondering how I'd get through a whole day without Jack, my now-college-enrolled boyfriend and superpower, weather-wielding sidekick. I wasn't even inside yet and the place felt fundamentally altered: empty, lifeless, and lacking.

"Please," Penny pleaded. "It won't take very long. Besides, it's a privilege and an honor. *Come on.*" If she batted her lashes at me any harder, we'd need a home base and an umpire.

I sighed. This would be the third time she roped me into one of her extracurriculars. Already last year, I'd been shanghaied as the fashion editor of the school paper and pressed into singing and dancing for the musical production of *The Snow Queen*. No wonder I was a little wary around the girl.

"How long will it take?"

"Thank you. Thank you. Thank you." Penny hopped up and down and was through the front doors and bounding down the hallway without even answering me.

I scowled and pulled on the massive wooden door. *Happy flippin' first day of school.*

I found Penny in the front office. She had her back to me and was filling out some kind of paperwork. I made a quick note-to-self not to sign anything. She'd have us shipped out with Doctors Without Borders by lunchtime. Triage unit. War zone. Front line. And she'd claim it a privilege and an honor, no doubt.

Ever the what-would-I-wear type, I was mentally tricking out bulletproof scrubs when I caught sight of a guy sitting in one of the waiting-area chairs.

Holy crap. I almost dropped for cover. And now, by comparison, foreign service didn't sound half bad. Here in Norse Falls, not ten feet from me, sat none other than Marik.

Marik as in the messenger from Vatnheim.

Vatnheim as in the otherworldly realm where mermaids, mermen, and split-tailed sirens are healthy, happy, and in pursuit of an heir to Queen Safira.

Safira as in the queen who believes — because of my impulsive Stork prophecy — that an heir exists here on our earthly Midgard and is none other than Leira.

Leira as in my born-too-soon, still-frail, five-month-old sister, whose name — pre-chosen by our long-dead grandmother — is one from a selkie legend and an anagram of Ariel, like in *The Little Mermaid*. Not to mention she was born with webbed fingers and toes.

Yeah. That Leira. That Safira. That Vatnheim. That Marik.

I wanted to hurl.

Penny, turning, must have noticed my greenish hue.

"Kat, are you all right?" she asked.

"Sorry." I put a hand to my tummy. "My mom put a shot of wheatgrass in my smoothie this morning." She had. It was nasty. "I think it and the acai just started a turf war." It really had left an aftertaste, one that had, if nothing else, provided a tip-of-the-tongue alibi for my puckered cheeks.

"Should you go to the nurse?" Penny asked, hugging the clipboard to her chest.

And leave Marik unattended? No way. "I'll be fine," I said.

Like I had a choice. Like I intended to let Marik, who was eyeing me playfully, out of my sight for a second. Unsuspecting Norse Falls had more than its share of the para-abled pounding its streets. Besides my own clan of soul-delivering Storks and my Jack Frost–descended boyfriend, we'd come up against Wade, an evil Raven, and Brigid, the power-hungry Snow Queen from land o' snow Niflheim. The last thing we needed was—

"Jinky?" I said, steadying myself against the front-office counter.

Jinky, the second of our new kids, arrived and now stood just a few steps inside the office waiting area. Jinky was the tough-chick, rune-reading gypsy girl (Roma, if we're being PC) who swiped my runes last spring in Iceland. With the help of her Laplander (Sami if we're *still* being PC) grandmother, she launched me onto some kind of sweat-lodge-induced vision quest, the one where I met Marik and wrested Jack out of Brigid's frigid fingers. Uh-huh. That Jinky. And as back-to-schools went, this one was sizing up to be epic in all the worst ways.

"Do you two know each other?" Penny asked, confused. She thumbed through the papers of her welcome packet as if she were out of the loop.

I knew the feeling. Except it wasn't so much that I felt out of the loop. Rather that it was cinching around me — my neck, to be specific.

"We met in Iceland," Jinky said, "at the festival. Kat told me such great things about Norse Falls that I was intrigued. So intrigued I talked my cousin, Marik here, into joining me for a study-abroad program."

OK. So that was the story. It didn't seem like I had much choice but to go along with it. "What a surprise," I said, taking a step toward Jinky. "You should have let me know you were coming."

Penny, still baffled, watched us. By now, she knew me better than anyone around here. And if Jinky had come halfway across the world to see Norse Falls at my — albeit inadvertent — recommendation, I'd be pretty stoked. So stoked I'd — ugh — hug the girl. Wouldn't I? I took the final step separating us and threw my arms around Jinky. Judging by the way she stiffened, she wasn't the PDA type.

Marik rushed forward, too, extending his hand, thank God. "So nice to see you again, Katla." We shook. At least he didn't try to embrace me. Penny was still looking at me like I was big-time holding out on her.

"Wow," I said, shaking the hair out of my face. "This is turning into one wild morning," said the human Stork to the merman and the rune-reading gypsy. Not knowing what to do with either of these unwelcome visitors, I was stalling for time.

Penny pulled two sheets of paper from the clipboard. "Here are their schedules. We should split up and—"

"I'll take Marik," I said, fast. Too fast. It earned me another odd once-over from Penny, though this one had a tinge of disappointment to it.

Taking a moment to breathe and survey the situation, I could understand her letdown. To the not-dating-anyone Penny, Marik would be the preference. He wasn't pretty-boy handsome, but—just like I'd intuited that first time we'd met—there was something appealing about him. His nutmeg-brown hair was shaggy chic with the odd stray swatch tumbling over his broad forehead. His kelp-green eyes were mischievous, his lips were pouty, and, despite his height and muscular frame, he gave off a light-and-nimble vibe. And he was dressed like he stepped right out of an Abercrombie ad, with a distressed sweater over a tails-pulled-out crew shirt, jeans, and sockless loafers.

Jinky, on the other hand, was still into the all-hell-no-angel look with heavy motorcycle boots, leather jacket, teased black hair, and heavily lined eyes. She was, as always, a little scary. Who could blame Penny for the droop in her shoulders?

"I mean, I figured you'd like to tell Jinky about the school paper," I said to Penny, scrambling. "Jinky's into photography."

Jinky chopped me a look, one that could roll a head, and mine was first on the block, judging by the glint in her eye.

"Oh. We *are* looking for another photographer," Penny said. "Our best one just graduated."

"If only I had brought my camera," Jinky said, still staring at me.

"My dad has one," I said. "A good one." I was asking for it, I knew. Jinky did not look like the capture-the-moment type. She probably hadn't snapped a photo in her life. Necks, on the other hand . . .

Penny handed one of the schedules to me. "Marik has biology first period. Mr. Serra."

"Got it," I said. Wasting no time, I signaled for Marik to follow me, leaving Penny with the paper's new photojournalist.

There were still a few minutes before the final bell. The hall was a zoo. I headed in the direction of the science wing but took the first detour—and private space—I came upon. Marik and I ended up at the back of the auditorium. The room was being prepped for a school-wide assembly later that day. A lone janitor was onstage setting up the PA system.

"What are you doing here?" Arms crossed, I rounded on Marik.

"As you may well guess, I've been sent to ensure you fulfill your end of the bargain."

The bargain. The damn bargain: *Leira to whom the waters are home must be returned to the sea.* It haunted me day and night and was a low-down double cross.

"It's not fair. I was tricked into the deal. I thought Leira was the redheaded selkie who lent me her skin. And, of course, there'd be no harm in returning *her* to Vatnheim. I had no idea that Leira would be the name of my unborn sister. I'd never have made the pact if—"

"Ah, but you did," Marik interrupted. "You made the pact." His eyes focused on the ground, not me. "And Queen Safira brooks no disobedience."

Feedback from the microphone filled the room.

"She's too weak, anyway. She's only been home from the hospital for a few weeks. She'd never survive any sort of ordeal—"

"I have been instructed to be patient," Marik said, cutting me off again.

I bit my lip. There was, I was still certain, a way out of this. All I needed was more time to devise a plan. All summer, fear had gnawed at my insides, but I was still determined. Marik's presence, despite his mention of *patience,* was a setback. And it started the clock.

"Katla, it is good that we take a moment here to talk. I must remind you that the agreement is secret. We know that you have . . . friends, many who would be willing to aid you in protecting the child. Be forewarned that this would only endanger you and those you seek to involve. Moreover, the pact is charmed with powerful magic. A potent spell connects the essentials of the agreement. Do you understand?"

I narrowed my eyes. "I think so."

"'Testing. Testing," the going-about-his-business janitor called out.

"Unlike the one who would jeopardize everything for revenge, Queen Safira is your ally and a voice of reason among the other realms."

No need to specify who he meant by "the one." Having foiled Brigid's domination plans, I had left her purpling with rage.

"And Jinky's presence here—"

"About that." It was my turn to interrupt. "What does *she* have to do with any of this?"

"Jinky and her grandmother, perceptive individuals, proved useful in my transition between the two worlds. Instrumental, you might say."

It occurred to me that Marik had first appeared during last spring's vision quest, my spiritual journey presided over by Jinky and her shaman grandmother.

"Jinky coming into her own intermediary skills has since been my envoy to all things earthly," Marik continued. "In seeking to understand her calling, she has agreed to continue in this capacity, understanding only as much as I deem necessary. Again, I remind you that the essentials of our pact are protected by powerful magic. Jinky's role falls outside of the spell binding your powers to my task and Leira's future." He paused, staring at me for an intensity-soaked moment. "I must ask you again if you understand the solemnity of our agreement. Of the the secrecy concerning its true nature. To enlighten anyone is to endanger that individual. Queen Safira will not hesitate in the face of interference."

While Marik's words were steeped in threats, his delivery was even-keeled and smooth. I understood immediately that he embodied the worst kind of danger, beguiling at the surface but with a nasty undertow.

"Yes, I understand." I modulated my own tone in harmony with his because Marik wasn't the only one who could pour it on.

"Good," he said, cupping my shoulder with his hand.

So Jinky was some kind of shaman apprentice. So Marik was a messenger-turned-collector. So Leira was currency. And I was on my own. The one-minute warning bell sounded, marking the beginning of more than another school year.

# CHAPTER TWO

Even knowing that Marik and I had the same second-period class, I was nervous to leave him at the science lab. I still didn't know who or even what he was at heart. Nor did I understand what he was capable of. Complicating these fears were my memories of being the new kid just one short year ago. No one had cut me any slack. They'd walked all over me and then just scraped their boots at the door. How would Marik, new to the planet, handle the looks and whispers and outright rudeness? Was he prepared for teen culture, a brand of human interaction that explained our ancestral need for clubs and extra-thick skulls? Had he ever been to school? Would he know to sit down, shut up, and let the teacher do the talking? Marik had described Jinky as "useful in the transition between the two worlds." Would that include basic societal norms and etiquette? And it was not lost on me that learning social skills from Jinky was like getting sensitivity training from Sue Sylvester. I was distracted by such worries all hour, as if, on its own, AP Econ wasn't enough of a brain fry.

Second period was Design, a class I was looking forward to. I was one of the first to arrive and grabbed a seat in the middle of the room, saving the two on either side of me with my satchel and a notebook. Penny walked in, and I called her over. She took the chair to my right. Marik entered next, flanked on one side by an all-smiles, blushing Abby Mills and on the other by the chatty, also flushed Shauna Jones. *Huh?* These two girls had given me the full-body shutout this time last year. And now that they were seniors—*top o' the mountain* as I'd seen it referred to on Facebook—it was clear that certain groups were scrambling for first-flag bragging rights. At any rate, the way Abby, class president, and Shauna, a track star, were pink-cheeked and giddy indicated some kind of thin air.

Marik paused just inside the doorway, pulling his schedule out as if checking whether he was in the right place. Both Abby and Shauna peered over his shoulder, pointing at the paper and nodding with big hair-plumping, you-belong-here-with-us shakes of their heads. *What the heck?*

I flared my eyes. It was, I knew, a gender thing. The girls were eyeing him as fresh meat. The guys, on the other hand, were sure to put him — the outsider elbowing in at what was already a small drinking hole — in his place.

John Gilbert walked in and braked, taking in the two girls panting over Marik. Uh-oh. John was a state-champion wrestler: big, brawny, and packing attitude. He rolled his head in their direction. I held my breath.

"Dude," John said, lifting his fist.

Marik turned, readying his own. And then they fist-bumped like best buds. I almost fell out of my chair. Marik knew those two stuck-up girls? Marik knew John Gilbert? Marik knew how to fist-bump? All by second period?

Their small party yukked it up to a cozy four-square of desks at the back of the room. I dropped my book bag onto the floor, catching a glimpse of Penny as I did so. Judging by her glum expression, I wasn't the only one who had expected Marik to join us.

Just as the bell rang, none other than Jinky came clomping into the room. She breezily surveyed the open spots, eyes fixing on the one next to me. Her graceless collapse into the seat was loud, and she reeked of cigarettes. A smoker; I should have known. Luckily, the arrival of Ms. Bryant spared me the chore of conversing with her. Ms. Bryant was my favorite teacher ever, because she was young and smart and hip. It didn't hurt that she was into art and design and could rock a belted sweaterdress and a pair of boots like nobody's business.

"If I could have your attention." Holding a single sheet of paper in front of her, Ms. Bryant took a seat at her desk. "Good morning, everyone. To begin, I'd like to welcome two exchange students from Iceland to Norse Falls High." She stabbed at the paper with her index finger. "Jinky Birksdottir and Marik Galdursson, welcome. Would you introduce yourselves and maybe tell us what you hope to take home from your study-abroad experience?"

Jinky folded her arms over her chest, while Marik popped to a stand.

"I am Marik. I'm from Hafmeyjafjörður in Iceland. My cousin Jinky and I are very happy for the opportunity to study here in America."

It wasn't so much that he spoke slowly, it was, rather, that his voice pitched at unexpected words and syllables. My classmates surely attributed it to an accent. I, however, felt something more physical at work. I was aware of my shoulders rocking from side to side, and my hands grasped the sides of the desk for balance.

"And I'm hoping," Marik continued, "that my time here will reward me with much more than just language and culture."

That last remark was meant for me, and I dug my

nails into the underside of the desk in reaction. The girls in the room, on the other hand, purred their approval of the handsome foreigner. Even Ms. Bryant's reaction was strong. While Marik was speaking, she pulled her hand to her throat and her eyes widened. She seemed to stammer, even, when next calling on Jinky.

Jinky, for her part, kept it short and to the point. Like the way her choppy black bangs came to a sharp V at the center of her forehead.

"My name is Jinky. I'm looking forward to studying here at your school." Her still-crossed arms didn't sell the message, nor did her scowl.

Next, Ms. Bryant, lover of all things collaborative, explained our first project. Working in pairs, we were to prepare a design package for an imaginary start-up business, including company name, logo, a website landing page, and promotional materials. The rub was it had to be a business for which we saw a need in either Norse Falls or Pinewood. That last detail got a few "Huhs" and "Why them?"s from the class.

Dating way back, the two towns were rivals. Penny once told me that the tensions began with two feuding families. Whatever its roots, the fact that our two schools, due to budget constraints and falling enrollments, were considering a merge did nothing to improve relations.

"Because," Ms. Bryant said, "the projects are to be

displayed at a joint By Student Design Show that our class and their high school Design class will plan together. Seven weeks from Friday, all projects will be displayed at Pinewood as a partnership. No matter what comes of the consolidation proposal between the two schools, it's time the two communities focused on something cooperative, not just a football rivalry."

A few more grumbles floated in from the back of the room, but Ms. Bryant ignored them, continuing with a description of the assignment.

"This semester, I think I'll let you pick your own partners." Ms. Bryant paused, consulting her notes.

Penny and I locked eyes and gave each other a small nod. No deliberation required; Penny and I had the term-project thing down to a science.

When she glanced up and resumed, a strange look passed over Ms. Bryant's face. "Sorry. I don't think we will do it that way. Not this semester, anyway." Again, her finger trailed down the page of her lesson plan. "Katla Leblanc . . ."

Funny, Ms. Bryant knew I preferred Kat. Not so funny was my foreboding that I'd get Jinky.

". . . will team with Marik Galdursson," Ms. Bryant continued. I gave Penny a small shoulder lift before turning to receive Marik's broad smile. Just a few names later, Penny was saddled with Jinky. I couldn't help but notice

Penny's slump; even her lobes hung lower. Though, guessing by her glances to the back of the room, I wasn't her first choice of partner, after all.

Once all the groups were assigned, Ms. Bryant distributed handouts and talked us through the entire semester's coursework and timeline. For the last five minutes of class, she suggested we sit with our partner and look over the list of sample businesses. It was clear Jinky was not going to budge from the chair she was in. Penny, therefore, eyed my seat expectantly. I gathered my things and headed to the back of the room and a spot that had opened up next to Marik.

Abby and John, another assigned team, occupied the seats in front of us. Abby, who I thought was dating a basketball player, spent the bulk of the remaining class time turning and addressing Marik.

"So where does your host family live?" she asked.

"On Spruce Street."

"That's nice and close," Abby said, "and walkable to school and downtown."

"Good thing," Marik said. "We don't have a car."

"We . . . meaning?" Abby asked.

"My cousin Jinky and I are staying with the same host family," Marik said, pointing to where Jinky sat stone-faced and an ambitious Penny chatted away.

"Your first cousin?" Abby leaned in closer.

"Yes."

"If you ever need a ride anywhere, just let me know," Abby said.

John, a buddy of taxicab Abby's basketball-player boyfriend, had been busy texting during their little gabfest. No doubt sending his friend a heads-up on the potential situation.

"No wheels is a serious problem around here, dude," John said, dropping his phone into his backpack. "Don't worry, though, we got you covered."

*Got you covered? Seriously?* Already two of the school's finest were open-arming Marik, whereas one year ago I was Leper City.

"Should we take a look at this list?" I asked Marik, fully aware of the glare Abby shot me before turning in her seat. Because Marik on his own wasn't enough of a handful. And like I needed a situation in which he had more friends than me.

# CHAPTER THREE

Third period was an all-school assembly. Penny and I entered together. Marik, I noticed, was already camped out with Abby, John, Shauna, and their kind. Spotting a group of our fellow school-paper writers, Penny pointed and led us to the front of the auditorium. Jinky arrived a few minutes later and sat by herself in the back. I wondered at her aloofness. Why had she come if she wasn't going to make an effort?

Following the principal's annual welcome, the senior-class officers were called to the stage. Abby, our president, delivered a by-the-cue-card speech. What it lacked in spontaneity, it went for in dramatics. The save-our-school message revisited last year's rumors and Ms. Bryant's mention of a merger between our school and Pinewood. With a year's worth of attachments to the place—and to a guy named Jack—I, too, was now in the SOS camp, but I couldn't help think that Abby's remarks were all hype, no content. Plus, I imagined it was the school board that needed convincing, not the student body. Finally, lowering her voice from its helium-sucking heights, she dropped her note cards onto the podium. "Finally, I'd like to take a moment to welcome our new kids, especially our two exchange students."

I noticed Abby looked over to where Marik sat, not Jinky.

"Let's all do our best to make their year one to remember," she finished, clapping her hands above her head in a do-as-I-do gesture.

The room detonated in cheers. *Seriously?* And was it the anti-merge message or the special welcome they were responding to? In irritation, I scratched at my neck.

After the assembly, Penny hurried to catch up to Jinky, inviting her to walk through the lunch line with us and to follow us over to the journalism room. I was more than a little surprised when she fell in step behind us. I'd half expected her to bail on the photographer thing. Then again, I remembered how lunch had been my least favorite thing about being a new kid. During the rest of the day, you could keep your head down and not draw too much attention. But in the cafeteria—all cafeterias, I'd assume—the true pecking order was revealed. Though I figured Jinky could give as good as she'd get, Abby, Shauna, and their gang would shun her the way Monique, last year's senior queen, had done me. As much as Jinky's perpetual scowl irked me, I still kind of owed her for last spring. She and her grandmother had helped me save Jack's life, after all. I even handed her a tray and steered her away from the fish croquettes. *No one* deserved that particular brand of cruel and unusual.

Just as we exited the line, I saw Marik. Holding his tray in front of him, he wavered back and forth, looking confused. I took a step toward him and he lifted his chin as a sign of acknowledgment, possibly even relief. I wondered then if this all wasn't a little overwhelming for him. Pulling me from this internal debate was a whistle, followed by John Gilbert hollering, "Yo, Marik. Over here." Marik gave me a nod and a coy smile as he sailed off for his lunch with the top o' the heapers. Whatever.

Our first lunchtime journalism meeting was an all-business affair: partly because Mr. Parks was putting in one of his rare appearances, and also because Penny, the new editor in chief, had some ambitious goals. She wanted the paper to have an online presence with a blog, Facebook page, and Twitter feed. She, too, mentioned the merger and the paper's role in reporting the events. I was proud of her, although I wondered what my traditionalist, former-editor-in-chief boyfriend would have to say about the web branding. He hadn't even wanted a Starbucks to open up in town.

I did not see Marik, Jinky, or revolutionist Penny as I closed my locker on day one of my senior year. I bounded down the front steps of the building with an Iced Peppermint White Chocolate Mocha on my mind when a figure leaning against my VW bug came into focus.

"Jack," I said, skipping the remaining ten feet that separated us, "shouldn't you be at Walden?"

"I finished my lab work early so I could surprise you."

"Mission accomplished." I slipped into his arms, sensing my burdens ease. Only Jack had this effect on me.

"So how did it go?" he asked, resting his chin on my head.

Despite sharing three near-death experiences with the guy—something other couples might take as a sign of incompatibility—I believed in our unique connection. Given this conviction, a part of me wanted to tell him everything right then and there. I felt words collect in my mouth; they pooled under my tongue until I had to force a dry swallow. Coming in with only the slightest of majorities, my cautious side remembered that the guy had once plunged into an icy lake after me. Recognizing I triggered this reckless, self-sacrificing trait in him, I knew I had no right to involve him in my current mess. So how much was, therefore, wise to reveal? Norse Falls was too small a place for the presence of two Icelandic exchange students to go unremarked upon.

"So do you remember that girl I told you about? The one I met at the fair in Iceland and who read my runes?"

"Yeah. Why?"

"Funny enough, she's here. As an exchange student. With her cousin. It seems my descriptions of Norse Falls were pretty enticing."

"She's here?" Jack pulled back, holding me at arm's length.

"Yes."

"But she's the one who helped you—"

"I know."

"Isn't that kind of strange?"

"A little, I guess." I tried to keep my tone breezy and flipped back a strand of my hair.

"What cousin?" Jack asked, narrowing his eyes.

*Ugh.* I should not have attempted body language. Jack knew me too well.

"His name is Marik. I met him briefly. On the boat."

I knew I was leading Jack to assume I was talking about Hinrik, Jinky's real cousin who boated us over to her grandmother's nub of an island. I had *not* told Jack anything about Marik, nor had I given any details as to how I came about the gift of a selkie skin that was so key to my survival in Niflheim. To have done so would have necessitated an explanation of why the Water World was involved. All Jack knew, all Jack had to know, was that Jinky had helped me get to him. Given Marik's warning—threat, really—it was a topic best left intentionally vague.

"Oh," Jack said, questions still clouding those gem-blue eyes of his.

I felt something in my gut pouch with regret: liar's tummy. And then I wondered how Marik or Safira would ever know what Jack and I whispered to each other. As it was, we practically had our own language. A single twitch of his mouth or bite of his lip and I, for instance, knew exactly where his thoughts were headed. What chance did I stand of keeping the existence of a landlocked merman and a shaman-in-training from him?

"And cool that they've come all this way," he continued. "I guess I'll be meeting them sometime or other, then."

With that small act of graciousness, of calling the situation "cool," all thoughts of involving Jack in my mess gusted away. I couldn't do that to him.

"I'm on my way to the factory," I said, inventing a change of subject. "I need to borrow my dad's camera. You wanna come along?"

Jack's phone rang. I unlocked my car door and threw my book bag over to the passenger seat during his brief brow-scruncher of a conversation.

"I can't." Jack pocketed his phone. "That was my dad; he needs me. Plus, I've got an assignment due tomorrow."

The assignment alone would be enough to distract him. I knew also that harvest was their busiest season.

"Will I see you tomorrow?" I asked.

"Not likely," he said with a shake of his head.

"How much longer will it be like this?" I asked.

"We grow different varieties, all with different grow cycles. The worst should be over by Halloween, I'd think."

"Halloween?"

"And by Thanksgiving, we're just sitting around waiting for it to snow."

I could tell he was goading me now. Best to redirect. Besides, Thanksgiving made me think of something.

"For Thanksgiving, my dad and I are planning a trip to Santa Monica to visit my grandmother. You should come. She said she'd like to meet you."

"What? To California?"

"Yeah."

He swiped at his brow as if mopping up sweat. "The beach. Sunshine. Temps in the 70s or 80s. Am I painting an accurate picture?"

"Well, sort of."

"Nothing personal, but summers around here are

torment enough. You know I barely go out. Southern California is not my idea of a vacation."

"Ever?"

He shook his head. "I really don't think so."

As much as I knew all about his Jack Frost heritage, this was somehow news to me; bad news, to be specific. I had a secret fantasy of showing him my old stompings, parading him in front of my old friends, kissing him as the surf crashed over us. This was a serious buzzkill.

"Hey," he said, pulling me from my sulk. "I'll see you on Friday."

"OK."

"Count on it," he said.

Watching him walk away, I couldn't help feeling that our gifts were more often than not burdens. And on top of it all, we still had the full complement of household chores, schoolwork, financial obligations, and all the rest of the load that came with life. And Jack took on more than most. The only upside was that just maybe, with his own preoccupations, he'd be too busy to further question the Marik issue, at least until I could devise a plan. It was a reprieve, at best. One I'd take for now.

# CHAPTER FOUR

Balancing a carrier full of Starbucks offerings, I strode
the short distance across the reception area and set the
drinks down.

"Just what the doctor ordered," Jaelle, my dad's
office manager, said, getting up from her desk. She
boxed me into one of her hugs and then initiated a hand
slide, a gesture so jive I laughed out loud every time I
was on the receiving end. As always, Jaelle had a way of
making anyone and anything look cool. Case in point,
the thick zebra-print headband, nubby green cardigan,
knee-length corduroy skirt, and scuffed cowboy boots
she presently sported. Jaelle had been my very first friend
here, a kindness for which I would always be grateful.

"Is my dad busy?" I asked.

"He's on the floor," Jaelle said, sipping from her Grande bold drip with a shot of skim foam and *ah*-ing in appreciation. "I'll help you find him."

I followed Jaelle down the hallway that separated the quiet office space from the assembly area. The moment she pulled open the door, a din of machinery and voices hit me like a rogue wave. My dad's wind turbine factory had been in business for less than a year, but already it was in full swing, with more orders than they could handle.

As we passed various stations, I noticed one or two of the workers snap to attention. It wasn't for me, the boss's daughter. My dad, a big softie, had done well to hire the clever and capable Jaelle. He liked to joke that she had even *him* kowtowing around her. Proving my point, her husband, Russ, a brawny former logger, saluted as we walked by. I inwardly preened. When I'd first met Jaelle, a little over a year ago, she was underemployed as a waitress and lamenting her husband's travel-required back-buckler of a job. Convincing my dad to open his factory here instead of California was admittedly a self-serving act; nonetheless, I couldn't help but gloat a little at how much it had done for Jaelle. Even though she had been one of my very first vessels — prospective mothers considered as candidates to receive a hovering soul — and I'd recommended against her, I knew it had been the right decision. At the time, Jaelle simply wasn't ready. She'd come a long way since then, however.

We found my dad near the shipping dock. He signed a paper, handed the clipboard to his foreman, and walked toward us.

"Atta girl," he said, taking the coffee I held up for him. "I was just thinking about how nice a little of the mermaid would be right now."

While he enjoyed his first sip, I shrugged off the jitters brought about by his casual mention of a water creature. To him, Ariel was simply his nickname for the split-tailed siren that was featured on the Starbucks logo. Little did he know that it was responsible for the ad-lib prophecy that I'd made during my very first Stork assignment and for the difficult situation I was in now.

"A little bird must have told me," I said, recovered enough to make a private joke. My dad had no idea that his daughter was a member of an ancient flock of soul deliverers.

"So how much is this cup going to cost me?" he asked.

Busted. Kind of. It was true enough that the last time I'd come bearing beverages he'd ended up out two hundred bucks for my car's tune-up.

"It's more of a trade than anything else," I 'fessed up.

"A trade?" he asked, arching his brows.

"Can I borrow your camera for a while? Well, technically I'll be lending it to an exchange student, our newest member of the school paper."

"My good camera?" he asked.

"Yeah."

"And you're lending it to a stranger?"

"Well, not a complete stranger. I met her briefly while I was in Iceland." I left out the part about her pickpocketing my runes as well as any kind of physical description.

"It's in my desk drawer," he said with resignation. "Jaelle, would you get it for her?"

At times like these, I super-loved the way my easygoing, surfer-dude dad just rolled with things.

"Sure can," Jaelle replied.

I walked behind Jaelle back across the factory. The afternoon sun was streaming through the west-facing windows; it cast a slanted shaft of light over our path. In this illuminated patch, dust motes danced like first-of-the-season snowflakes. It was fascinating, like a peek under a microscope, but they weren't the only things catching my notice. Above Jaelle's head, corking spirals of energy bounced. Finally. I'd been waiting a long time for the signal that Jaelle was *all systems go.*

As we stepped back into the calm of the office space and Jaelle retrieved the camera from my dad's desk drawer, I, again, saw the vibrations above her head. I took it as the very best of vibes.

# CHAPTER FIVE

Driving home, I was so excited about Jaelle's ready-for-baby signs that I almost didn't register the summons to a Stork meeting. Our means of announcing a same-day, nine p.m. council gathering was a scalp rash: a barbaric method of communication and my least favorite part of the job. Thankfully, it wasn't nearly as painful or as noticeable as it had been the first few times. I irritably dug through my bag looking for something to cover my head. Dreading the next few pre-meeting hours, I decided to reroute.

The door chimes above the Norse Falls General Store, my grandfather's shop, clanged as I entered. I was surprised to find him, rather than his employee and one of my sister Storks, Ofelia, behind the counter.

"What's up, Afi?"

"Canada," he said in that croaky voice of his and pointed to what I presumed was due north.

"Where's Ofelia?"

"She went to the Kountry Kettle to pick us up some dinner, but you had to know that already."

"I did?"

"She said she was getting you the mac and cheese plate."

Ofelia had an unsettling ability to read minds and intuit things. Sure, kinda good when you had a hankering for a warm and gooey bowl of comfort food. But bad—very bad—when you had secrets to keep. Despite my barking tummy, the latter was my more pressing concern.

"Leave it to Ofelia to remember I'd promised to come by and tell you both about my first day back."

I hadn't promised any such thing. Moreover, I was more the I-miss-summer-already type.

"There you are," Ofelia said, coming through the door with a large brown sack in her hand. "I hope you're hungry."

"I am," I said. Did she already know that?

"And how was school?" She set the bag on the counter.

"Interesting. As a matter of fact, there were a couple of new exchange students from Iceland. One of whom you met while you were there, Afi."

"I met?" Afi asked, his milky blue eyes widening.

"Remember the girl who sold you this necklace at the fair?" I lifted the icicle-shaped crystal from under my collar. Though it was a painful reminder of the ordeal Jack and I went through, I wore it as a present from Afi and as a reminder that there were forces out there, bad forces.

"No, not especially," Afi said, receiving the white Styrofoam bowl that Ofelia handed him.

"At the festival, I had chatted with the girl about Norse Falls. I must have made quite the impression, because she's here. Brought her cousin, even."

Ofelia's brow raised in slatted lines like a venetian blind. Not a good omen. With forced concentration, I focused on Jinky, her tough-chick appearance, and her real cousin, Hinrik the fisherman. For almost a full minute, Ofelia and I locked minds like this until, finally, she rubbed her temples, as if fatigued, and resumed passing out containers of food.

I myself hadn't been the least bit wearied by our tête-à-tête. I was, however, hungrier than ever and forked a big scoop of mac and cheese into my mouth.

Afi, I noticed, took only a few bites before he closed the lid on his dinner.

"Not hungry?" I asked. Then again, given his order, who would be? Oxtail stew? Gross. Any tail, for that matter. Except it was normally one of his favorites.

"I'll take it home with me," he said, "and try again later." He drew a wheezy breath.

"Why don't I run you home?" Ofelia said, dropping a napkin over her own container. "My car's right out front."

I watched Ofelia steer Afi out the front door and was grateful for about the hundredth time this month that she was around to keep an eye on him and the store. That mind-reading thing, though — I could do without that.

While finishing up my dinner, I pulled out the handouts for a few of my classes. Judging by the length of time it took Ofelia, she had seen Afi into his house and had probably run a load of laundry and swept his kitchen floor. Grateful moment number 101. Frowning at the inclusion of Faulkner on the Honors English reading list and blowing my bangs up in frustration, I was startled to find Fru Hulda, our Stork leader, standing near the doorway to the store's back room and our transformed-come-meeting-time council crib. Truly, "startled" hardly did justice to my state of shock. Not only had she appeared without triggering the door chimes or owning — to my knowledge — a key to the back door, but also, and more importantly, she had been away on top-secret Stork business since I had uttered the word *Ragnarök* — the Norse equivalent of the End of Days—to her three months ago on the night of my mom's marriage to Stanley.

"Fru Hulda!" I was off my stool like a bottle rocket. This time she opened her arms to invite the hug she knew was coming her way. I took it easy on her. Now that she was back, I intended to keep it that way. As second chair, I fulfilled my obligation to lead in her absence, but there were other things I'd rather do. Like read the torturous Faulkner or gnaw on leathery oxen, for instance. "I'm so glad to see you."

"Likewise, child, likewise."

"So is there something I should know?" I asked, biting my bottom lip in anticipation of her reply. Within moments of hearing the *R* word from me, she'd skittered off for the World Council, not much of a rest-easy or all-clear signal. To my relief, there had been no large-scale disasters during her absence, but I still got the willies every time I heard Anderson Cooper's voice.

"The council recorded many disturbing events but is most pleased to report a lull in such activities. We have all been sent back to our home districts with the reprieve."

The whole calm-before-the-storm phenomenon came to mind, but I wasn't about to bring it up. "That's kind of a good sign, right?"

"I think so," Hulda said. "And in keeping with what is possibly a Stork's most important attribute."

"What's that?" She may as well have hooked a worm to that statement the way it begged a question.

"Patience. And belief in the fullness of time."

Patience. Ugh. Not often linked with my name.

"Did you call the meeting to announce your return?" I asked, changing the subject.

"No. I am answering another's call to order, as are you, I presume."

"That reminds me," I said, jumping to attention. "I better unlock the back door."

The moment I twisted the dead bolt a quarter turn to the left, Storks began filing past me. Once assembled and with roll called, Fru Grimilla informed us that she had called the meeting. Despite the fact that she was Penny's grandmother and guardian, Grim and I weren't exactly chummy. With glares, stares, and scolding remarks, she made it her mission to expose my inexperience and challenge my authority as second chair. It usually made for the kind of tension that could launch nukes.

That night, I tried a new approach; I wouldn't allow the messenger, Grim, to detract from the wonder at hand. To do so, I refocused my sensory attention. Sound and sight faded to the background while smell and touch became sharp and clear. It was at moments such as this that I felt my magic as an alternate aperture through which the cosmos and I communicated.

I sensed a pillowy down as my shoulders melded into the honor and responsibility of our mission. We delivered souls. Not all souls. Only those who came to us for guidance. Beyond our small piece of the equation, an unquantifiable number of souls teemed in perpetual ebb and flow of transition.

Now, in one of those rarefied cocoons of awareness, I felt them surround me like a starry sky and pulse with life at its purest essence, which was, of course, our Stork term for a hovering soul.

I had no idea how long humans such as myself had been charged with ushering the undecided. I had no idea how others, of their own volition, slipped into that suspended moment between oblivion and conception. I didn't want to know why some alighted upon the unwilling or unprepared. Nor did I understand how that journey for others was compromised with physical or mental challenges or, worse, cut short entirely.

I only knew that, on occasions such as this, an individual essence petitioned our magical sisterhood for placement with one of a small selection, usually three or four, of potential mothers.

I was snapped from this reverie by Grim's pronouncement of tonight's soul as "a rambunctious but well-intended boy." Though this description described pretty much the entire male population from toddlers to teens, some atmospheric static or pressure clapped me to attention.

Nothing in Grim's description of the first two vessels resonated but when she described the third as "gung ho, brassy, and thriving in her new job," I knew via some crackling alternate frequency she was describing Jaelle. I was instantly alarmed and fell into a sulk. Why hadn't I received this assignment? I was so distracted by my brooding that I was slow to react to Grim's recommendation of vessel number one.

"Not number three?" I asked much louder than I intended to. In my defense, there were some weird acoustical properties to the room once it assumed the function of clandestine command post, as if it, too, swelled with purpose.

"I believe my endorsement of number one was perfectly clear," Grim said with that uppity clip of hers. "Shall we vote?"

"Wait!" I had to do something. This would be the second time that Jaelle was passed over by our council. Deep down I knew this was a bad omen. When new to these responsibilities, I was often overwhelmed and reluctant to trust my instincts. Now, coming into my abilities, I had an odd sixth sense about these things. Being passed up again would cloud Jaelle's aura with a dark mark; I was certain of it. "Can you elaborate as to what vessel number one offers that number three does not? If you would be so kind, please, Fru Grimilla." That last suck-up part was pure Fru Dorit: our expelled-for-divulging-Stork-secrets, now-on-the-lam former member. Maybe not the best choice to emulate, but resistance had never worked, either.

"No. I cannot," Grim snapped. "Will not, rather. I believe my presentation was fully formed."

So much for the kiss-ass approach. "It's just—"

"Just what?" Hulda asked.

"I kind of liked the sound of number three," I said, deflating like a blown bicycle wheel. "And otherwise put, 'brassy' could be described as confident or assertive, good qualities for the mother of a high-spirited boy."

"Honestly, Fru Hulda, am I to be interrupted for such inanity?" Grim may have been addressing Hulda, but it was me she shot with a look that could puncture a lung. I heard a small burble in my chest.

"Fru Grimilla has, indeed, adequately presented the involved parties. We will proceed to the vote without further delay," Fru Hulda said in a much kinder voice than Grim's. Gentle tone or not, I'd been schooled. It smarted; too bad I didn't feel any wiser.

"A show of digits, please." Grim raised her single index finger, as did many in the group—Hulda included—but not everyone.

I wagged three fingers, as did Ofelia, as did others among us.

Grim's face grew stony with the realization that I'd led some sort of uprising: Mutiny of the Birdies. And, man, did she make for one blistering Captain Bligh.

"Hold your votes until recorded," Fru Hulda said.

Fru Birta—another of my mutineers—scribbled furiously into the ledger, bobbing her head up and down as she transcribed our hand signals into our Stork version of election results. "Vessel number one passes by a two-vote margin," Birta said, lowering her eyes.

Even though she'd won, Grim cawed some sort of outraged reaction. In all honesty, it was the first time I'd witnessed one of our votes pass by such a slim margin.

Hulda closed our meeting with a reassurance to our group that her time away had been fruitful and successful and that it was her great honor to resume her first-chair duties. I, for one, was glad to have her home and wanted nothing more than to hand back the reins and get away from that room and Grim's menacing stare. For once, Hulda did not ask me to stay, and I was up and out of there like a pardoned-by-the-guv electric-chair escapee. Though, when passing Grim on my way out, I got a sample of the kind of zap pure hatred could generate.

# CHAPTER SIX

On Friday of that week, I woke up with a rumble in my belly, and it wasn't the result of my late-night nacho-rama. It was, rather, a something's-coming premonition. Though I was on high alert, the school day was routine. Jinky continued to skulk through the halls, skunking equal parts boredom and belligerence. She showed up for our school-paper meeting, which always surprised me. I would have pegged her for more of a ditcher. It also went against type that my dad's camera was frequently strapped over her shoulder. I'd even seen her, earlier that day, lining up a rather artful shot of a dozen or so open lockers. She appeared to have an eye, even if it was penciled to a Cleopatra-like point with coal-black liner.

Nothing seemed amiss with Marik, either. He continued to be Mr. Popularity, gushing charm like a severed artery. Abby and Shauna still groveled around him like he was some kind of mountaintop oracle. I supposed, for a couple of summit-minded social climbers like them, it was all part of the daily uphill battle. Penny was the one who surprised me the most. I watched her go all fluttery when Marik complimented her sketchbook. As much as he was the undeniable school crush, I wouldn't have figured Penny for one of his hangers-on. I thought she had more of an individualist streak to her.

When the final bell rang, I headed to my locker with a sense of relief and excitement. The end of day signaled not only the weekend but just a few hours remaining until my date with Jack. So maybe I should have cut Penny a little slack on the whole moon-eyed thing. As I was spinning to the last number of the combination, none other than Penny appeared at my side.

"Are you coming to the game?" she asked.

Jack and I had talked about it. It was a home game, and our football team was supposed to be decent again this year, even after losing Jack, the star quarterback. I had argued in favor of a real date night: a movie and a bite to eat. Jack, on the other hand, didn't want me to miss out on my senior year.

"Maybe. We haven't really decided."

"You have to come," Penny said. "It'll be weird

enough without Tina. I can't lose you, too. Who would I sit with?"

Though I had only known Tina for one short year, whereas she and Penny had been hanging out since their monkey-bar days, I missed her, too. She was a freshman at Iowa State — a Cyclone (which, as far as mascots went, was nothing short of twisted).

"There's always Jinky," I said, joking.

"Actually . . ." Penny scrunched her mouth to the side. "Jinky will be there. I told her I'd show her around the field and explain the game a little bit, so she can get some photos for the paper."

"Dinner and a movie is sounding better and better," I said, leaning down to get the jacket that had fallen to the floor of my locker.

"Please," Penny pleaded.

"Please what?" I heard a male voice ask. A slightly accented male voice.

"Please come to the football game," Penny said, her voice going all singsongy.

"I'd love to," Marik said.

Standing and folding the jacket over my arm, I shut my locker with an echoing bang. The "please" had been for my benefit, I wanted to clarify. I didn't. I held my tongue. One look at Penny's cherubic expression, and I decided to play along.

44

"Great," Penny said. "Jinky's coming, too. And you and Jack, right, Kat?"

"The boyfriend?" Marik asked. "Good. A chance to meet him."

*And while we're on the subject of twisted ideas . . .* I thought.

A few hours later, when Jack picked me up, I was sporting a palette of gold and green, our school colors.

"I thought you'd said no to the game," he said.

"I had a change of heart. Do you mind?"

"A minor change to the evening's itinerary I couldn't care less about. But a change of heart . . ." He raised one eyebrow and tilted his head forward. "Not my favorite expression."

I shoulder-bumped him. "You know what I mean."

"I just wish I hadn't dressed up."

I had to cough back a laugh. What he considered dressed up was Levi's and a dark gray polo shirt. Casual was something in the T-shirt family, genus NFL, species Vikings.

"Good thing you did. As a returning alum, you have an image to keep up," I said, climbing into the passenger seat of his old beater of a truck.

"This ride will do the trick." He smiled and turned

the key in the ignition. The engine gunned to life with all the subtlety of a garbage disposal.

I had decided not to prepare Jack for meeting Jinky and Marik. The goal was to give them — Marik in particular — as little buildup as possible. More and more, I was realizing how crucial it was that Jack did not sniff out a secret between me and Marik. Any hint of trouble, and a caped Jack would fly in. The guy could throw storms, after all. Who could blame him for a teensy hero complex?

As we approached the entrance gate, I saw Penny off to the side with a camera-slung Jinky and a tall, bouncing blur of green and yellow.

"Look. There's Penny," I said, my voice a study in practiced nonchalance.

"Who's she with?" Jack asked, his registering hesitation. And it wasn't Jinky giving him pause. Her black leather jacket and ripped jeans were tasteful compared to the cartoonish being that bopped up and down beside her.

"Didn't I mention she invited Jinky and her cousin, mostly because Jinky's taking pictures for the paper?"

"No," Jack said, taking my hand. "You didn't mention it."

As we approached, Marik waved and leaped like some kind of dancing bear. "Over here, Katla." For all his silly antics, he was still roguishly handsome.

Jack squeezed my hand tighter.

"Hey, guys," I said, still moderating my voice. "Go Falcons," I added by way of acknowledging Marik's over-the-top school spirit. "Jack, meet Jinky and Marik, exchange students from Iceland."

Jinky gave Jack a beady-eyed once-over. If I had to guess, I'd say he passed initial inspection. She didn't sneer, anyway, and shook the hand he offered. Marik pumped Jack's hand vigorously and even dropped an arm over his shoulder like some kind of costumed bighead making his theme-park rounds. Marik was several inches taller than Jack, who was no runt at six-two, which made the impression all the more comical.

"It's very nice to finally meet Katla's boyfriend," Marik said.

I watched for a beat or two, wondering if Jack would have some kind of spooked reaction to the merman or shaman in front of him. He didn't. Instead he gave me a quick pump of his brows. So far, Marik was more theater than threat.

Right on cue, Marik pointed to his chest and said, "Look, Katla, we match." Indeed, we wore the same Falcons T-shirt, on sale every Friday at the school's spirit shop, technically a folding table from which the marching band sold school-logo apparel. My T-shirt was under a denim jacket and had a fluffy gold-and-green scarf cowling its neckline. His was over a white thermal undershirt and tucked into a pair of what could only be described as plaid golf pants—knickers, more specifically—circa turn of the century: 1900, not 2000. They were in the right color family, anyway.

Marik noticed me scrutinizing his outfit. "Penny said to wear as much green and yellow as I could find."

How he had found some of the more unusual articles, the coordinating argyle socks, for instance, I hardly knew, but figured I had no room to judge, especially as I was currently wearing striped tights, green high-top Converse sneakers, and yellow pom-poms at the ends of my two braids.

"Should we get seats?" I said. "It looks like the stands are filling up."

"Save us two," Penny said. "I'm going to walk around with Jinky and help her get some shots of the crowd."

Jack, Marik, and I climbed up the steep steps of the home-side bleachers. Once again, I noticed the overall lightness of Marik's bearing, despite his size. His crazy getup didn't help. He was like a big stuffed animal. I was sure, regardless of the inroads he'd made with the school's *it* crowd, that his outfit would invite teasing, if not outright mockery. Just my luck to be his seatmate. About halfway up the climb, someone called out, "Hey, Marik."

He stopped, lifting his head in the direction of the voice. Meanwhile, Jack had found us an open row of seats with enough room for five.

A whistle again drew our attention to the upper ranks of the crowd. "Marik," a male voice bellowed, "we've got a seat for you up here." Gazing up, I noticed Abby, Shauna, and John in the group.

"Thanks, but I'm with Katla tonight," Marik said full throttle, turning more than a few heads in our direction.

"Nice outfit," a girl's voice, closer than the other, called out.

Marik performed a small jig in the aisle, which earned him a round of applause and more whistles, all good-natured and well-meaning, as far as I could tell. As Marik took a seat next to me on the bench, Jack dropped his arm over my shoulder, and I felt his own shake. Turning, I realized it was laughter rocking him. Go figure.

Penny and Jinky didn't join us until well into the first quarter, and they were both up and gone again from halftime until the start of the fourth quarter. Jinky, I noticed, was dangerously close to smiling when they got back; Penny, it seemed, could coax a curl out of the most stubborn of cowlicks.

Our team won by a field goal. It took Marik a while to sort out the rules and the concept of partisanship but ended up as one of the Falcons' biggest fans. Even I had to tee-hee at his enthusiasm. It looked like Penny had competition for Most Spirited.

We were standing just outside the exit to the

stadium, sorting out rides to the Kountry Kettle, when Jack's phone rang. He stepped away to take the call and returned with an odd expression on his face.

"What's wrong?" I asked.

"I've gotta go. Something's up at the farm," he said, pulling me out of hearing range of the others. "Can you get a ride home with Penny?"

I didn't like the sound of "Something's up," mostly because I'd had more than my share of *up* since moving to Norse Falls.

"Up how?" And where the heck was gravity when you needed it, anyway?

"Midas is acting strange. He's howling and pacing and clawing at the door to get out. My dad's never seen him like this. And since he's my dog, my dad wants me to come and settle him."

Midas was a huge yellow lab, an old one, so mellow he'd earned the nickname Old Meller. If he was spooked, it had to be something. My heart was already racing so fast it was halfway to the parking lot. I remembered my premonition from earlier that day.

"I'm coming with you," I said.

Jack exhaled one short puff through his nostrils. I loved it when he went primal on me.

"Why?" he asked. "What are you thinking?"

"I'm not thinking anything yet, but I want to come

along," I said, already stepping toward Penny and formulating an excuse for her.

Jogging through the parking lot, Jack tugged at my arm with urgency. I could do without a lot of the baggage that came with our abilities, but having Jack pull at me insistently . . . Yep, that part of it made me all kinds of mad-happy.

## CHAPTER SEVEN

At Jack's, his dad, Lars, met us at the back door, where he stood holding an exuberant Midas by the collar. Seeing Jack, the hulk of a dog barked and jumped, pushing off Jack's chest with his front paws. It was an act of affection, but one that would have knocked a smaller person — me, for instance — back a week.

"Down, boy," Jack said.

Midas returned to all fours, spun three times, and then leaped at Jack again, this time stretching his front legs onto Jack's shoulders and baying at something outside.

"See what I mean?" Lars said. "But he's obviously relieved to see you."

Jack rubbed the dog's shaggy head and ordered him down. Even I could see that Midas in a clearly agitated state was a danger to no one, but it didn't tamp down the something's-wrong sensation in my gut.

"We'll walk him," Jack said. "It's probably a skunk or an opossum. You know how he hates trespassers."

A few minutes later, Jack and I set out carrying a couple of Maglites with beams that could guide tanks. Though mine was a foot long, heavier than my own arm, and clublike, and though we were accompanied by a very large, overly protective dog, I still had the feeling that we were under-provisioned.

As we trekked along a hard-packed dirt path, Midas pulled at Jack impatiently. At first, Jack's spirits matched the dog's; both were giddy and pumped with adrenaline. Soon, though, Midas's feverish behavior grated on Jack, and he stopped, more than once, to scold and heel the unruly animal.

The path led us deep into their back property. Much of the Snjossons' land was planted in orderly orchard plots according to species. Sweeping my light left and right, I knew we were still skirting these tidy sections. We fell into a comfortable pattern, and even Midas seemed to relax with the even pace of our march and the harmony of nature's nighttime music. I was particularly heartened by the chorus of birds overhead, and their songs were in perfect accord with the whoosh of wind as it ruffled leaves and branches. It seemed to me a symbol of the way Jack and I complemented each other.

We came to the old stone bridge that crossed a brook. Behind it was a wooded area, too cragged and hilly to farm. Though I knew it was the shortcut to the back plots, something about the woods — the wildness in the diversity of size and type of trees, the density of their shoulder-to-shoulder stance, and the darkness they harbored — reawakened my misgivings.

"Maybe we should take the road," I suggested. The property was crisscrossed with a system of interior roads over which trucks were able to pass. It would be a longer route but more civilized, in my opinion.

Jack stopped at a fork in the path. "Midas is pulling this way." He pointed toward the woods. "As odd as that is."

"Odd how?" I asked.

"He doesn't usually go this far. Getting old, for starters," Jack said, reining Midas in with a gentle tug of the leash. "He normally tires out about halfway through the first plantings. But even when he was a pup, there was something about the back plots he never liked."

"What do you mean?"

"For whatever reason, the area always spooked him."

I swept my flashlight back and forth as if scouting for Midas's bogies.

Again, the dog strained to keep going.

"Calm down, boy," Jack said. "We'll get there."

We started up again, heading for the woods. Taking deep breaths, I told myself that it was the back orchard, not the woods, that rattled the dog. It wasn't much reassurance, but it kept me from visualizing the trees' branches as snatching fingers and hearing threats issue down from their heights. As to Midas's nervousness, I reminded myself that dogs were worriers by nature, operating on some kind of perennial Code Red, where everyone from the UPS guy to the cookie-peddling Girl Scout was up to no good.

"How long has your family owned this land?" I asked, my voice taking on a breathy quality. This wooded area felt very different to me, as if thrumming with something ancestral. Plus, crazy as it was, I wanted the press of trees to know we were there, as if somehow conversation would quell other forces. Forces that had Midas now howling in some kind of doggy-distress signal.

"He's really agitated," Jack said. Ahead on the path, our lights illuminated the dog's snout-lifted-to-the-heavens yowl. "Sorry, did you ask me something?"

"About the property."

"Right," Jack said, coaxing Midas to continue. "We've owned it since the late thirties."

"And what was here before?"

"Prairie, mostly. These woods are probably just as they were. Other sections were cleared, of course."

Above me, I heard a sudden snap of branches. Underfoot, I stumbled upon an arterial root contorting across the narrow path. As I shone my Maglite down on its tentacle-like spur, I had the creepiest, though fleeting, image of it throbbing.

I was relieved when, up ahead, the trees thinned and patches of moonlit clouds became visible. I allowed myself a full, lung-expanding inhale. Only then did I realize how sharp and ragged my breaths had been. With the express of air, my ribs rattled.

Weird.

Midas howled again.

Jack, pulled by the dog, increased his pace. They set out across a small open field to where a plot of trees loomed in the distance. I jogged to keep up. The prospect of being left behind made my legs quiver until they ached. It was the oddest response, until I realized that it wasn't a reaction, that the reverberations weren't being produced by my legs. They were, in point of fact, absorbing shock waves emanating from the ground.

I caught up with Jack. He, too, was feeling the vibrations and held his hands up to the sky as if they were something to be caught like raindrops. Midas had begun running in a circle, yapping at the air.

"What is that?" Jack asked.

You don't grow up in California without feeling the earth shake a time or two, but there was something different about this tremor, though I couldn't have explained it at the time. I took a step past Jack to where a row of apple trees began a neat sentrylike formation and shone my light on their trunks. It was curious the way the silvery limbs were rippling as if themselves in fear. As I touched the rough surface of one, it seemed to shrink away, until I realized it wasn't shrinking, it was slipping.

"Jack!" I screamed, now holding on to the trunk and hopping from one foot to the other.

My light fell to the ground and provided a single swath of illumination into the area thick with apple trees. They were, dozens of them, dropping before my eyes.

As I clung to the tree in terror, I could hear Midas's frantic barks as he bounded away and Jack's urgent "Kat, oh, my God, Kat!"

Now the ground beneath my feet was rocking like a rowboat. I felt something grab at my jacket collar, and I looked up to see Jack's hand tugging at me. I released the tree and clasped his arm just as everything beneath me went as liquid as pancake batter.

"Hold on!" Jack yelled.

Instantly I was swept down with the collapsing ground. I screamed, though the roar of the shifting earth had me beat by a landslide—a real landslide, in this case.

Self-respecting Californians know what the tug of the tide feels like, too. At least with a wave, you know it will break. I sensed with whatever it was at work here that it would be a one-way trip down.

My hands slipped from Jack's forearm to his palm, and rocks and dirt sprayed my face and caked my mouth with soot. My legs flailed wildly until finally catching the trunk of the tree I had so recently been standing next to. It was — crazily enough — now at a right angle from where I dangled, clinging to the side of the chasm, and it offered me a momentary support. Because I was no longer a dead weight, Jack was able to readjust his hold on me, grasping me under my arms. He grunted with pain, a cry so visceral I feared for us both, until I was able to swing a most unladylike leg over the side of what had become an abyss.

We scrambled away from the hole and collapsed in a panting tangle of arms and legs.

"What the hell was that?" Jack asked, clutching at me like I might again be wrenched away.

"Did the earth just open up in front of us?" I asked, hacking up dirt and spilling tears.

Ever the precautionary type, Jack lifted me back farther away from the area. We took many more moments to recover, and he held me as rolls of shock left me shaking uncontrollably.

When I had recuperated enough to sit up, Jack, on

all fours, crawled to where his flashlight lay emitting one forlorn shaft of light. He lifted it and swept it over the area, what was left of it, anyway. Midas returned, whimpering and ducking his head submissively.

"I think we just witnessed a sinkhole open up," Jack said, standing.

"A sinkhole. Is that what it is?" I accepted Jack's offer of assistance in getting up.

"It has to be," Jack said. "We've studied them in geology." Again, he trailed his light over the collapsed area. "But this one looks bigger than the slides we looked at."

As his flashlight shone into the caved-in bowl of land, I noticed its edges were sheared off, as if carved away with a sharp instrument, and the depth was staggering. Especially considering how close I had come to plummeting into it. Seeing apple trees toppled like matchsticks upon its floor and others dotting the bowl's sides like bent nails made me shiver.

"We should go," Jack said.

Before we could start back toward the woods, headlights barreling down the interior road came into sight. Lars swung down from the pickup truck and walked briskly toward us.

"I heard a crack out here, and that dog's howl was probably heard clear down to Iowa," he said. "What's going on? Are you kids all right?"

Jack raked his light over the hole. "This is what

Midas was fussing about. A sinkhole. He must have sensed some early vibrations and dragged us out here. Crazy dog nearly got us sucked down into that thing. If I hadn't grabbed Kat at the last moment . . ." He dropped his head, and it was his turn to shudder.

For many moments Lars walked back and forth, mumbling and shining his own light onto the damage. "Let's get you two back," he said finally. "Get you cleaned up, and maybe a hot cup of tea or something to settle your nerves. There's nothing we can do until morning. In the daylight, we'll get a better look. And I'll get a geologist out here for an opinion." He scratched at his chin. "It's the darnedest thing," he said.

I didn't stay long enough for a hot cup of anything. Once I'd cleaned up enough not to frighten my mom, I asked Jack to drive me home. Thoughts were spiraling through my head faster than the earth had shifted below my feet, and I needed some alone time to sort a few things out.

On the ride, Jack apologized for not taking Midas's warnings seriously. For dragging me out into the dark. I did my best to reassure him that I didn't hold him responsible and that it was just one of those things. The first part was true, the latter, not quite.

"I don't think we should share that we were at risk," I said after a long pause.

"What? Why?"

"Even you have to admit, we have enough I-shouldn't-be-alive stories to start our own TV show. To say we were there will invite gossip and speculation."

"I see what you mean," he said, ten-and-two-o'clocking the wheel.

"Your dad wouldn't say anything, would he?"

"I'll talk to him," Jack said. "He won't want too much attention over the whole thing, anyway."

For once, Lars's taciturn nature came in handy.

While saying good night, Jack had to pause before choking out the words, and his eyes were haunted. He also had a hard time letting go of me. As always, I enjoyed the ferocity of his affection, but I could do without it coming on the heels of a life-threatening situation. We'd had our share of those.

# CHAPTER EIGHT

The next morning, Saturday, after receiving a *Busy. Will call later* text from Jack, I shambled down to breakfast, with a fitful night's sleep having earned me the crazy bedhead that had my hair looking like dandelion fluff. Besides reliving my near fall into a muddy abyss, I had heard Leira crying off and on through the long night, so I understood the desperate slurps and full nasal inhalation with which my mom was ingesting her coffee.

"Oh, hon, did Leira keep you up, too?" she asked. "I know your room gets the worst of it, which brings me to this morning's plans: we want to show you a house."

Even if the lease on our rented property wasn't about to expire, a move was overdue. My bedroom shared a razor-thin wall with Leira's; last night was a good example of why that wasn't such a perfect floor plan. And what had been an already cozy space for my mom and me had become a shoe box with the addition of Stanley, his gazillion books, rowing machine, and more sports equipment than I'd have figured for a pocket-protector type. With Leira finally home from the hospital and the pile-on effect of her carrier, high chair, rocker, and bazillion toys, the current situation possibly qualified us for a feature on A&E's *Hoarders*.

"You found a place?" I asked. I had left the house-hunting trips to my mom and Stanley, opting, instead, to watch Leira and give them some alone time. Besides, I would be graduating in nine months and had always planned on an away-from-home college experience. My opinion wouldn't matter for long.

"Maybe," my mom said. "We're going back for another walk-through today. It's our favorite so far, and we both got . . . I don't know . . . really good vibes, or something, from the place."

As much as I wanted the 411 on the earth opening up over at Snjosson Farms, Jack's text had delayed any news on that front for a while. I was not scheduled to work at the store, nor did I have any pressing schoolwork. And, heck, when my mathematics-minded mom threw around words like *good vibes,* I was in.

"When are you going?" I asked.

"How soon can you be ready?"


En route, I briefly explained the previous night's scene at Jack's farm, downplaying the danger we had been in. My mom simply thought it was odd. Stanley, on the other hand, was intrigued.

"How big did you say it was?" he asked.

"It was dark, but maybe a hundred feet. That's what Lars estimated, anyway."

"It's unusual to have one so large."

I was starting to hate words like *unusual*.

"I'll make a few calls later today, see if there are any theories as to cause. Sinks are often due to human interference."

I noticed we were just a few blocks away from Afi's house, Penny's, too, for that matter. "What street are we on?" I asked as Stanley's car rounded a corner.

"Spruce," he said, pulling to the curb in front of a large Victorian.

The name tinkled some familiar key, but my brain was too busy taking in a first impression. The house was big: two floors plus a third-story attic with dormer windows. As for the downside, it was painted a brazen shade of pink with scalloped white trim. I knew the painted ladies in San Francisco could get away with such girly colors, but in this neighborhood—this town—it stood out like a ball gown at a hoedown. And make that a frayed, tattered, and seen-better-days gown. Peeling paint gave the home an abandoned look, compounded by the weedy and overgrown lawn.

I stood on the small strip of grass between the curb and sidewalk, bug-eyeing the place.

"Now, don't prejudge," my mom said, taking my arm. "We know it's a fixer-upper. And it would not remain pink."

Stanley, who had Baby-Bjorned Leira to his chest, waited for us on the cracked and sagging driveway. "Wait till you see inside, Kat. She's a beauty."

A suit-clad woman, the real estate agent, met us on the front porch. "You've brought your daughters today, I see," she said, extending her hand to me. "Margaret Simmons. Pleased to meet you."

After gushing over Leira, Margaret ushered us into the wood-paneled foyer, where she figured I could do with a history lesson as well as a house tour.

"Built in 1904 in the Queen Anne style—though, of course, the original Queen Anne of England had died in the early 1700s." I followed my private docent into the first room to our left. "This would have been called the parlor and was the formal space in which the family would have entertained visitors."

It was a high-ceilinged, bay-front-windowed room

that we'd call a living room but probably have very little use for. Next, I followed Margaret and her sensible heels into the room behind the *parlor.*

"The dining room," she said. "Notice the lovely built-in corner cabinets and the separate butler's pantry."

They were nice, I supposed, if you had a bunch of patterned china to display. Or, say, a *butler.* Margaret's all-business walk-through continued into the next room to the right of the dining room.

"The sitting room," she said, "an informal space where the family would have spent the majority of their time. And, finally, the kitchen."

I struggled to keep up as she stepped into the rear-most area, a separate and small-by-today's-standards space.

"This would be one of our first projects," my mom said, probably noticing my grimacelike reaction. "The walls between here, the dining room, and the sitting room aren't load bearing. We could open it up to create a more modern flow. "

"That sounds like a lot of work," I said, running my hand across a cracked tile countertop.

"Stanley has always wanted to renovate an old house," my mom said, using a strange, chipper-sounding voice.

"This place would be a wonderful challenge, then," commission-based Margaret pointed out.

"Let's have a look upstairs," my mom said, heading back toward the staircase.

I trudged up the narrow steps.

The three upstairs bedrooms were OK, but as far as I could see I'd still share a wall with Leira, which, no fault of her own, would be an ongoing detriment to my beauty sleep.

"Has she seen the best part yet?" Stanley asked, catching up with us after tending to one of Leira's exploding diapers.

"I was just about to mention it," my mom said with a sly look on her face.

"What?" I asked.

"Follow me," she said. "We were thinking this could function as your own private space."

We ascended an even narrower staircase to the attic, where a now-we're-talking renovation had already been undertaken. The smell of fresh paint permeated the U-shaped area. There were two dormer windows, new carpeting, a wall of built-in closets, and three separate spaces, which I was already mentally setting up as bedroom, office, and my own personal lounge. I might even call it a parlor to keep with the *This Old House* theme. I was sold before I even peeked into the shiny white bathroom.

"I love it," I said. And I did.

Back downstairs, my mom and Stanley got into the nitty-gritty of an offer with Margaret. I stepped outside and started walking toward the car, thinking that with my little third-floor hideaway I could put up with a little reno dust, when, across the street, someone stepped out of the front door.

Was fate truly this cruel? Was I never to catch a break? Exiting the house—my soon-to-be neighbor—was none other than Marik, which meant Jinky wasn't far behind. I tapped my toe irritably, and, yep, the door opened again and Jinky, flying her full-black colors, joined Marik.

"Katla." Marik waved and headed over. "What are you doing here?" He came to an all-grins stop in front of me.

"My mom and her husband are putting an offer on this property," I said.

"What? The gingerbread house?" Jinky asked, joining us.

"With any luck, it won't look like a frosted cake for long." My cheeks felt warm, as if I already self-associated with the place.

"What happened to you and Jack last night?" Marik asked.

I gave him a long, tight look. Despite Stanley's opinion that sinks were usually man-made, I had a few theories of my own. And they all involved warnings of one kind or another.

"There was this . . . thing . . . that happened at his place. We took off to check it out."

"The sinkhole?" Jinky asked.

"How did you know about that?"

"Penny called me. It's all over the local news, and she wants to know if we can get some pictures for the paper."

I pulled my phone out of my bag. I had two voice-mails and three texts from Penny and one missed call from Jack. Per Jinky's report, Penny was angling for access to the site. It took a back-and-forth volley of messages between Penny, Jack, and me before I had sorted out an impromptu field trip to the spot.

Marik was uncharacteristically quiet but hanging around like his participation was assumed, wanted even. Still reeling from last night's narrow escape, I wasn't so sure anymore about that keep-your-enemies-close theory. Because close meant access, as far as I was concerned. For the time being, I didn't see any options. When Penny pulled to the curb to pick us up, I stood aside and watched him squeeze into the backseat.

# CHAPTER NINE

Just a short while later, approaching the turnoff to Jack's farm, I surveyed a changed scene. Several occupied vehicles, including a police car, were parked at the top of the long driveway to the house. Penny came to a stop, and I rolled down my passenger-side window and watched a policeman walk over.

After a brief call up to the house, we were given permission to turn into the driveway. Which meant the other cars were not. I noticed one guy aiming a large camera out his window.

Jack met us out front.

"So what's going on?" I asked, accepting his assistance getting out of the car.

"Two geologists have been out today, as well as our insurance agent. No one is ready yet to speculate as to a definite cause. All they'll say is that it's very large, and we're lucky it hadn't been up here near the house or in a busy residential area, for that matter." He pressed his eyes closed and squeezed my fingers. I appreciated the moment of solidarity and was grateful not to have to describe my own "lucky" escape.

"And the place has been crawling with reporters," Jack continued. "My dad let a few down for photos earlier this morning, but our insurance agent got a little nervous about liability and public safety."

"What about us?" pen-in-hand reporter Penny asked.

"Don't worry. I have permission to take you guys out there," Jack said, "but we'll have to be careful."

Jack and I got into the cab of his truck and the three of them climbed into the back for a winding and bumpy, off-road trek to the family's back acreage. It was a warm early-September afternoon. Overhead, leafy branches, many already sporting this fall's colors, flapped with the day's light breeze, and birds chirped their approval of the blue sky and crisp air. For a moment, I forgot the nature of our outing.

It came rushing back the instant we arrived at the scene. In the daylight, I could clearly see the drop-off. It was as if the bottom had simply fallen out of the large circular area. And it was deeper than I remembered. The trees snapped and disfigured at the bottom took on eerily human shapes with their outstretched limbs.

"Whoa," Penny said, joining me at a safe distance from the chasm.

"That's a big hole," Jinky said, already snapping photos.

"Both geologists have classified it as a karst or a *tian keng,*" Jack said. "A Chinese word that translates into 'heavenly pit.' China is famous for some of the largest sinks known."

Someone had been doing his homework.

"So is it really dangerous around here? Could it open up further?" Penny asked.

"At the very edge, yes, some more soil could give way," Jack said, "but it's unlikely the hole will widen from within, if that's what you're asking. The real danger would, of course, be someone falling into it."

I took a step back. Jack's mention of a fall tripped my memory of the two times and places where a physical location had dropped from under my feet—the power places, or Álaga Blettur, as Hulda called them.

"How do I get to the other side for a photo?" Jinky asked. Indeed someone had been out with cones and tape roping off a good portion of the area.

Jack hesitated and then waved with his hand. "I'll show you, but we have to be quick. My dad is really nervous about the liability of this thing."

Newsgal Penny followed the two of them around the side of the pit.

Once I was sure we were out of earshot, I asked Marik, "Did you have anything to do with this?"

"What? No," he said.

"When I say 'you' I mean the collective you, as in Vatnheim."

"To what end?" he asked.

"As a warning."

"As far as I know," Marik said, keeping his voice to a whisper, "this has nothing to do with my assignment. And why would a warning be necessary? You're cooperating, right?"

"Yes," I said quickly.

"Moreover, this is an apple farm, correct?" Marik asked.

"Yes. Why?"

He looked around, his head stretching side to side. "I could feel it as we drew near." He tapped his chest.

"Feel what?"

From the ground, Marik picked up a battered apple and held it at eye level with me. "Apples are the life-giving fruit of all the realms. This is, therefore, a place of great symbolism. To destroy such sacred land would be a very bad omen, especially given the plight of our queen."

This particular apple hardly looked like anything

special. Something had nibbled or pecked at it, leaving it exposed to its core on one side and bruised and scraped on the other. Still, there was something in his grotto-green eyes that pooled with sincerity. And he did seem to have some kind of reverential reaction to the place. Moreover, I didn't want to discuss the topic of my cooperation.

"OK. Fine," I said. "Because I'd hate to think —"

"Think what?" Jack asked, startling me from behind.

"That Marik and Jinky would sit around on a Saturday night. I've invited them to hang out with us." Penny was the last to catch up. "Penny, too. It'll be fun."

From the looks on their faces, Jinky and Marik were free. Penny, I noticed, plumped with the prospect of a Saturday night in Marik's company. Only Jack seemed to go a little hangdog with the news. We had talked about going on that *real* date.

Jack looked at the rotting apple in Marik's hand. "Hungry?" he asked.

Marik glanced down at the specimen. "More like fascinated." He dug with his thumbnail into its flesh, popping out the hard seedpod. "From one small seed, all this." He swept his arms open.

"Actually, that's one of the five carpels you've got there," Jack said. "The seeds or pips are still inside."

Marik nodded his head in appreciation before lobbing the apple back toward the woods; it landed with a soft thump. Back at the truck, science-guy Jack grabbed

74

an apple—a perfect pink specimen—from a wooden crate, shined it on his jeans, and tossed it to Marik.

Marik's eyes grew large, and he held the rosy orb upon both palms as if it were something rare and fragile. "Thank you. Thank you very much."

While swinging into the driver's seat, Jack shot me another of those crooked smiles. It had me wondering who was the true fool: Marik or the rest of us?

# CHAPTER TEN

Later that afternoon, my dad called.

"So, Kitty Kat, it's Saturday night. Any big plans?"

"Actually we're heading your way, into Walden."

"It just so happens I'm free. Can I buy you two some dinner?"

I laughed. "You may want to take that invite back. There're five of us."

"Five of you!"

"Yep."

"I guess I forgot you kids run in packs."

"Like dogs," I said.

"What the heck. A few pizzas and a couple pitchers of soda aren't going to set me back too much. What do you say?"

It was no secret that my dad had relocated his company and his life to Minnesota for me. And as much as business was booming, I knew his social life was currently a bust. In LA, he had a whole roster of friends he could call on a Saturday night. Here, not so much. I knew he and his foreman were friendly and went out for the occasional beer, but the guy was married with young kids and had the kinds of obligations that came with both. Still, I wasn't too sure that my friends would be as sympathetic to his situation as I was. It was a Saturday night, after all. And Walden had a hip, university-town scene. Not too many of the college crowd were out with their parents.

"Don't worry," he continued. "I'll cut and run as soon as the check's paid. Let you kids finish the night on your own."

That part sounded all right. Walden did have a pedestrian street where people just kind of hung out on their way to or from the shops, bars, and restaurants.

"Sure, as long as you're buying." It was kind of our running joke that I was the handout kid.

I drove my mom's Explorer so we could all pile in. We picked Jinky and Marik up last. While pulling up, I pointed to the Victorian house.

"So my mom and Stanley did put an offer on this place."

"No way!" Penny said.

"It's certainly colorful," Jack said.

"They've promised to repaint it," I added quickly.

"You know what it is, don't you?" Penny asked. She was definitely worked up about something.

"Uh. No."

"It's the gingerbread house."

"That's what Jinky called it."

"Because that's its name. It's kind of famous, you know. Actually, infamous is probably the better word choice."

*Ho, boy.*

"Why?" I asked.

"Because of its former owner: the Bleika Norn."

"Who?"

Penny unbuckled and leaned forward, filling the space between the front bucket seats. "More like 'what.' It translates to the 'Pink Witch.'"

"Pink? That doesn't sound very infamous."

"I think 'witch' is the operative word," Penny said.

"So why did people think she was a witch?"

"It's not like I know any of this firsthand," Penny said. "She died a few years back at the ripe old age of a hundred and three, but she was supposed to be some kind of healer."

Which would explain the longevity.

"Again, 'healer' doesn't sound very scary," I said.

"But she did it with spells and the laying on of hands."

The delicious irony was that I'd seen Penny's own grandmother heal Jack at a power place with herbs, chants, and her touch.

"Why pink?" I asked.

"The house, of course. She had it painted pink. Plus, people say she wore a lot of it."

"It is a pretty color, though it might be a bit girly for a centenarian."

"You know," Penny continued, "you and I have a small connection to the Bleika Norn."

"We do? How?"

"The fight between our *amma*s was over a cameo that once belonged to her. Both of our grandmothers contended it had been promised to them upon her death. Way back, they were all members of a garden club, and the Bleika Norn was a bit of a local celebrity and had a small following. I don't get it, myself. She sounds kind of spooky, but maybe that was the draw."

More and more, it was sounding to me like the Bleika Norn was a former Stork. I'd guess she was the group's flamingo. Quite possibly she had been first chair pre-Hulda. The way Penny described her as having a "following" would suggest as much. The "healing" I'd witnessed myself among our current flock. And Hulda had once described a Stork as a type of good or white witch. But pink? Regardless, none of it rattled me.

"How is that spooky?" I asked. "Doesn't your *amma*

make you a special hot drink when you have cramps? It could very well be something she learned at the garden club."

With the sight of Jinky and Marik heading for the car, Penny sat back, pulling at the shoulder strap of the seat belt. "I never really thought about it, but she does have quite a few home remedies."

"What happened to the cameo?" Jack, Mr. Practical, asked. He'd been so quiet during our talk, I'd almost forgotten he was there.

"My *amma* has it," Penny said with an apologetic roll of her shoulders. "She says it's part of my inheritance."

Jinky and Marik piled into the backseat with Penny, bringing all talk of pink witches to an end.

We met my dad in front of the Pizza King, one of Walden's most popular eateries, even if the *king* was a fat guy named Nick, who didn't take credit cards or reservations. With a thirty-minute wait quoted, we opted to head outside, where King Nick lined the sidewalk with plastic chairs for his lords- and ladies-in-waiting.

Jinky, I noticed, had given my dad a full-body scan. Whether he noticed or not, it didn't deter him from singling her out for a chat. My dad always said he liked a conversational challenge. He didn't get a smile out of her, but she had partnered more nouns and vowels for him than she had for the rest of us. She may have even thrown in an adjective or two. My dad had a way of oiling modifiers out of the rustiest of hinges.

Marik, on the other hand, was a spew of words. He talked nonstop about the pleasant evening, Walden's busy streets, the sense of community he felt in Norse Falls, and about how much fun being neighbors would be. That particular remark made my tongue swell. I couldn't help think it was a rather lucky turn of events for him — my bounty hunter — that I would be right under his nose. I also wondered about what Penny had said about the house. Did its odd history have anything to do with the feelings my mom had claimed for the place? Needing a moment to think, I stood, stretched, and walked to the corner.

"Ms. Bryant," I said, catching a glimpse of a belted red coat go by.

"Kat, how nice to see you," she said, slowing and turning.

Penny, another of Ms. Bryant's biggest fans, jumped up from her chair. "Hi, Ms. Bryant."

Ms. Bryant noticed Marik and Jinky and stepped toward the rest of our group.

My dad soon recognized Ms. Bryant, too. "Sage, right? We met last year when Kat was in the musical."

"Of course, Greg, nice to see you again," Ms. Bryant said.

My dad eyed the shopping bags in Ms. Bryant's hands, possibly also taking in her bare left-hand ring finger. "I see you've been busy. Have you eaten? Our table should be ready any minute."

"Oh, no, I wouldn't want to intrude," Ms. Bryant said.

"You'd be doing me a favor, really. I'm solo here with all these kids. A little help with crowd control would be welcome," my dad said.

*Crowd control?* He was smearing it on thick, but who could blame him; it was Ms. Bryant.

"Please," I said, turning to her. A chance to see her outside of the student-teacher setting intrigued me.

"I *have* built up an appetite," Ms. Bryant said, lifting her packages with a couple of bicep-curling motions.

I sighed. She was smart, funny, and gave shopping the cred it deserved. It was official; Ms. Bryant was perfect.

Our name was called and we, Ms. Bryant included, were shown to a table.

The restaurant was one of those places that encouraged smack-talking employees. The waiter, a small guy with a chiseled soul patch, took one head-back, eyes-up look at Marik and pulled from his large apron pocket a roll of paper and a fat blue crayon. "I see a children's menu is in order," he said, unrolling the sheet to reveal a place mat with a crossword puzzle and a long list of word scrambles.

We all had a good laugh, and Marik picked up the menu to return it to the waiter.

"I'll take that," my dad said, reaching across the table.

"And you called *us* kids a few minutes ago," I said.

"It's not the chicken nuggets I'm after," he said.

I recognized his cheeky grin, the one my mom called his "game face," except in his case the "game" had nothing to do with a field, court, or diamond. He took both the crayon and menu, and before I even had time to formulate another thought, never mind sentence, he whipped through the list, a dozen at least, of word scrambles.

"Done," he said as if it had been a race or we'd been timing him.

"That's impressive," Ms. Bryant said, leaning over in her seat next to him to scan the list. "Some of those words were tricky: kingdom, knighthood, majestic. I remember this talent of yours."

"You're so funny, Mr. Leblanc," Penny said. "I never even knew *Penelopa* scrambled to *one apple* before I met you. Though I'm not too sure Tina liked her *Kerstina* becoming *a stinker.*"

"And I reworked *Sage* into *ages,*" my dad said. "I remember it was interesting, given your talent of guessing how old someone is."

"You guess ages?" Marik asked, sitting forward in his seat. "How do you do that?"

"I don't really know," Ms. Bryant replied. "I just . . . know somehow."

"How about me, then?" Marik asked.

Ms. Bryant bit her thumbnail, watching Marik closely. She didn't answer for a long time.

"Well, you're a senior, so seventeen or eighteen is logical. But for some reason I want to guess older." She paused, steepling her hands. "I'm going to say eighteen."

She hadn't specified years. I personally thought it was more like centuries.

As if confirming my suspicions, Marik chuckled through his reply: "An excellent guess."

The waiter returned, asking, "So are you people gonna order, or what?"

I was grateful for the interruption; I had become wary of the previous topic: one that could have led to Leira's name being an anagram, the back-to-front spelling, even, of Ariel. Nor did I want Marik to expound on the fact that although he appeared to be an eighteen-year-old senior, he was, in fact, an ageless, soulless creature from another world.

"I for one am starving," I said. "Pepperoni–green pepper, anyone?"

The green pepper earned me a grumble from my dad until Marik suggested anchovies, which got a groan from everyone.

We ordered, going with a few different combinations,

after which my dad turned to Jack. "What's this about the earth moving out at your place?"

Another topic I wasn't crazy about.

"One of those things, I guess," Jack replied.

Ms. Bryant had heard about it, too. She and my dad focused on the loss-of-trees aspect of the story. Only Penny, so sweetly oblivious to who she ran with, had a "weird the way the earth just opened up like that" comment. *Weird* was not one of my favorite words anymore.

I was relieved when the conversation meandered to much more generic topics: disgusting pizza toppings like hamburger, the disgusting hamburgers at our school cafeteria, and then the perennial adult-to-child safe subject: school in general. My dad had started this one; the rest of us — Ms. Bryant included — were on weekend-avoidance mode.

"So what do you think of Norse Falls High?" My dad singled out Jinky with this question.

"I like it," Jinky said.

"Do you have any classes with Kat?" my dad asked.

"Ms. Bryant's design class. We all have it together." Jinky gestured to me, Penny, and Marik.

"Who's your partner for the project?" Jack asked Jinky.

Earlier, when I had shared that Marik and I were assigned team members, Jack's "that should be entertaining" comment had said it all.

"Penny."

"You got lucky," Jack said.

"What project?" my dad asked.

"The one for which we still need parent volunteers," Ms. Bryant said.

"Where and when?" my dad asked.

I inwardly cringed. The volunteer form, smashed at the bottom of my book bag, had been neglected — abused even — for several reasons. First of all, although I was keenly aware that I was fortunate to have two involved parents, I was a senior now and felt a little independence was healthy. Second, I would be plenty busy keeping an eye on Marik — and Jinky, for that matter — and didn't need my dad underfoot, too.

"At Pinewood High School for the By Student Design Show. Because the show itself is off property, I need chaperones the day of the event. I'm also looking for some help with a few basic building projects: easels, a display case, etc. Mr. Derry, the Design instructor over at Pinewood, is in his fortieth year of teaching. Suffice it to say, he's left the entire undertaking up to me."

Ms. Bryant could sell a school outing just as much as she could an upturned collar.

"I'm your man," my dad said. "Sign me up." This without ever getting the "when."

I swallowed a big gulp of root beer and my hopes of the show being uneventful. Something about my dad

thrown into the mix—another player on the field—
foretold of complications. And, the "I'm your man" comment was cheesier than the still-bubbling pizza that had
just paraded past us. Ms. Bryant hadn't seemed to mind
it; she was all smiles at the prospect of having snared a
parent helper with construction experience, a factory,
and its full floor of handymen. How had I—given the
turmoil of my life—ever thought that *uneventful* was in
the realm of possibility? *Realm:* another of those loaded
words I was coming to seriously hate.

# CHAPTER ELEVEN

I woke Sunday to Leira's plaintive cry, more of a bleat, really. I hadn't closed my door. With Leira's open, every sound resonated with intensity. Already I was painting the pink house white and reveling in my one-floor-above hideaway. Singing soon replaced Leira's mewlike wail, and I drifted in and out of consciousness to my mom's high and clear voice. The lullaby was familiar. I was sure she'd sung it to me, and she'd hummed its tune — one reminiscent of the John Peel hunting song — for years:

> While you sleep, my sweet,
> Wrapped in love so tight,
> May your watchman be

The brave gale of the night
And the lark your reveille
At dawn's first light
Be thee safe in my love until morning.

Leira continued to fuss. My mom then went into a second verse, one that was less familiar to me.

Do you know, my pet,
What the wise ones say?
That the swan's snowy span
Is but a wish away.
May this comfort you
As you wake to this day
Full of love, full of hope, full of glory.

I sat up with a bolt. It was such a beautiful song. Was this the first time I'd really listened to the lyrics, the second verse in particular? If I had heard them, how had I not processed them before? I quickly padded into the hallway, pausing at the door to Leira's room. My mom had her on the changing table; her tiny legs kicked in defiance. I took it as another sign of her strength, a quality that would come in handy: later rather than sooner, if I had any say in the matter.

"Mom, that song you were just singing, what was it?"
She pulled the disposable diaper's plastic tape snugly

across Leira's concave belly. "I'm not sure I know the name of it. It's something I learned from your *amma,* something I sang to you when you were a baby."

"I don't remember hearing the words before now. They're pretty," I added. "Do you know where Amma learned the song, or how old it is?"

My mom looked up and out the window, as if trying to pull memories from the sky. "No, and no, though I suppose it's quite old and that the English is a translation. Almost all of Amma's lullabies were. Leira seems to like it, anyway."

Indeed, she had settled and was bicycling her legs in a more playful show of vitality. Another good sign, if you asked me.

"Now that you're up," my mom continued, "Stanley said there are some news reports you might be interested in. He's been glued to the TV all morning."

*Uh-oh.*

"What kind of news?"

"More sinkholes like the one out at the Snjossons' property."

I didn't stick around to hear it from her. I headed downstairs and straight for the family room, where Stanley was — coffee cup in one hand and remote in the other — camped out in front of the television.

"What's going on?" I asked.

"The weirdest thing," he said.

Again, the *weird* word. I almost growled.

"Three more very large ones, like out at Jack's place, have been reported: one in Australia, one in Chile, and another in British Columbia. The timing is odd, almost like a cluster, but they're too far apart to be related. Luckily, they've all been in remote areas. No injuries, thank goodness."

I left Stanley channel surfing and grabbed my phone out of my backpack. Jack picked up on the second ring.

"Have you heard?" I asked.

"Yes. We're crawling with reporters again. My dad's at the site with a news crew as we speak."

"So what's their angle?" I asked.

"There isn't one, really. Just that it's a coincidence."

His mom called him outside, cutting our conversation short. Next I retrieved a text from Penny. Her *More holes. Freaky huh?* message didn't do much to muzzle the sirens going off in my head. Jack claimed Midas had never liked that area. What if it had been a power place? What if they had all been power places? Were they portals? Vulnerable portals? If Marik was to be trusted and it wasn't Vatnheim, no need to ponder who else would try to get through. The fury we'd wrought in Brigid had been apoplectic, a word that shared a whole lot of letters with apocalyptic. And I left nothing to coincidence anymore.

# CHAPTER TWELVE

That evening, as I gazed through Afi's front window about to flip the sign to CLOSED, a face pressed up against the glass.

"Jesus!"

I stumbled backward, twisting my ankle in the process.

Jinky opened the door and stood in front of me, while I braced myself against the nearby newsstand and rubbed at my already throbbing foot.

"What the hell?" I said. "Are you trying to scare me to death?"

"Hardly. Just thought it was time we spoke alone." She swallowed a smile, obviously oblivious to my colorless cheeks and physical injury. "Can we take a walk?"

To my way of thinking, "a walk" was the prelude to bad news, a breakup, or the pirate's plank. Besides, my ankle hurt. "We're alone here."

"There's somewhere I have in mind," she said.

Stranger Danger 101: Never willingly go to a second location.

"And you're done here, right?" she continued.

"Yes." My hesitance made the word sound like more of a question than a reply.

"Then get your things and let's go."

A few minutes later, I was following Jinky down the darkened Main Street.

"Should we take my car?" I asked, struggling to keep up.

"It's nice out," she said, which — as far as I was concerned — was a non sequitur.

An evident proponent of the work-it-off school of pain management, she took the corner at Fern gaining speed. Something in her long, purposeful strides announced that conversation was curtailed until arrival. It set an ominous tone. I was surprised, therefore, when our destination turned out to be . . .

"Big Turtle Park?" I asked, which wasn't the name of the dead guy on the playground's official sign, but it was what townies called the place, owing to the large, green, climb-on structure that was its main attraction.

"I have my reasons." Jinky dropped into one of the swings facing the concrete turtle.

I took the one next to her. She seemed content to drift back and forth gently. More relaxed given our location, I pumped my legs a couple of times to get a little momentum going. Growing up, I was a swing kid. You could keep your slides, your seesaws, and your merry-go-rounds; give me a sling seat and a starting push and I was sky-high happy.

"I am here," Jinky said, "to complete what began in Iceland."

I planted my feet so suddenly that I retwisted my bum ankle. "Uh, could you be a little more specific?"

"When I first spied you at the festival, I knew you were different. With just a simple rune reading, I saw that a journey lay ahead of you. And, of course, a true vision quest is the mark of one with strong ties to the other worlds. And even my grandmother, a powerful shaman herself, was stirred by your visit."

"Uh. Thank you, I think." Stirred was one of those hazy words. You stirred up trouble, resentment, and the occasional martini.

"Soon after, Marik came to see us on his own voyage."

"Voyage?" I bristled at the suggestion that he was on some kind of pleasure cruise or adventure. My tone earned me a look from Jinky.

"Look, I may not be privy to all the particulars.

Neither one of you is exactly an open book, but, as my grandmother has strongly advised me, as a shaman, I'm to act as a conduit only."

"A conduit?"

"A shaman is an intermediary. One who can communicate with the spirit world, and if the magic is strong enough, beyond."

"Beyond?"

"I do know that Marik isn't from Iceland, you know."

"I guess you would." I ran my hand up and down the swing's chains. I was getting into dangerous territory here.

"Occasionally, I assist him to *visualize* his natural habitat. It's therapeutic, he claims."

"So you're a shaman in your own right, then?" I asked.

"Well, not exactly. That's kind of the point." Jinky unwedged her butt from the swing and stood in front of me. "This is my initiation, my rite of passage."

"What?" I was up out of my swing now, too. "I'm your test run?" Her role was becoming clear to me as well. And she wasn't just a conduit, she had wings to earn.

I walked in the direction of the immense green turtle.

Jinky followed. "Hey. You, more than anyone, should get it."

"Get what?"

"That it's not a choice. As spiritual beings, we have to act on our premonitions. To ignore a gift, to not rise to the calling, is a willful defiance of our true purpose. For us, there is no coincidence, no chance."

That last bit got me. It's what I'd thought yesterday about the holes. I turned my back on Jinky and braced my arms against the monster turtle; my fingers landed in something sticky, the residue of some kid's snack, no doubt. I stepped back, wiping my hands on my jeans. When I looked back up, Jinky was holding something highly suspicious in my face: a bundle of weeds and a lighter.

"I'm not into that stuff," I said, holding up my still-gooey hands.

"It's sage, for smudging," she said, communicating both her impatience and condescension with a shake of her head.

"And what are you going to do with that?"

Jinky ducked down, way down, and crawled below the turtle. "I felt a strong vibe that I had to connect with you tonight. Around here, this was the closest thing I could find to a domed sweat lodge. I'll have to improvise."

"What, here? Now?" I had to stoop and address the underside of a big green turtle.

"Have you got somewhere else to be?"

I sighed, a big huffy thing. And though I couldn't

believe I was doing it, I bent down and scrambled below the belly of the concrete reptile, jettisoning a juice box out of my way.

In the cramped and dark space, Jinky sat cross-legged. I did the same. With a click, she lit the bundle. I coughed; she shot me a look. All was proceeding normally. Even her motions were just like last time. She held up the smoking bundle, waved it over her head and around her shoulders.

"We pass the smudge wand," Jinky said, "to cleanse the space and to purify our bodies and minds."

She handed me the burning sage, and I copied her smoke-bath routine.

I remembered there had been more to the giving of thanks that first time. Improvising meant the abridged version, I assumed.

The smoke collected under the curve of the turtle's back. It burned my nose, and I felt sick to my stomach.

"We call to the spirits on behalf of one whose journey crosses into the ancestral realm and beyond."

It was clear to me why I was not a smoker. The stuff was nasty. My eyes were watering. I couldn't clear my throat. And I was getting light-headed.

Next thing I knew, Jinky was two inches from my face, asking, "What about Frigg?"

I coughed and rubbed my eyes. "What?"

"You said: 'From the goddess Frigg, one seeks

forgiveness and the other offers life.' And that 'within *them* lies a solution.'"

"I did?"

"Yes. Do you remember anything else?"

"Frigg?" I repeated groggily.

"Do you know what that means?"

"That I need to get some *friggin'* air," I said, crawling from under our improvised sweat lodge. I took a deep, cleansing breath of clear air and staggered to my feet.

Jinky followed me.

"Do you even know who the goddess Frigg is?" she asked.

"No."

"Frigg is the queen of Asgard. Only she and her husband, Odin, sit upon Asgard's highest seat and look out over the universe. She is the goddess of marriage, childbirth, motherhood, and wisdom."

"Now, that's a résumé," I said, "but are you sure I said Frigg?"

"Yes. But it was only a moment of clarity. Obviously we need to find a real *savusauna,* and a place of concentrated ancestral energies, if you're to walk with the spirits again."

I was on board with the walking part. I wanted out of there.

"Can we call it a night?" I said. "I think I'm quested out for now."

We headed back in silence and at a humane pace. My ankle felt better, but it was my head's turn to twist. Had I said Frigg? Did I have a brief vision? Despite my confusion, it felt like progress. And I now knew Jinky's role. But what did Frigg have to do with it? And where would we find a *savusauna* around here?

# CHAPTER THIRTEEN

I had only the vaguest recollection of arriving home Sunday night. Either I was already half asleep or whatever altered state shaman Jinky had enabled had been more powerful than we'd thought.

The next morning, I woke early and went straight to my computer to Google Frigg. Jinky had been correct in the goddess's basic bio: Queen of Asgard, home of the Warrior Gods. Scanning a few different sites, I found a few more details of interest. She had an inner circle of nine faithful handmaidens, a tenth — Idunn, the Goddess of Eternal Youth — had been booted for incompetence. I also focused on Frigg's role as the goddess of childbirth and motherhood. In one saga she is said to have sent a magic, fertility-boosting apple to a childless King Rerir and his queen. It seemed important, given Marik's claim that apples were the "life-giving fruit of all the realms." Nor was it lost on me that a third queen (after Brigid and Safira) was making her presence known. Great. At this rate, I could host a state dinner. Except I feared I'd end up as the main course.

Leira's crying jarred me back to the here and now. I closed my laptop, walked to the closet, grabbed a pair of jeans, and ran a hand across the selection of tops. I elected to go with a peasant blouse; it seemed to mirror my predicament.

Thankfully, school was uneventful. In Design, Ms. Bryant handed me a chaperone form that my dad needed to fill out and return — by tomorrow. I sighed and jammed it into my book bag. At least it was one of Ms. Bryant's assignments where neatness didn't count.

If nothing else, it was an excuse to visit Jaelle after school.

She gave me a full-flash smile as I walked into the office.

"Well, hey there, Ice," she said, using her own personal nickname for me, a reference to my white-blond hair. "What gives?"

"Santa, if you're good," I said, borrowing a line from Afi.

"Oh. I like me some sass," Jaelle said. "Kind of like a mini me."

Her mention of a "mini me" reminded me that I'd failed to sway Grim into changing her recommendation at our last meeting. I still felt that it was a bad sign, one leading to fertility issues for Jaelle and Russ. I found it all so maddening. They'd make excellent parents; any child would be lucky. Again, I wondered why I hadn't received Jaelle's second bestowment assignment. As with Jacob—a soul I had placed last year—I could have guided things, steered the essence gently toward Jaelle. It wouldn't have been without its problems, however. From his past life, Jacob had been drawn to his former-mother Julia's familiar presence. Jaelle wouldn't have that advantage. I clung to the hope that there had to be a way to stack things in her favor next time—if there was a next time—the contemplation of which frustrated me.

"Kitty Kat, why the pout?" my dad asked, emerging from his office.

"Just my Monday face," I said, snapping to. I retrieved the chaperone form from my bag and smoothed it against Jaelle's desk. "Ms. Bryant needs you to fill this out."

"Anything for Ms. Bryant." My dad plucked a Sharpie from the desktop pencil cup and began filling in boxes. "Any more cave-ins out at Jack's place?" he asked without looking up.

"Not that I know of."

"I heard about that," Jaelle said. "What a shame about all those trees. I just hope it was those tart green ones, not the sweet pinks I like so much."

I hadn't thought about which variety had been affected. Jack's family did grow quite a few different types.

While inking his name to the dotted line, my dad asked, "So who's your partner for this project again?"

"Marik."

"You mean the big hunky guy from Saturday night?"

There was no correct way to answer that question. To say yes was to agree that Marik was hunky. To say no was to infer that Marik wasn't my partner or hadn't been present on Saturday. Moreover, since when did my dad call other guys hunky?

"Yes, the big guy."

"What about Penny?"

"She's partnered with Jinky."

"Now, there's an odd couple," my dad said.

My dad stepped away for a phone call. I sat down in the chair next to Jaelle's desk. While leaning down to her lowest desk drawer, she groaned.

"Are you OK?" I asked.

"Fine. Just a little sore from the weekend's home-improvement projects."

"What did you guys do?"

"We painted the spare bedroom."

Jaelle and Russ had recently purchased a house, one with a swing-set-containing backyard and just a block away from the elementary school.

"What color?"

"Pink."

"Pink!" I had a hard time modulating the surprised tone of my voice. "Is there something I should know?"

"Not yet, but I believe in the power of positive thought and in being proactive. And I want a girl first."

"Wow."

"You think I'm crazy, don't you?"

"Not at all. I think you're right, in fact. Proactive is the way to go."

"Precisely," Jaelle said. "I've got it all planned out: pink curtains, pink comforter, pink shaggy rug, and a menagerie of pink stuffed animals. It will be adorable."

A few minutes later, I left Jaelle with a gurgle of hope in my chest and ideas 'shrooming like spores. It felt great.

## CHAPTER FOURTEEN

At home there was a stack of flattened boxes near the back door.

"Is there something I should know?" I asked, entering the kitchen.

"We got the house," my mom said, bouncing Leira on her lap. "We were even able to negotiate a short closing."

"Congrats," I said, "but how short?"

"A week from Saturday."

"What? That's not enough time to—"

"It will have to be. The papers are signed," she said, snapping a lid on the baby bottle and our conversation.

I sulked off to my bedroom and flopped onto my bed. I didn't have time for homework, working at Afi's, breaking a magical pact, *and* boxing up my life.

I was about to let such negativity cloud my plans when my cell phone rang and I saw Jack's name on the caller ID.

"Hello," I said.

"Hey." It was a simple word: expendable in most sentences, but the way he delivered it, growly with affection, undid me.

"What's up?" I asked.

"Just checking in. I thought you were going to call last night."

Ugh. Forgot. Plus was underneath Big Turtle.

"Sorry. I worked and then . . . had a bunch of homework. We got that house, by the way." I was happy for something newsy as a change of subject. "We move a week from Saturday."

"That's fast."

"And will be a lot of work."

"Then we should do something fun this weekend. We've got an overtime crew going out all day Saturday, but my dad will have to give me some time off on Sunday."

"What should we do?" I asked.

"There's a hike I haven't done in a long time: Alpenstock Conservation Area."

I should have known his idea of fun would be a nature outing that took stamina. Personally, I'd have preferred a department store that took Visa; my dad's, of course. I must have gone too long without commenting.

"Did you have another idea?" Jack asked.

*A movie. A play. A restaurant. Bowling. Putt-putt golf. A scenic drive. A pumpkin patch. Or even a corn maze, for goodness sake.* But it occurred to me that it was his turn to pick.

"A hike sounds pretty."

"The forest is old-growth. It feels like stepping back in time."

*Better than through time or to another realm,* I thought after hanging up with him, reluctantly, as always.

Contact with Jack gave my mood, and confidence, the boost it needed. While in the bathroom getting ready for bed, I turned my attentions back to Jaelle. Why not paint a room pink if your heart is set on starting a family with a girl-first preference? Made sense to me. And it inspired me. I had been proactive in placing Jacob with Julia. Why not Jaelle? The only small snafu was that with Jacob I had a specific soul to beckon, thus I could tailor my efforts to his personality.

I spat toothpaste into the sink and looked up at my reflection.

How would I begin such a thing with Jaelle? Also troubling was the pesky issue of the other potential vessels. If the soul had no previous attachment to Jaelle, how could I guarantee that she would prevail as the chosen vessel? As with Jacob, I was willing to explore the reach and sweep of my powers, and even employ subtle manipulation, but I wouldn't lie during the council meeting. Even without a rule book or set of Stork laws, I sensed such a maneuver would be the kind of transgression like the one that got Dorit booted. I also knew an incompatible placement wouldn't benefit either Jaelle or the soul. So what were my options? One thing I knew for sure, the child I placed with Jaelle would do well to have an easygoing personality; Jaelle had the strength of will for two, or more. And to sign on with this renegade mission of mine, a sense of adventure was a must. And given the palace that awaited her, an affinity for girly things wouldn't hurt, either. These criteria were, if nothing else, a starting point in my search. I plinked my toothbrush into the sink-side cup and pulled the headband from my hair.

Sitting on the edge of my bed, I whispered, fanning the words with a whisk of my right hand, "A soul, a girl, is sought. She should be a lover of pink, sweet-natured, and an explorer at heart." I slipped under the covers satisfied with my appeal.

# CHAPTER FIFTEEN

Barefoot and in a coarse and tattered dress, I awake at the edge of a great forest. Before me, a serpentine path twists between two watchmanlike trees and continues into the dense woods.

I set off with a sense of urgency, stumbling once, and then again, over sharp, white pebbles, whose regularity indicates the marking of a trail.

I follow the stones for a very long time. Darkness settles like mist from the forest's canopy, and strange grunts and screeches announce the presence of feral creatures. I am cold and scurry with arms drawn tight to my chest. Hunger pounds in my belly like a drum.

Weak with fear, exhaustion, and starvation, I stagger around a curve in the path, when before me appears a cottage. From within, it glows, revealing a white-capped roof and thick russet-toned walls. And it smells delicious; my mouth pools in anticipation. Advancing quickly, my hand brushes over its low stacked-stone garden wall. The stones, to my surprise, are springy, cakelike, and they, too, smell delectable.

Weak-kneed, I hurry along the cobbled front path. The smells of nutmeg, cinnamon, clove, and — above all — ginger are so strong that I am borne upon them like a wave. At the front door, I pause, studying its strange surface. It glistens with a sheer glaze and is sticky to the touch, and it, too, smells wonderful, like caramelized sugar. I swing the door open. From its lintel, a fat morsel crumbles into my hands. I lift it to my nose, sniff, and take one exploratory lick, after which I gobble up the chunk of gingerbread greedily.

From inside, I hear a baby's laugh. I stoop to pass under the low doorway and find myself in a tiny space. Flames dance and leap from a massive fireplace. A mouse skitters across the floor, drawing my eyes to a corner-hung cage. Within its iron bands lies a baby girl. As I approach, she coos contentedly. Tripping the latch, I gently lift her out of the horrible contraption.

The black-haired bundle pokes at me with a fat finger, and I giggle at her playfulness. My own laugh, however, is soon drowned out by another, one that is haunting and wicked. Someone is coming, and I must get the baby out of here. The cackle reverberates through the cottage, causing the rough-hewn beams—pretzel logs?—to shake; granules of salt fall like hail. The raven-haired child's face crumples, her heart-shaped lips tremble, and she lets go a desperate wail. I spin, clutching the girl to my chest and knocking the hanging cage; it groans on its rusty chain.

I spy a back door: thick strips of black licorice banded together with ropes of red. I move toward it, passing a low cupboard. Its biscuit-shaped door swings open to reveal a very young boy. He sits cowering with his arms wrapped around pudgy knees.

From the front of the house another peal of laughter erupts. I gasp. The girl leaks fresh tears; the boys eyes widen. I extend my hand to him, urging, "Quick."

I watch the tot take a large gulp of air and fill his dumpling cheeks with courage. He puts squat fingers in mine, and I hoist him from the cubby and onto his bandy legs. Clutching the girl and tugging the boy, I storm out of the strange house and into the pitch of night.

# CHAPTER SIXTEEN

I woke confused and flat-tired, not a good sign. Normally, I felt a sense of elation following one of my Stork dreams. This time, however, it felt incomplete. Not only had none of the vessels — not even Jaelle — been present, but there had been two essences. Of course, multiples were not unheard of. But from what I understood, twins and triplets (and up) presented together, in a like location and as the same age. I remembered Svana had once described a set of identicals in a hollowed-out pumpkin shell. An older child, such as the boy, happened occasionally, too. It indicated a soul that had hovered for some time without selecting a mother. The two anomalies — their separate locations and different ages — were, thus, puzzling.

Nor could I help thinking of the similarity between my dream and the classic "Hansel and Gretel" fairy tale. While it certainly had all the markings of a Stork dream, I wondered at the borrowed imagery—complete with evil witch—that was so recently suggested to me with our new "gingerbread" house. Despite this, I knew the children were essences, so where were the prospective mothers? And why the element of fear? Unfortunately, none of it put me any closer to helping out Jaelle. But it was, if nothing else, a lesson in that *patience* Hulda had so recently preached.

At school I dragged my two-ton limbs to first period, where I had a hard time keeping my head in an upright position. Thank God for educational videos, lowered lights and blinds, and head-in-laptop teachers.

In Design, my walking coma made Penny's effervescence all the more crackling.

"You seem awfully chipper," I said. "Even your hair is having a good day."

It was. Her natural curls were normally just a kink or two away from frizzdom. Today, however, they seemed tamer, more gentle wave than churning foam.

"Thanks." She fluffed her bangs.

"Did you use some kind of relaxing product?" I asked.

"No."

And now that I was hawk-eyeing her head, the

shade seemed brighter, too. I had always loved Penny's hair color, all redheads for that matter. Today it was even more flaming, like something alive.

"Did you do something with the color?" I asked.

"No." This time, with all my attention, she patted down her hair, which — come to think of it — seemed longer.

"Good morning." Marik passed between us and eased into the desk behind Penny. I noticed she sat up straighter. Had her shoulders always been so angular? And her boobs, had they always been so perky?

From her backpack, Penny pulled a spiral binder and turned to hand it to Marik. "You left this in my car last night."

*Huh?*

"Thank you," he said. "I'll need that next period."

I knew Marik was a quick study in the social game and that Penny was a willing subject, but it was the first I had heard of them spending time together without . . . me. I felt oddly strange about it. I trusted Penny more than I trusted anyone else in the school, myself included. Nonetheless, there was something that nettled about this new information. And exactly what was it? A study date? They had American History together. Or was it a *date* date? Penny would have told me about that; I would have thought so, anyway.

Abby arrived, making a point of walking down our

aisle. She stopped to chat with Marik on her way to the back of the room. I could sense her disappointment that he had settled near Penny and me today. Unlike the rest of us, Marik was a floater, taking various desks around the room with no apparent rhyme, reason, or rotation. He hung just as easily with the stoners in the far right corner as he did with Abby and her social climbers as he did with the math-club types. I'd even witnessed Mean Dean, a guy who talked to no one and had—according to school lore—coined his own nickname, lend Marik his latest *Manga Club* magazine.

With Marik and Abby involved in a conversation, I took the opportunity to ambush Penny. I leaned across the aisle that separated our two desks and whispered, "So what's up with you and Marik?"

She went cherry-pie red; even her freckles tinted with crimson. "I don't know," she said, keeping her voice low. "He could have his choice of any girl; still, I just can't stop thinking about him. And it may sound weird, but"—she swiveled in her seat, bringing her head to within inches of my own and cupping her mouth with her right hand—"I feel like we have something."

I snuck a glance backward to where Abby was perched on the edge of Marik's desktop. She, from the looks of it, was working on her own *something,* and *it* involved her chest being right at his eye level.

Ms. Bryant walked in the room, bringing our

conversation to an end and sending Abby back to her own seat.

While Ms. Bryant distributed a handout, I sat brooding. How could Penny not see that Marik had something with everyone? Even Mean Dean, for Pete's sake. And I felt fairly confident that if the Pete of Pete's sake walked in, he'd be Team Marik, too. I made a mental note to keep a close eye on her and Marik. The guy was already after my sister; no way was he getting my best friend, too.

# CHAPTER SEVENTEEN

"Can you feel it?" Jack asked. He stood rooted to the damp earthen path under the million-leaf canopy of the Alpenstock forest. The air thrummed with the ticks and clicks of living things, and the light, filtered through the prism of swaying greenery, cast an emerald sparkle over everything.

"Feel what?" I asked, afraid of the answer.

"Our loads lighten."

I relaxed. He was in his element, a primordial forest on what was presumably once a glacial ice field. On an individual basis, Jack's adjustments to his surroundings were minute: his eyes darkened a half shade, his voice rang an octave deeper, and his stride loped an inch, at most, longer. As a whole, however, it was like watching a salamander meld into a pebbled backdrop. His harmony with the environment seemed to suggest the restoration of a withheld sustenance. I thought about the way an indoor activity — shopping, for instance — dulled his eyes and slowed his pace, and I vowed to be more open to this off-the-grid passion of his.

When he pulled me in for a kiss so swift and as feral as our hinterland setting, my approval rating for our backcountry adventure climbed to the treetops.

"I feel lighter now," I said into the steam of his still-nuzzling mouth, "but I don't think it was the woods."

"But it's all — we're all — interconnected," he said, taking me by my shoulders. "I feel that here especially."

I had to admit the place was teeming with energy, and as proof of Jack's chain-of-life theory, a mosquito plunged his greedy proboscis into my calf. My swat at him and consequent stumble backward broke the intensity of the moment, but I took three things away from that instant in time: Jack's rapport with this environment, the beautiful and mystical tapestry of life, and one big, honkin' welt of a nasty skeeter bite.

An hour or so later, when we circled back to the park entrance, I noticed an area with a visitors' center and what looked to be tepees and other simple structures; one, in particular, caught my eye.

"What's that?" I asked.

"An interpretive center. School groups come here by the busloads. If I remember from my own fifth-grade field trip, this was once the site of a super-old—like prehistoric or something—Native American settlement. They've recreated what the site may have looked like."

"Can we take a quick look?"

"Sure," he said. "I love stuff like this."

It was late afternoon; only an elderly couple and one park ranger remained. Fearing vistors' hours were coming to an end, I made a bee*line* for what looked like a giant bee*hive*.

"Leave it to you to head for the source of heat," Jack said.

Though it wasn't in use, I could see that the small bark-covered structure was, in fact, a working sauna. Its low profile and domed shape was similar to the *savusauna* I'd visited at Jinky's grandmother's place. A pile of rocks and logs and the remains of a fire were consistent with a hot-rock process of generating steam.

"Sorry, folks." The ranger came up behind us, almost tumbling me out of my Timberlands. "We're closing up for the day."

"Do you use this for demonstrations?" I asked him.

"We have a staff member of Ojibwa descent who, on occasion, leads select researchers and small groups through a sweat lodge ceremony."

"Cool," I said.

"Actually, it's pretty darn hot," the ranger said, laughing at his own joke.

"It'd kill me," Jack whispered into my ear with a shudder.

A few minutes later, as Jack and I pulled out of the parking lot, I cast a glance backward toward the sweat lodge. *See you soon,* I thought.

# CHAPTER EIGHTEEN

Operation Vision Quest, OVQ, was a four-phase plan: breakout, stakeout, abduction, and break-in. I wore an all-black ensemble, as would be expected.

The breakout was from my own home, of course, and the easiest of the four. Having parked my car down the street earlier and claiming homework and aching muscles from the afternoon hike, I said an early good night to my mom and Stanley, who barely glanced up from their *Masterpiece Mystery* and shared popcorn bowl. It also helped that my mom was, in general, a respecter of the closed door.

Phases two and three were necessitated by the fact that Jinky didn't have a cell phone, something to do with an exorbitant international plan. Nor did her host family have Internet or a listed phone number. Besides, I feared that any overt contact—a call to the house or knock on the door—would alert a meddlesome Marik. I'd had no choice, therefore, but to insert steps two and three. It was a delicious irony that they would be payback for a similar adventure last year in Iceland, one in which I was the victim, not the mastermind.

The stakeout wasn't too difficult, either. In singling out Jinky's window, I'd caught an eyeful of a shirtless Marik and a teeth-removing old man. Jinky's, I therefore surmised, was the one with the closed curtains. A few stone throws—and dang if my aim and velocity weren't dead on—and two flashlight pulses to the dark bob of hair in the window, and OVQ was moving on to phase three.

OK, so abduction may have been a bit of an overstatement. It wasn't like I threw a bag over Jinky's head or anything. But it was me at the wheel and with all the answers as we drove out to Alpenstock.

"And Jack said it was the site of a prehistoric settlement?" Jinky asked.

"Yes."

"And the rocks, logs, and even the prayer bundles were all there?"

"Yes."

"Good and good, but we'll need to stop at the store."

"For what?" I asked.

"Cigarettes."

"Cigarettes! What? No way. We don't have time. Besides, there's no smoking in my car."

"I'm not going to smoke in your car. But it's a nonnegotiable point. We need to stop."

I pulled into the next gas station and flicked my fingers against the bottom of the steering wheel as Jinky clomped into the convenience store. It pinched that my captive had "nonnegotiable demands," but at least I was still in the driver's seat.

I parked on an access road some distance away from the front entrance. It necessitated a small hike but would call far less attention to our presence. I cut the engine and lights and was more than a little surprised to be on the receiving end of instructions.

"Once we're over that fence, I do all the talking," Jinky said. "You got that?"

*Uh, no.* It was *my* mission, after all.

"I hardly think —"

"Exactly," Jinky interrupted. "And what do you know about the hilly terrain in front of us and respect for spirit ancestors?" She didn't even let me guess before continuing. "We're about to set foot upon sacred land. Those look to be burial mounds. We will make our disruptions few and with a pureness of thought and action. And you will follow my lead in all things, OK?"

"OK," I said, after which I clamped my mouth shut and breathed bull-like through my nose. The pureness of thought didn't start until we were over the fence, which we weren't yet. And I couldn't wait to get on with the vision quest, phase four of *my* operation, because, besides hopefully providing some valuable information in saving Leira, an out-of-body experience would be preferable to stumbling behind Jinky in the black of night and abiding by *her* gag order.

Once over the fence, I did embrace a pureness of thought. I would have, anyway. From this approach, the place was *om*ing with energy. Jinky took a zigzag course to the site, remaining at the lowest points of the terrain and never once stepping across or onto any of the hills.

At the recreated village, she set to work building a fire and, eventually, heating a few select melon-size rocks. It took a long time. As much as I was willing to assist, I didn't know what to do, so I sat nearby thinking of my purpose in pursuing another vision quest. Of course, I wanted to protect Leira from Queen Safira. I also wanted to know if Brigid of Niflheim was a true threat. And, last, I sought to make sense of the brief message I'd relayed: "From the goddess Frigg, one seeks forgiveness and another offers life. Within them lies a solution."

Finally, Jinky motioned me over to the fire. She silently pulled a cigarette from her pocket. I came very close to breaking my vow of silence to enact a no-smoking policy, but when she tore the paper and crumbled the tobacco onto her palm, I stood down.

Approaching the fire, she said, "Great Spirit, to this sacred fire we offer a gift from the Great Mother. May the smoke carry forth our request for guidance." With this, she tossed the tobacco into the fire.

She next lit a prayer bundle of sage and performed the smudging ritual. When done, she passed it to me, and I copied her movements. I followed her to the entrance of the tiny tent, where we both removed our clothing. She went down to her bra and panties. I did the same, electing to retain my black cami as well. I was relieved when she made no sign of disapproval. We next ducked under the open flap and sat cross-legged facing the five hot stones that Jinky had already placed in the small center pit.

Pouring water onto the rock farthest away from the doorway, Jinky said, "We call to the Stone People Spirits of the West and welcome them." With a hiss, steam poured forth and the tiny space was bathed in a cloying mist. She next poured water on the stone in front of me. "From the Northern Spirits of Courage, we seek guidance."

More hot, hazy air filled the space, and I felt groggy and had a hard time focusing on even my hands in my lap.

I heard another blistering sizzle as Jinky said, "To the Eastern Spirits we offer our prayers." Another spit of roiling vapors shot forth as she continued, "And may the Southern Spirits heal our bodies and calm our minds."

My mind was definitely feeling calm — blissfully calm.

"And, finally, of our Spirit Grandfathers we ask for permission to walk with them in order to seek knowledge and wisdom."

With the word "wisdom," it felt as if — in a gush — I was particulate and floating upon the churning mist and through the open flap of the tent.

# CHAPTER NINETEEN

I opened my eyes to a crosshatch of branches; they swayed back and forth at the wind's command. A piney bouquet filled my nose, and leaves crunched under my back. Disorientation had me fearful. As my raspy intake of air leveled, my eyes adjusted to the mottled light.

At the sound of a bird, I sat up. Before me, upon a low branch, was a yellow-breasted lark. With my attention secured, he began a longer song. *Tee, tee, hoo. Tee, tee, hoo.* The flute-like warble was followed by a quick succession of *kerr, kerr, kerr, kerr, kerr.* The song was joyous and youthful. It thus seemed natural when a giggle erupted from behind me.

I turned in the direction of the voice. Again the lark chimed: *tee, tee, hoo.*

"Hoo," a voiced mimed, except that with a human inflection, I heard it as *Who*.

Before me the brushy undergrowth parted and a girl a year or two younger than me appeared. I was struck by her beauty: wavy honey-toned hair fell to her waist. Her gown was long and cinched with interwoven ties and she carried a basket. She gazed at me, her tawny brown eyes rounding with a mischievous expression before she released the foliage, after which I heard a scurrying retreat.

*Who is she? And what does she want?* The two questions formed on my lips as I struggled to my feet. I could hear her ahead of me, her feet alternately plodding on a dirt path or trampling crackle-dry leaves. I ducked into the scrub of bushes and set out in the direction of the sounds. When I crashed through a particularly dense hedge of thistle, thorns pricked at my skin and grabbed at my black cami. While rubbing at a long scratch on my forearm, I heard a rustling, this time from above. The girl sat in the scooped-out bowl of a tree's lower limbs. She held the basket upside down and proceeded to shake it with a frown as if disapproving of its empty condition. She reached up into the tree as if to pluck or pull at something, but instead her hand opened to reveal a crumpled ball of white paper. Smoothing it against her lap, she poked at three things. She then lifted the paper to show me three large words in a childish block print:

PARCEL DINKY PAL. Swinging her legs playfully, she reversed the paper, ripped it into careful squares, and released them. They rained down like confetti.

I picked one up; it was a *P.* As I stood there examining it, the girl nimbly hopped down from her post and took off running.

By then I was getting a little annoyed. It was obviously all a game to her. I dropped the scrap of paper and sprinted after her. I could play, too.

Once through another stand of trees, I chased her across a field. I ran full out, my thigh muscles clenching with every jarring thud. To my great disappointment, she was freakishly fleet of foot and had no difficulty with the increasingly rugged terrain. I, on the other hand, was losing sight of her. Soon the ground shifted under my feet, and I was splashing through a large puddle. No sooner was I out of that one when another dipped in front of me. I found myself skirting increasingly larger pools of water until before me stretched a swampy terrain, the kind of mossy marshland where everything — the sky, the water, the land — took on a jade-green tone.

I feared I'd lost my empty-basket-bearing, paper-tearing giggler until she stepped from behind a tall growth of rushes, pulling a small boat by its prow. She next leaned across it and patted its center bench in a get-in gesture.

I wasn't much of an oarsman, and I didn't yet have a

good read on the girl, but I'd come in search of answers, and she appeared to want to help me. I waded through the knee-high water, climbed into the small skiff, and took hold of the oars. I expected the girl to climb in, too; instead, and with surprising strength to go with her foot speed, she pushed me away from shore. All thoughts of her wanting to assist me were replaced with the worry that she wanted to get rid of me. Too late to turn back. Her shove had launched me into a fairly swift current. Once the rapids finally transitioned into a smooth run, I'd given up all hope of seeing the girl again. The waterway wrapped around gentle curves; hanging trees fanned long tendrils into the pea-green brook. The effect was like moving through one draped doorway after another, never getting a clear look at what lay ahead.

It was fairly relaxing, given my overall sense of caution and nervousness and the perfect setup for when, without warning, I plunged down a waterfall, a vertical drop of an organ-scrambling distance. I landed with a teeth-shattering splashdown and shot out of the boat like a popped cork. Surfacing out of breath and aching from the impact, I was still struck by the beauty of the scene. The natural pool was deep and so piercingly blue it shone as if faceted like a gemstone. And it was as warm as a hug.

I spied my boat, intact and upright, a few yards away, and dog-paddled toward it. While grasping it and taking a moment to recover, I heard a voice. In a sheltered grotto, not far from where I'd landed, there was a woman half-submerged in the water. What registered first was her hair. It was so silvery white it was opalescent, picking up the sparkling blue of the water and the fern green of the cavern's foliage. And her dress was fantastic, even though I had only a waist-up view. It was formfitting, willow-green, and made of such intricate glittery sequins that they seemed to ruffle in accordance with the movements of her lithe frame. What I'd first taken as beauty, however, was soon tainted by her behavior. A manic desperation contorted her features as she wailed, seemingly to herself. Upon closer inspection, I noticed before her, in what was otherwise a glassy pool of water, a small whirlpool. It was this swirling rotation that she was, for all appearances, addressing.

"I have no reason to doubt the success of this mission. The girl knows what's at stake. To break the pact would be to risk everything."

*Uh-oh.*

When, next, up from the spinning vortex, Brigid's icy voice rose, I felt the water ripple around me from my pounding heart.

"You and King Marbendlar are fools, Safira, if you think that girl will cooperate. She's headstrong and rash and too young and foolish to comprehend the enormity of the situation. You'd do best to throw in with me now."

*Safira? As in Queen Safira? OVQ* had just gone *OMG* scary. Dread pressed the oxygen from my lungs. "I do grow impatient," Safira replied, her voice carping and bitter. "Though I've dispatched one of my most loyal servants, I admit to misgivings. My forbearance will not last much longer."

"Together we have the power to revisit missed opportunities, to change the universe. Why do you not seize this opportunity?" Brigid was raging. The waters' rotation intensified, and an icy mist rose from its core.

"Should the pact fail, Marbendlar and I do not deny the necessity of such recourse. But until then—"

"You disappoint me," Brigid snapped. "It is my tolerance that is now tested. My offer does not stand for long."

With that, the vortex spun downward, creating a recessed bowl, until it snapped back to a glassy surface with a splash. Safira slapped at the water with such fury that the force of her action caused a tidal wave upon which my boat and I were borne like flotsam. I don't know how I managed to hold on to the side of the skiff, but I did, knowing probably it was my lifeline through this treacherous ordeal. The wave did eventually break, and I managed to catapult myself back into the boat. I lay on its hard, cold hull recovering and replaying the two queens' exchange.

Finally I coasted onto a sandy bank and was surprised

at the sight of a group of women at the base of a large, silver-trunked tree.

What on earth now? Until it jarred me like flying glass, this wasn't *earth* at all.

I slipped from the boat and padded across sand and then grass. The women took no notice of me even as the reeds and rushes swished at my feet.

The oldest of the group, a woman with long white hair, spoke with an air of authority. "Gather, maidens. I have need of your divine counsel." She perched on a velvety stool. Women assembled before her — nine, by my count — and sat at her feet.

"First my box, please, Fulla, for I have heavy burdens to store," the older woman continued.

A beautiful young woman with long golden braids stood. "Yes, Goddess Frigg."

*"Frigg" as in the queen of Asgard, surveyor of all the universe, and Odin's wife? Where the heck am I?*

The braided blonde, bearing an ornately carved box upon her open palms, approached Frigg. The box was opened. With bent heads, the two of them whispered for several minutes.

While they conferred, I studied the others. They were an interesting group: young and physically beautiful. Each was dressed uniquely and wore or bore an object of distinction. A very dark-skinned, raven-haired hulk of a woman wore a shield and carried a sword. Another, pale and freckled and boyish of figure, wore loose-fitting pants and strapped a leather satchel across her chest. A heavy book sat upon the long-skirted lap of a third, a full-figured redhead. A golden bowl rested in the elbow crook of a high-cheekboned, lively-eyed brunette who whispered with another of similar features and holding a mortar and pestle. Another clad in all black wore a veil from under which only the shadow of her face was visible. The final two were identical twins and seemed younger than the others. Their white-blond hair — a shade much like my own — matched their all-white gowns, over which they sported capes of white feathers.

Frigg and the one she called Fulla concluded their private conference, after which the box was snapped shut. The commanding Frigg then clapped her hands. "We proceed, for all is amiss, and I have need of your talents." The maidens drew closer to her. Suddenly, she cocked her head to one side, stating, "Silence! Did you hear that?" She stood abruptly from her stool. The women turned in unison to where Frigg was looking, right in my direction.

*Holy crap.* I froze. Had I done something? Made some kind of disturbance?

The women stood now, also peering in my direction and chattering nervously among themselves.

"Silence," Frigg said with a slash of her hand.

I heard it, too, then. It was a distant howl so eerie and discordant, my heart throbbed with an irregular beat. The sound of it—*caterwaul* defined—became unbearable. Frigg and her maidens scattered, disappearing behind tall grasses. I began to shiver and pulled my arms across my body, rocking back and forth and feeling as if I were dissolving into subparticles.

When I awoke, I was outside the sweat lodge, and Jinky had thrown my jacket over me on the ground.

"Are you all right?" she whispered.

"I don't know," I said through chattering teeth.

"Can you dress and walk?"

"I can try." My upper and lower jaws felt like slabs of cold marble slamming together uncontrollably.

She helped me with my clothes, even tying the laces of my boots for me. We trudged back in silence. I couldn't have talked if I'd wanted to. It was all I could do to hold my racking frame together and get one wobbly step to follow the next.

When we were finally over the fence, Jinky asked, "What happened to you?"

I bit my trembling lip. I knew I was playing with some powerful stuff. Whatever that shriek had been, it had jarred me to my marrow. If accepting Jinky's shaman services was a gray area, confiding in her was not: Marik had been clear on that point.

"I don't think I can say."

She gave me a look that could skin a rat. "You and Marik both, huh?"

I twitched my mouth to the side.

She stomped off in the direction of the car, lighting a cigarette and blowing back a huff of smoke. It probably wasn't good karma to piss off a shaman, even one in training; I had enough figures in my "foes" column. But there was nothing I could do about it right now. And I didn't care how mad Jinky was or how much I owed her; she still wasn't smoking in my car.

# CHAPTER TWENTY

The next morning was a grind. I was exhausted from two treks out to Alpenstock, and it was a Monday, never my favorite to begin with. OVQ had provided me with information; I was pleased with myself for initiating it, but it hadn't been quite as empowering as I'd hoped. Two things were for sure: Safira was getting restless, and Brigid was keen for a co-conspirator. Even if I resigned myself to Hulda's fullness-of-time mantra, it sure didn't sound like that was the two queens' MO. One thing I was in no hurry for was meeting up with the source of that ungodly howl. I couldn't get it out of my mind. Thinking about it made my stomach drop and my body spasm as if the temperature had suddenly plunged.

In Design, Jinky arrived late and took a seat in the back without ever glancing my way. She was always late and never one for eye contact or acknowledgments of any kind, but I couldn't help reading more into it on that occasion. She wouldn't tell Marik what we'd been up to last night, would she?

"Penny and Jinky, would you like to go next?" Ms. Bryant's voice tugged me from my reverie.

Jinky stood quickly, which surprised me. She was usually the eyes-on-desk, non-participatory type. Penny's jutting chin and tiny huff indicated that she had expected to be the team's spokesperson.

"The name of our business is the Sage Hand."

Jinky paused. I wondered at her timing; it seemed for dramatic effect, but that didn't seem her style. The small delay gave Ms. Bryant the chance to cock her head to the side in interest; Sage was, after all, her first name.

"It's a kind of New Age market," Jinky continued, "offering homeopathic remedies, books, artwork, jewelry, crystals, gems, and candles. Our slogan is 'Where open minds meet healing hands.'"

While Jinky spoke, Penny shuffled through the note cards in front of her as if trying to catch up.

"Very original," Ms. Bryant said with an appreciative nod of her head. "And definitely not on the list of suggestions. I look forward to your final project."

Judging by the vigor with which Penny tapped her

pencil against her notebook, she wasn't sharing Ms. Bryant's enthusiasm. I noticed that Jinky had nothing in front of her, not even a single sheet of paper, while Penny had now turned her stack of cards facedown. Not only had Jinky hijacked the project, Penny had put a lot of work into the original topic.

I was relieved when Ms. Bryant called on another team next. Marik and I weren't adequately prepared. We'd had a hard time agreeing on a business. My original idea of a hat store had met with little to no excitement from Marik, the guy who liked everything. Even Penny had rolled her shoulders when I'd run the idea past her. You'd think in a climate where protection from the elements was necessary that people would be keen to combine fashion and function. Guess not. Marik's idea, the one we'd settled on, was a toy store. Now *this* he did get excited about. I'd come up with a name, the Toy Box, but we'd still yet to create a slogan and had only the bare minimum of a proposal.

The bell rang, and I stuffed my things into my book bag. Abby and Marik walked down the aisle and through the space separating my desk from Penny's. Abby had her hand on his shoulder, pulling at him playfully.

"Wait up, goofball," she said, her hand now slipping into the crook of his elbow.

"Yes, Abril Julianna," he said, continuing his forward progress. Neither of them looked my way, which was fine by me. I didn't want Marik picking up on the dark circles under my eyes, my distracted state, or the goose-flesh that sprung to my arms every time that horrible screech came to mind.

Abril, I mused. I'd have guessed Abigail. It reminded me of the way Marik always called me Katla, never Kat. Furthermore, it spoke of a deeper friendship, one where he knew her full name, middle included.

I glanced at Penny. She didn't look any better than me. That little spark that had been growing in her like a hidden ember was gone. She didn't even seem all that mad at Jinky; she just appeared ashen and beaten down. And Abby had the glow that had gone out in Penny. I drummed my fingers across the desktop as I stretched to a stand. What was it about Marik that was so alluring? No one, not even Mean Dean, seemed immune. Even Jack was amused by the guy. And given his mission, my relationship with the guy should have been adversarial. But it wasn't. Not really. He was too damn pleasant all the time. A slump-shouldered Penny, not Penelopa, heaved herself out of her desk and shambled toward the door. I wondered what kind of homeopathic remedy the Sage Hand would have for a broken heart.

# CHAPTER TWENTY-ONE

Between my schoolwork, preparing for the move, working at the store, missing my busy college boyfriend, worrying about a two-queen scheme, and hearing bone-buckling howls in every dog bark, the week stampeded by. As proof, I had hoof marks on the side of my face when I woke up on Saturday.

A packing crew had spent the previous day boxing up our shockingly numerous belongings. That morning, a parade of moving dollies made its way out the front door, down the driveway, up the ramp, and into the huge van. Watching from a lawn chair on the front porch as the house emptied out, I felt oddly sad. It made me think of our move from California just over a year ago and of the fear and misgivings I had in leaving my home and neighborhood since birth. As if in counterpoint to this melancholy, Jack, in his old truck, rolled to a stop at the curb in front of the house. It was a nice reminder that things had a way of working themselves out.

This happy buzz was short-lived; a few minutes later my frenzied mom dispatched Jack and me to the new house with a mop, broom, and bucketful of old rags and cleaning supplies. "Kitchen first. No goofing off," was her directive. She was not in the mood for my "KP duty, no fun allowed, copy that," message into an imaginary walkie-talkie. At least Stanley thought it was a little funny, though he probably bought himself an extra hour or two on diaper patrol.

At our new-to-us, still-pink house, I pulled into the detached garage, a feature I knew I'd hate come winter. Jack and I unloaded the cleaning gear and were en route to the front door when a crazed and waving Marik came rushing toward us.

"Hi, there!" he called from the driveway.

So much for avoiding the guy now that we were neighbors.

"Hey, Marik," I said.

"Today's the day." Marik caught up with us on the steps to the porch.

"Yep. The moving van will be along soon. We're on

janitorial duty until it gets here." I hoisted the bucket and swung it from its handle.

"I can help." Marik pushed the sleeves of his denim shirt up over his forearms and made a muscle of his flexors.

"What's going on?" Jinky walked up behind Marik.

Regardless of my skittishness around both of them, a Tom Sawyerish scheme began to take shape in my head. Four people could certainly knock this thing out faster than two. "A cleaning party. One of those quirky American traditions."

Jinky jutted her chin forward. I figured she'd seen right through my ruse. Instead, she motioned with her head toward the house. "Let's go, then."

I led the way; Jack, behind me, was snorting with laughter. OK, so someone was onto me. Inside the foyer, I stopped and put down the supplies. The broom clattered to the floor. Jinky jumped as if poked.

"Are you OK?" I asked.

"This place," she said, circling the foyer with her head tilted upward. "What was this place?"

Jinky had not been in the car when Penny had told me about the Bleika Norn, the Pink Witch; her reaction, therefore, was without bias.

"Why?" I asked.

"I sense a presence," Jinky said. "Do you mind if I look around?"

Gack. The last thing I needed was for the rune-reading shaman in the crowd to go all poltergeist on me.

"I guess not," I said.

Jinky moved into the sitting room but quickly returned to the foyer. Moments later she started up the stairs.

"Wait for me," Marik said.

I was not about to let them out of my sight. I was on their heels; Jack swung me a confused look, but he, too, fell in line.

Jinky paused briefly on the landing of the second floor, but then—like some kind of whiff-frenzied bloodhound—made for the attic. My attic. *Just great.*

On the third floor, my new space, she walked from one dormer window to the other, touching the walls as she explored the area. Marik and Jack were quiet, as if hesitant to break her concentration. I, for the record, was more in too-freaked-to-speak mode.

"I've lost her," Jinky finally said, throwing her head back in frustration.

"Lost who?" I asked.

She gave me one of those pure-Jinky scowls and said, "She didn't exactly introduce herself."

What I wanted to sass back was: *My house. My ghost. Be nice or go home.* Instead, I asked, "How do you know it's a her?"

"By the smell," Jinky said.

"What smell? I don't smell anything," I said. Technically, I did smell mold and age and neglect, but those were hardly gender specific.

"It's gone now," Jinky said.

"What did it smell like?" I asked.

"Pink," Jinky said.

It was an awkward moment. Did I respond as if I believed that some kind of ghostly presence — one that reeked of some sensory short circuit — was a real possibility? Granted, the four of us were *Fringe*-cast material, but I was operating on so many secrets and cross-pacts and intentional misleads that I stood there with taboo tongue. It felt an awful lot like swallowing a bee, post-sting, which, by the way, I've experienced firsthand.

"My mom will kill me if she gets here and I haven't even started yet," I said, making for the stairs. If nothing else, my taskmaster mom was a good diversion.

The nice thing about a paranormal work crew was that they didn't mind getting their hands a little dirty. Jack stuck a wet rag and his head into a kitchen cupboard. Jinky took off with the Windex bottle. Marik swept the kitchen. I took a scouring pad to the kitchen sink.

"Now that we're neighbors," Marik said, "we'll be seeing a lot more of each other. We could walk to school together."

"I usually drive," I said.

"Even better," Marik said. "I can catch a ride."

I noticed his subject had been an *I* rather than a *we*.

"What about Jinky?" I asked.

"She gets picked up most mornings," Marik said. "I know when I'm not wanted."

I coughed and then sprinkled Ajax cleaning powder into the sink, creating a toxic cloud as cover for my reaction.

"Picked up by who?" I fanned the space in front of my nose.

"A friend," Jinky said, stealthing her way into the room. She grabbed a clean cotton rag. "Who's asking?"

"Katla can give me a ride to school now," Marik said, whisking a pile of dirt into the dustpan.

"I thought Abby drove you," Jinky said.

"Not necessary anymore." Marik rested the broom against the counter. "This is so much fun. What's next?"

The three of us — Jack, Jinky, and I — scrunched our brows in unison. Marik's enthusiasm for football games and downtown Walden were one thing, but grunt work?

"What?" Marik asked, picking up on our vibe. "Am I doing a bad job?"

"Oh, no, you're doing a fine job," Jack said. "So fine, in fact, I could just sit back and watch you. All day."

Jinky pursed her lips in an attempt to override a smile. I lifted my eyes quickly at Jack.

"Really?" Marik puffed up with pride. Pretty scary on a guy who was probably already an XXL. "That good?"

146

With a groan, the moving van pulled up front. I was glad for the distraction. Marik's zeal for even the most mundane of life's chores was odd. And soon someone besides me was bound to comment. Ask questions. Except that smart people, like Jack, Penny, and Ms. Bryant, seemed to find him sincere, if a bit of a goober. That kind of exuberance wasn't an easy act to pull off without coming across as an annoying cross between Ned Flanders and Forrest Gump. But Marik managed somehow.

Even Marik's spring-to-it-ness went down a notch once my mom arrived. She was in full drill-sergeant mode. And despite most of the workers being volunteers, she kept one and all busy hauling, heaving, and deboxing.

By early evening, we were sufficiently unpacked to eat takeout Chinese on plates — real, from-the-cabinet chinaware — while seated at the dining-room table. With the discarded to-go boxes pushed to the center of the table, I passed out our cookie-spun fortunes. The doorbell rang, and Stanley, the eager new man of the house, sprang up to answer it.

"Mine says, 'Adventure is around the bend,'" I said, ripping the paper in half.

"What does yours say, Marik?" my mom asked.

"'One's happiness spells another's discontent,'" Marik said.

"I think it's safe to assume Abby will be the happy one, even with losing her chauffeur job. She gets what she wants, I hear," Jinky said.

"Am I interrupting?"

I looked up to discover Penny standing with Stanley under the archway to the dining room. She looked hurt and embarrassed, with her eyes downcast and her arms clutching a foil-covered plate to her chest.

I looked quickly at the scene. For all appearances, it was a party she had not been invited to. I felt awful and popped to a stand.

"Of course not," I said. "Marik and Jinky saw the truck pull up earlier and just fell in step with the work crew."

"I made cookies as a housewarming gift, but I see you've already had dessert," Penny said, eyeing the cookie wrappers scattered across the table.

She had to have heard what Jinky said about Abby getting what she wants: Marik, in this case. Penny's colorless cheeks and halting tone hinted at as much. Crap. Why had Jinky said that? The strength of feeling was on Abby's side. To Marik, we were all a source of curiosity and entertainment, I guessed, one as interchangeable as the next.

"So, I told you about my new room, right?" I asked.

"Yeah," Penny said, her voice still faltering.

"Let me show you. It's the best thing about this place."

Behind me on the stairs, I could hear the *fwomp fwomp* of her Keds, as if they too had had the air let out of them.

Once we were up in the space, *my* space, I finally sensed a slight shift in her mood.

"So this *is* cool," she said, looking around.

Even with a bare mattress, no curtains, and a jumble of boxes, the space oozed potential.

I didn't believe in letting things fester; my approach, like stain removal, was to treat immediately. "You're not mad, are you?"

"No. I guess not. It just kind of looked like a party."

"Party? Hardly. I scrubbed toilets, and Jack went after some serious cobwebs in the basement. And Jinky and Marik coming over was entirely spontaneous. I mean, seriously, why they even volunteered is beyond me."

"I would have helped if you'd asked," Penny said.

"Is that what this is really about? About missing out on washing windows and sweeping floors? Or was it the company?"

Exhaling, Penny's head dropped forward. "I'm pathetic, aren't I?"

"No. Of course not."

"It's useless, anyway. I heard what Jinky said. It

149

wasn't a complete surprise, I mean, it's obvious that Abby has her hooks in him. And she pretty much *does* get what she wants. And no big secret whose name she'll be feeding to the Asking Fire."

The Asking Fire. Ugh. A local tradition that took place the Saturday prior to Homecoming. Girls fed the name of their hoped-for date to a supposedly mystical bonfire. OK, so it had kind of worked for Jack and me last year, but I didn't believe there was enough magic in all the realms to transform Marik into the right guy for Penny.

"He's an exchange student," I said. "Temporary. So maybe it's best."

"I know, but I can't help it. I really like the guy."

Footsteps on the stairs brought the conversation to an end.

"Your mom sent me up with a load," Jinky said, entering with a laundry basket full of my sheets and blankets. She set the linens on my mattress, all the while surveying Penny oddly.

"I should read your runes," she said finally.

"My what?" Penny asked.

"Your runes," Jinky said. "I mentioned them briefly during our project summary. They're an ancient system of divination. In the right hands, they have magical properties: fortune-telling and psychic knowledge."

"Uh. No, thanks," Penny said with the kind of

hesitation that would indicate that she saw this on par with drawing pentagrams on the floor or beheading a chicken. She was probably also still smarting from having the project topic snatched away from her like a cat toy on a string.

"Don't worry; it doesn't hurt a bit," Jinky said. "And I won't charge you, because I sense an important turning point in your life, one you should be prepared for. Kat, do you have your runes?"

Penny looked at me like Jinky had just asked me for my wand and spell book.

"They're a bag of stones I got from Jack's grandmother," I said to Penny by way of explanation. I turned to Jinky. "As if I could find them in this mess."

"Next time I'll bring my own," Jinky said, running her thumb along her bottom lip. "This could be very interesting."

Again Penny's eyes flared wide. The sound of my mom calling from the first-floor landing brought all talk of fortune-telling to an end, but I couldn't help but notice that Penny lingered, following behind me and Jinky as if taking an opportunity to view us with fresh eyes.

## CHAPTER TWENTY-TWO

There were times when my mom's work ethic was tolerable, beneficial even. Sunday after the move was not one of those occasions. She was in full manic mode with a goal of being "out of boxes" by sundown.

I was relieved to have a shift at the store as a hall pass on another day of labor and even a little sorry for Stanley, who gave me a small help-me bulging of his eyes as I headed out the door.

I opened up as scheduled but was surprised when, a half hour later, a slightly listing Afi came through the door.

"Sorry I'm late," he said.

"You're not," I replied. "You're a day early, actually. You had today off. Remember?"

Afi scratched at his chin. "Nope."

"You wanted to get the leaves raked up in your yard."

"Damn things," Afi said. "It's like this every . . ."

"Fall," I finished for him when he appeared to have lost his train of thought.

"Just a small one," Afi said. "Someone moved my ottoman again."

I blinked my eyes. At this rate, we'd need orange cones and a traffic cop for all the detours this conversation was taking.

"You fell?"

Afi backhanded the air in front of him. "Pshaw. And don't go blabbing to that mother of yours. She'll make a fuss, and I don't want it or need it." A hacking cough punctuated his spirited remarks.

I might have pursued the topic except a beat-up green truck rolled to a stop in one of the parking spots out front. Jack.

I bounced out the front door, meeting him as he planted his old work boots on the pavement. "This is a surprise," I said. "I thought you had to work today."

"I do. And am." He pecked me on the cheek. Afi's presence at the window was surely the reason for such a chaste greeting. "I'm out on deliveries."

I followed him to the rear of his truck, where he lowered the back gate.

"That's no fun," I said. And judging by the load in the back of his cab, he'd be at it for a long time.

"It never is." He grabbed a bushel by the handles and started for the store. I scurried ahead and opened the door.

"Good morning," Jack said, dipping his head to Afi.

"Working on it," Afi said, snatching an apple off the top of Jack's delivery and cracking into it with a loud crunch. "Yep. Best darn apples in the county."

The compliment made Jack smile, sparking the blue in his eyes and tautening the ropy muscles in his neck. "Thank you. My dad never tires of hearing it."

"Tell you what I'm tired of," Afi said. "That yappy dog next door barking all hours of the day." He took off for the front of the store, muttering something about a muzzle.

"Afi's in rare form today," Jack said.

"Tell me about it. He wasn't even scheduled to work. I think he has his days confused. And apparently he fell over that footstool in front of his chair. Should I be worried?"

"Nah," Jack said. "It's clear what his problem is."

"What?"

"He hadn't had his apple-a-day."

I gave him a look. "Says the apple peddler."

"True. And I'll be peddling these things until at least three. What time do you get off?"

"Three, as it just so happens."

"I have homework but could get away for an hour or two," he said, closing the space between us.

"About two hours is all it should take," Afi said, startling us both and reversing Jack's course.

"What should take?" I asked.

"Raking up leaves at my place. I sure do appreciate the offer." Afi clutched at the small of his back. "After that fall, I'm not sure I'm up to all that bending." His eyes, I noticed, were particularly glassy at that moment.

"Of course," Jack said. "You shouldn't be out there. We'd be happy to help." With his "we," Jack gave me a small roll of his shoulders.

"Thank you kindly," Afi said, taking another chomp of the apple and heading back up front.

Passing me, he lifted his eyebrows. Had Jack and I just been conned? If so, I had to hand it to the old codger; he'd managed to turn yesterday's dupers into dupees. Or just maybe there was something to that old apple-a-day wives' tale, after all. Either way, Afi looked a little more sure-footed as he walked off.

I wasn't too put out. A couple hours in Jack's company on a gorgeous fall day sure beat returning to the sweatshop my mom was currently running. The afternoon had potential. But I still didn't know if I should worry about Afi, scold him, or thank him.

# CHAPTER TWENTY-THREE

"We have a breaking story," Penny said, getting our Monday lunchtime journalism meeting under way. "It seems that our school board and Pinewood's are voting tonight on the consolidation proposal. If the measure is passed by both boards, it goes to voters in November."

The room erupted in chatter and cries of surprise. Although Abby's speech on the first day of school had hinted that the topic was still hot, I'd hoped that my father's factory and the new businesses along Main Street had brought enough jobs to the area. While there had been a dozen or so new kids last winter, even I knew it obviously wasn't enough to offset the two schools merging.

"So what does that mean for us?" someone asked.

"It's not good news," Penny said. "The two districts hired a consulting firm whose newly released report favored retaining Pinewood's high-school building and closing ours."

Jeers and boos ensued. I had always known it was an unpopular topic but was still surprised by the level of animosity.

"We need to cover this," Penny said, quieting everyone down with waves of her arms. "Plus, it will look good to fill the seats with supporters of Norse Falls. Let's get out there on Facebook and Twitter to spread the word on the meeting. And then tomorrow we'll get to work on a special issue. I expect to see you all tonight. Seven p.m."

As the fashion columnist, I hardly thought my presence was required. Plus, I was a senior; the earliest the actual merge could take place was next fall. "You mean those who do news stories, right?" I interjected.

"Everyone," Penny said with an odd glint in her eye. "We're going to attack this from a variety of angles. And if it means touting our cheerleader uniforms over theirs, we'll do it. Mark my words: If there's going to be a building put out of service, it isn't going to be ours."

Jinky coughed, a big, hacky bark stripper.

The bell rang, and I gathered my things, turning a shoulder on Penny. She'd been a little harsh on me. She, of all people, knew I wasn't a hard-boiled gonzo journalist like her. She'd been the one to drag me into it, after all.

Jinky waited until the room had emptied, leaving only Penny, me, and her. "So now I have to read your runes more than ever."

"What? Why?" Penny asked.

"You finished with a prophecy," Jinky said.

"Hardly a prophecy," Penny said. "More marching orders. If we get our community rallied, we get more voters to the polls. It's not too late to turn the tide on this thing."

"I don't know," Jinky said, tugging on her eyebrow ring; the effect looked like a caterpillar inching across her face. A skewered caterpillar, that is. "I can't put my finger on it, but there's an interesting aura about you."

I knew I had to slash the tires on this runaway conversation. After Jinky read *my* runes, I ended up slapping on a selkie suit and facing down the Snow Queen and her Frost Giant henchmen.

"You want me to pick you up for the school-board meeting?" I asked Penny in a deliberate subject-changing ploy.

"Sure," she said.

"What time should I be ready?" Jinky asked.

I pursed my lips, exhaling through my nose.

"We need to get there early," Penny said. "I want

seats up front and I want Jinky getting arrival shots of the crowd. You guys pick me up at six-thirty."

"I'll be ready," Jinky said. She moved to leave, but then pivoted. "Your runes or mine, Katla?"

"Neither," I said. "We'll be too busy tonight."

"Another time, then," she said, hitching her bag over her shoulder.

*Not if I can help it,* I thought.

"Do you think Marik would want to come?" Penny asked, catching up with me as I headed out the classroom door.

"I wouldn't think so," I said. "He's an exchange student. Local politics are hardly his business." Besides, until I figured out what Frigg had to do with it all, what that shriek was, and how to get out of my pact with Safira before Brigid enlisted her, I was trying to keep Marik at bay, not worming into every little facet of my world.

"You're probably right," Penny said, her eyes focusing on the ground. "I just thought it might be something interesting for him to see, you know, from a visitor's perspective. It wouldn't hurt to ask him, would it?"

I didn't answer, hoping she'd drop it. I'd be busy enough coming up with my own angle on the developing story and keeping Jinky's runes in her pocket without having to worry about Marik.

# CHAPTER TWENTY-FOUR

When Marik scrambled into my car with Jinky, I knew, somehow, that the evening was going to be about more than school consolidations.

Penny swallowed a smile as she gladly hopped out of the front seat and squeezed into the back with the titanic-size merman. She scooched back in the seat, pulling the seat belt across her white sweater, which made her boobs look big, bigger than I ever remembered them being.

On the short drive to the high school — Norse Falls wasn't large enough to support a separate administration building — Penny passed out index cards. "I did some research and put together a few questions for the board."

"Very impressive," Marik said. "You're quite the go-getter."

In the rearview mirror, I could see Penny squirm with pleasure.

"I'm to ask if they were aware that one study shows that post-merge stress levels among both teachers and students approached PTSD levels," Marik said. I could hear the flick of his finger against the card. "What's PTSD?"

"Post-traumatic stress disorder," Penny said. "It's the clinical name for anxiety following a highly stressful event."

"What an amazing concept," Marik said. "Does that really happen? Are people truly so overcome with emotion that it has a lasting effect?"

"Uh. Of course," Penny said.

"Incredible," Marik replied.

I took another peek in my rearview mirror. I expected to find Penny eyeing Marik like he was nuts. As usual, she—like everyone else—accepted his unabashed novelty for what should be both routine and obvious as a kind of Marikism.

At a red light, I picked up my card from the center console. I was to ask about the impact longer commute times would have on farm families, given that many of these students had obligations before and after school. Of course she had picked a farm question for me, and I felt a stab of panic. Having worked two after-school hours

161

at the store and whipped off a Spanish assignment, I'd neglected to return Jack's text message from earlier.

We were indeed early for the meeting. While Penny got us seats up front, I tried to call Jack. No luck. It wasn't like we had plans for tonight; our weekday schedules were too busy for that kind of couples' glue. We did, generally, return messages, however. I dropped into a folding metal chair next to Penny. Marik took the seat next to me, leaving Jinky the seat on the other side of Penny.

I had the school board figured out the minute the meeting began. Their tactic of defusing the larger-than-normal, ready-to-grumble crowd was to numb us to death. Talk about agony. And never again would I proclaim Mr. Harper, the guidance counselor at Norse Falls High, the world's most tiresome orator. The president of the school board spoke with the kind of thrumming drone that the CIA should clearly consider using as a torture device. The budget reports were all doom and gloom and hardly helped with the overall heavy atmosphere.

Finally, the meeting got around to the topic of consolidation. Things got under way with a to-date summary of events: after the initial approval by both school boards to go forward with the merger consideration, a joint committee had been formed. A consulting firm was then hired, and their newly released report did indeed find in favor of retaining Pinewood's building.

This news triggered a wave of murmurs and grumbles rippling over the crowd.

The board finally opened things up for questions and comments. Penny was the first to approach the free-standing microphone set up in the center aisle. Looking around, I was surprised to see Jack leaning against a side-wall with other latecomers. I took advantage of the short break to join him.

"I didn't know you were coming," I said.

"I texted you."

"Just to call you, not to tell me you were coming here. I figured you'd be busy."

"Never too busy when it comes to the future of our town."

Penny was given the go-ahead to address the board, and the room fell silent.

"I better get in line," I whispered. "Penny has assigned me a question."

Jack held me back with his arm.

"What?" I asked.

"Humor me. I'm just enjoying the moment."

"Huh?"

"You're on our side now. All in." He let me go with a small squeeze. My arm buzzed where he'd touched me.

Taking my place at the back of the line for the micro-phone, I couldn't help but reflect on my journey on this issue. When newly arrived, I'd taken a progress-minded, bulldoze-the-downtown stance. But now the idea of change scared the panties off me. And there was a lot more at stake than our high school. And you bet I was all in.

# CHAPTER TWENTY-FIVE

With all the mayhem that was my daily grunt, the very notion of the Asking Fire should have triggered apathy in me, at most. It had been nearly two weeks since my vision quest, and, although I was admittedly in denial over the Safira-Brigid conspiracy, I'd dearly hoped for a little more clarity on Frigg's involvement. Nor was I any closer to a placement on behalf of Jaelle. It was all on my mind constantly. A possible collusion of the first two was still a source of an unsettling chill, and the latter simply wouldn't come. Surprising even me, I was far from indifferent about the fire. I had been looking forward to it, in fact, and hoping it would be a little letup from the beat down of my looming bargain with Safira.

As Jack and I trekked hand in hand to the remote location, I felt as gooey as marshmallow fluff. It was a postcard-worthy evening. The Indian-summer temps provided a warm — almost charged — quality to the air, to the surrounding clusters of pines, and even to the buzz of the cicadas. The dirt trail was lit by hanging lanterns and cut in and out along the swaying bulk of a dense woods. As we approached the clearing and the already-crackling blaze, I flushed with the memory of last year's events. Jack and I had arrived as head-butting strangers but had departed as a Homecoming couple. And the fact that someone as grounded as Penny would suspend disbelief for the tradition of a magical fire steeped the evening with even more of a mystical glow.

I spotted Penny standing off to the side of the blaze with the camera-in-hand Jinky; Marik — praise be — was nowhere to be seen. As we approached, I noticed an unusual bulge in Penny's jacket pocket. I patted it, expecting mittens or a scarf or something else of a bulky nature. With my touch, the pocket crunched.

"What do you have in there?" I asked.

Penny looked quickly at Jack and Jinky, who had struck up a photography-related chat. "Papers for the fire."

As the full extent of this pronouncement — including its environmental impact — grew, my eyes widened. "How many?"

"A lot," she said, biting back her lips.

I had only been to the Asking Fire once before, but, as I understood it, girls fed the name of a single guy to the fire. Single as in one piece of paper. It looked like Penny had the equivalent of a shredded phone book in her pocket.

"Not taking any chances, are you?"

"I guess you could say that," Penny said.

The screech of a microphone filled the air. Abby, as class president, was ready to get things under way. I followed Jack and Penny to a spot near the temporary stage; Jinky took off with her camera.

By now, I had endured a few of Abby's speeches. She used the upper register of her voice at all times and paused with an "umm" every third or fourth word, but we all got the message: On Monday, Homecoming-dance tickets would go on sale and voting for king and queen would begin. I noticed she looked to a specific spot in the crowd when she trilled the word "king." Glancing in that direction, I noticed Marik's shaggy head.

Abby then got down to the business at hand, giggling and sending her already high voice into chipmunk range.

"Should your mind be open
And your heart be true,
Then let the fire's magic
Make a match for you."

Of course, I'd been through it all before, but it still smacked of high fructose to me.

"So are you going to ask for me again?" Jack said, bumping me with his hip.

"Again?" I said, heading toward the table where the paper and pencils were set out. He followed me, his left thigh jostling against my right. "We both know that was a mix-up; you're just lucky it all turned out so well." I chose a pale yellow slip, cupped my hand over my work, and jotted down Jack's name.

"Let me see," he said.

I folded the paper and slipped it into my pocket. "Against the rules." I had no idea if it was, but I liked the pout it produced in him. It made his lips even more irresistible. I gave him a quick kiss and then jogged off for the fire. He followed slowly, affecting a little swagger. OK, so we had our corny moments, too.

I found Penny at the edge of the fire. She was dropping papers by the fistful into the flames. Sparks shot up into the air. I hardly knew what to say. This time last year, she'd asked for Jack; we all knew how well that one turned out for her. I was worried she'd be disappointed again. The rumor mill had Abby and Marik as a predicted matchup. I noticed Abby and Shauna just a few girls down from us releasing their chits of paper. Abby gave hers a kiss before letting it be swept away by the wind. Beyond them, to my surprise, I noticed Jinky.

She, too, had thrown something into the fire. Well, well, maybe it *was* magic, after all. Or just a trickster. I'd have given my knee-high suede moccasins to know who she'd requested.

Jack pulled me away from the flames by my waist. "So is it a date?"

"Dude, you're stuck with me for more than just a date."

The band's electric guitarist ran through a few warm-up chords and segued into a first tune. It seemed that the evening was progressing as planned, but then a kid with a picket-style sign jumped onstage. I didn't know his name, but I recognized him from school.

"Before we move on to the entertainment," he said in a booming voice, "a few words about the proposed merger."

The band stopped, the drummer the last to sound a few jarring beats. Judging by their confused looks, this was not a scripted interruption. I noticed that more kids with signs had appeared, crowding the area close to the stage. Obviously, some preparation had been made.

Jack, Penny, and I took a few steps forward. I figured it was a heartfelt display of school spirit.

"We won't sit back and watch our community get the shaft," the kid said.

"Who is that guy? What's going on?" I whispered to Penny.

"His name is Carter," she said. "I had heard he'd organized some kind of task force. I guess this is it."

"We're going to take action," Carter said, working himself up.

His fellow sign bearers urged him on with impromptu "Yes, now" and "You know it" shouts of agreement.

Watching him, I felt there was something about the Carter kid that felt off. His eyes were glassy and he was swaying a little onstage. I wondered if he was drunk, or if it was a nervous kind of energy from speaking in public. I took a moment to study his sign. An addendum to a neatly blocked SAVE OUR SCHOOL was a sloppily scrawled DESTROY PINEWOOD. I wondered at the wording. Pinewood would be our opponent at the Homecoming game; the rivalry was fierce. *Destroy* was definitely the kind of word a football team threw around with a harmless bravado. Still, one of our schools could have a wrecking ball in its future.

"Who's with me on sending Pinewood a message, one that shows just how much we like their school?"

*Uh-oh.*

I looked around. There was a strange energy coursing through the crowd. Kids were rapt with attention, the kind of attention no teen gives anything that isn't hooked up to a game system. And from under my thin-soled moccasins, the earth was drumming. I had to hop from one foot to the other to relieve the vibrations. It wasn't like what I'd felt over at Jack's place; this energy had a charge or live current. And more and more kids were pressing in close to the stage. Penny scooted forward. Jinky, I could see at the perimeter, was snapping photos. With Marik at her side, Abby had moved in also. She, too, had a strange glaze over her eyes. Marik, I noticed, looked at her oddly.

"I say we deliver part one of our message tonight," Carter yelled.

Another kid vaulted onto the stage to join Carter. His sign, which he jabbed up and down, said, HELL NO, WE WON'T GO. He began chanting this while removing a lighter from his pocket. With the Bic, he lit a corner of the poster-board sign. It caught fire, but it was a wimpy little thing. The crowd took up his cry. Abby had pushed her way to the very front of the crowd and was pumping her arms like it was some kind of political rally. As the crowd kept chanting, I felt the wind pick up. Except this was no ordinary breeze. It was more of a blast, something in the gale family with an icy bite.

The kid's sign, fueled by the gust, blazed now. Delighted with its sudden ignition, he jumped off the stage and jogged over to the Asking Fire, into which he pitched his sign. Other sign carriers followed suit, jettisoning their placards into the fire. Its flames leaped higher and higher, fueled by both the continued swirling drafts of air and the newly added kindling. People danced around the fire now. Abby and Shauna were two of the revelers. The scene was disturbing to me somehow. Their movements were graceless and primitive, more war dance than waltz.

The visiting wind rushed among the throng, lifting hair, scattering leaves, twigs, and scraps of colored paper about like confetti. I had spent enough time around my Jack Frost–descended boyfriend to know the difference between an ill wind and one of his inadvertent displays. This wasn't his, which made it all the more frightening.

"Something's wrong," I said to Jack, pulling on his arm. "Everyone's acting so strange. Like they're whipped into some kind of frenzy."

As if proof to my point, some kid let go a rebel yell that could have toppled Tarzan from his treetop. More kids pressed closer to the fire. Their faces, burnished by the pulsing glow, were grotesque and distorted. Some seemed hyperalert; others spun about giddy and dazed, while a few had a feral-eyed look of savagery. This latter group, joining the fire moshers, was the most troubling. I sensed it was all too sudden and too intense, as if some kind of mob mentality had taken hold. And *taken* was an important distinction. Kids I knew to be quiet and respectful were rushing about as if just waiting for a call to action. The only two who seemed unaffected were

Penny and Marik, who had her by the arm as if keeping her out of harm's way.

"We need to do something," I continued, tugging insistently at Jack's sleeve.

He shook his head as if he himself was struggling with some kind of confusion. "You're right," he said, his voice tight. "Something's very wrong."

"We'll meet up in their parking lot," I heard one of the guys yell. "Bring whatever you can find: sticks, rocks, and kindling."

I grabbed Jack's shoulder. "You have to do something now."

"Like what?"

"You know."

We both knew that he hadn't used his weather-wielding abilities since our showdown with Brigid in Niflheim. On earth, it had been since the record-setting snowfall that had led to Jacob's death and summoned Brigid. Not surprisingly, he considered his powers volatile and dangerous.

With comprehension, his face darkened. "That's not a good idea."

"I don't think you have a choice," I said, tightening my grip on him. Two kids ran past us with lit torches made from branches lashed together with vines.

Pulling away from me, Jack turned and rounded his

shoulders. Even from behind, I could sense the effort it required. His back muscles strained against the cotton of his light T-shirt, and I could hear him gnar with pain, though he tried to muffle it.

Within moments, the sky churned above us and jet-black clouds folded one into another until they were an angry boil. A slash of branched lightning rent the clouds and a whiplike crack of thunder was followed by a sustained boom as the ground shook. Fat drops of rain fell as if thrown by buckets, and it became very cold, very fast.

The scene was altered instantly. The bonfire hissed as if recoiling like a snake. Kids yelled and screamed, but their reaction, to my relief, was one of surprise. The band, waiting in the wings of the stage, scurried about, stowing their equipment. Cups of punch lined up on the refreshments table were toppled; open boxes of sugary donuts turned to a doughy mash. The remaining slips of pastel paper were plastered to the table or trodden underfoot. I watched as groups of kids grabbed their blankets and belongings and made a dash for the parking lot. With them, I sensed something else shrink and retreat as if it, too, were caught off guard. The distemper that had pervaded the area was dissipating.

Looking around, I saw Penny and Marik still standing off to the side. They appeared dazed; Marik, especially, seemed frozen with fear or shock.

When Jack finally turned to face me, his face was gaunt and hollow.

"What the hell was that?" he asked.

"I'm not sure." I shielded my eyes from the downpour. "But I have my suspicions."

"What suspicions?"

Again, I never knew what was privy only to my pact with Marik or, alternately, what qualified as preexisting information, thus open to discussion. Jack had been with me in Niflheim. He'd seen how enraged Brigid had been at our escape. He had to have his own concerns about her revenge. Furthermore, Marik had shrunk from tonight's small riot and still seemed shaken by the turn of events. Had it been of Safira's making, Marik would be aware, if not in cahoots.

"Brigid," I said, my voice uneven.

"Brigid!" He jabbed the word back at me as if rejecting it.

"I have reason to suspect that she'd like to revisit the events of last spring," I said, hesitating, "and you know I thought there was something odd about the sinkhole at your place. And what I felt coursing through the crowd tonight, it was an ill will, something cold. My guess is that she's having a hard time getting through. Whatever we did to close the portals, it's holding."

"For now," Jack said.

*Until she has help,* I thought.

Penny sloshed her way over to us. "What are you guys waiting for? You're getting soaked." She stood a few feet away, oblivious to the tension between us. "A bunch of us are going over to the Kountry Kettle. Should we save you seats?"

I looked around. Already the area was down to a few soggy members of the cleanup crew. The never-to-be-heard band was loading their gear into a van.

Jack swung a to-be-continued look my way, but with it, the smallest nod of his head.

"Sure," I said, "but we probably won't stay long." I was cold, and wet, and weirded out, but no way was I going to be able to sleep tonight unless I was sure that whatever had infected those kids was gone.

# CHAPTER TWENTY-SIX

The drive over to the Kountry Kettle was tense. Two keyed-up superpowers in a confined space makes for a highly charged atmosphere; I was surprised we didn't throw an air bag.

"Do you really think it's her?" Jack asked, finally breaking the silence.

"I do. We left her furious."

Jack didn't answer, but he pressed down on the accelerator.

"I hate to say it," I continued, "but I think we need to consider recent events as failed attempts to break through."

"One strong enough to pull the ground from under our feet, another vile enough to turn a few ramped-up kids into an angry mob . . . What's next?"

"Who knows? A part of me hopes she's out of ideas." ("And friends," I muttered, turning to the window.) Besides, no one ever said *hope* was the same as *belief.*

We didn't speak again until we were inside the Kountry Kettle. Looking around the restaurant, I anxiously scanned the place for signs of trouble. It had never settled well with me that *kettle* was a synonym for *caldron.* Knowing that my own clan was a brand of white witch, I'd always wondered about the genesis of the name. And Norse Falls was obviously some kind of special place, vortex, or whatever. There were days when my para-radar was triggered by some Joe Blow on the street. It made me scribble garlic onto random shopping lists and accessorize even T-shirts with chunky crosses. My fears were allayed; it was the usual scene, one where the school divided into its various cliques. From first appearances, there didn't seem to be anything *brewing* following the Asking Fire, though quite a few of the kids looked and smelled like wet dog. I passed Abby and Shauna's table, where they were cozily munching fries and sipping sodas. Spying Penny in a booth at the back, I braced myself for bad news.

Jack slid in next to Jinky, and I took the spot beside Penny.

"That was an Asking Fire to remember," I said, slipping a menu out of the tabletop holder.

"I'll say," Penny said, biting her lips back to keep from smiling.

I eyeballed her, dropping my menu; I already knew I was going to get apple pie à la mode. "Spill."

"I'm going to the dance," Penny said.

I couldn't help it; my eyes flickered to the front of the restaurant, where Abby was still, for all appearances, happy as could be. "Who?"

"Who do you think?" she said, as if it was a dumb question.

"Uh." Again my gaze roamed. "Does it start with an *M*?"

She finally unleashed the smile she'd had such a hard time controlling.

"Then where is he?"

"He took off. He wasn't feeling good. I, on the other hand, feel great." Penny said. Her smile had broadened; she'd have marionette lines if she didn't dial it down soon.

Jack and Jinky were discussing burger toppings. He recommended pepper jack to Jinky, who was firm in her conviction that Americans made cheese about as well as they made beer.

I took advantage of the moment to whisper to Penny, "So when did this happen?"

"On the dash for the parking lot through the pouring

rain." She lowered her voice and turned her head to my ear. "It was the fire; I'm sure of it. He said I hadn't turned ugly like the others."

Jack and I hadn't acted *ugly*, either, but it wasn't like I needed affirmation from Marik.

"We need to come up with a few dresses by next Saturday," Penny continued.

"A few?" A *couple* meant two, so a *few* was more than that.

Penny motioned across the table with her head. "Jinky needs one."

"I need one *what*?" Jinky asked.

"Homecoming dress," Penny said.

"Oh. Cool. Who are you going with?" I asked Jinky.

"It's a surprise," Penny said with a lift of her shoulders.

So this evening was getting weirder and weirder.

"Let's check out that vintage clothing store in Walden," Penny continued. "They have some nice stuff."

"I'm not wearing some dorky ball gown," Jinky said.

I sighed with relief. The world was not off its axis and careening through space. Though there was an alternate realm that I was pretty sure would like to see us roll.

# CHAPTER TWENTY-SEVEN

Arriving home, I realized I'd been mistaken in thinking all was temporarily OK with the world. I found my mom pacing the kitchen floor with a distraught Leira in her arms. According to my mom, Leira had been fussy all evening and hadn't eaten since breakfast. Stanley had already been on the phone twice with the doctor. They were in wait-and-see mode for now, but I noticed an overstuffed diaper bag at the back door.

I offered to give my mom a break while she ran out to the pharmacy for soy formula, which the doctor had suggested they try. Once I had Leira settled into her reclining rocker and she had calmed enough for her sobs to transition into a kind of blubbery hiccup, Stanley snuck off to his office to Google WebMD. Again.

Alone with Leira, I placed a hand on her birdlike chest. Her heartbeat was more fluttering than pounding, and her tissue-thin skin felt as dry as onion skin.

"Hang in there, sister," I said. "We'll get this figured out; we'll get it all figured out."

Leira looked up at me with her more-purple-than-blue eyes. Tears clung to her lashes and her thin bottom lip trembled. In moments like these, I perceived a wisdom beyond her years. Given everything I knew about the provenance of souls, it made sense. Did she remember her time as an essence? Was it preferable to the rough start she'd had in bodily form? And did she know anything of my role in it all?

"You know I'd do anything for you, right?" I continued.

She stretched, bringing her fist to her mouth in a self-pacifying gesture. She continued to fuss and fidget and spill fresh tears. I wondered at my mom's patience and strength through all that Leira had already endured. But how much more could she take? It was a question I didn't want the answer to—one that I made a fresh resolve to *never* find out the answer to. I was relieved when I heard the jangle of my mom's keys as she came in the back door.

182

Though I was exhausted after the turmoil of the day, I couldn't sleep. I continued to hear Leira crying, which meant—if nothing else—that she hadn't taken a turn for the worse, necessitating a trip to the emergency room. I dedicated the next few hours to prayer and positive thought.

# CHAPTER TWENTY-EIGHT

The next morning, Sunday, I was exhausted after a fitful night of sleep. I flopped into a kitchen chair.

"How's Leira?" I asked a nose-in-book Stanley.

"The good news is that she and your mom are sleeping."

"What's the bad news?"

"They were up all night."

I stopped feeling sorry for myself.

"What did the doctor say?"

"That sleep is a very good sign, but if she doesn't eat today, she needs to go to the emergency room."

"Oh," I said. "Sleep is definitely the good news."

Stanley situated his bookmark, closed his book, and got up to refill his coffee.

I looked at the title to his latest read: *The Painted Ladies*. On the cover was a row of Victorian houses in pastel hues of lavender, powder blue, mint green, and pink.

"Pretty racy title," I said, turning the book to face me. The name tugged at my subconscious; I heard the snap of neurons firing.

Stanly chuckled as he dropped a glug of half-and-half into his cup. "Just getting a few ideas on how to restore this old lady." He sat back down across from me, resting his steaming mug on a coaster. Leaving the book facing me, he fanned the pages; they shuffled like an animated strip. Something about the way they fluttered into place reminded me of my vision quest. The girl had ripped the pieces of paper into squares and thrown them into the air, scrambling them. On a hunch, I grabbed a notepad and pencil from the countertop and jotted "dinky pal" across the top of the paper. Crossing letters off one by one and reassembling them below, I ended up with a likely rearrangement: pink lady. Parcel from a pink lady. Could it be? But what pink lady? What parcel? At that moment, it didn't make any more sense to me than *dinky pal*. But, if nothing else, it was progress. In celebration, I voluntarily refilled the cup for big-gulping Stanley. What he lacked in café etiquette, he made up for in choice of reading material. OK, he was also a pretty nice guy. Yep, I was feeling *that* good about a first puzzle piece finally sliding into place.

# CHAPTER TWENTY-NINE

That same afternoon, Penny, Jinky, and I took a junket into Walden.

"I can't believe we have less than a week to transform these things into dresses," Penny said, dumping our day's haul—a jumble of vintage dresses and an assortment of belts, vests, notions, and one piece that we were calling chain mail—onto her bed. "It's going to be nothing short of magic."

"Magic, you say," Jinky said, raising her eyebrows at me.

I cut her a don't-say-a-word look. Like I needed the shaman-in-training to chime in on my abilities. If only I had those kinds of powers. As a girl, I'd been positively gobsmacked by the scene in Cinderella where all the little critters help her assemble her gown. But no "bibbidi-bobbidi-boo" was going to take the place of a seam ripper, sewing machine, and good ol' needle pulling thread.

"Where do we even start?" I asked. Not one of the dresses was to remain whole following what we were already calling *Project Homecoming.* I was going to pair a tea-length gauzy bone-toned skirt with a silvery tunic that, yes, in its current state had the look of a suit of armor. Once I scooped the neckline and cinched and belted the waist, there'd be nothing medieval about it. Penny had found a long dusty-rose dress in a taffeta moiré with a ruffled collar. She planned to add ribbon trim at the hem and cuffs and a wide, tied-at-the-back waist sash. Jinky's dress was the most original, a find for which I took full credit. It was a long silk, mandarin-style, embroidered midnight-black dress with a diagonal of three Chinese looped frog closures angling from chin to armhole. The plan — all mine — was to slit the skirt to waist level at both sides and for Jinky to wear black silk pants underneath.

Penny held the makings of what would be her dress against her and stood in front of the full-length mirror. "I hope you don't mind, Kat, but I have a piece of jewelry in mind for this neckline."

"Why would I mind?"

"Because it's that cameo I told you about. Its color,

its vintage style, just everything is perfect for this dress," she said. "I haven't asked my *amma* if I can wear it yet, because it's supposed to be saved for a special occasion. But if a formal dance your senior year isn't a special occasion, what is? Do you want to see it?"

"Sure."

From her top dresser drawer, she removed a small velvet box. After snapping it open, she gently lifted the pin from its cushion and held it against the high collar.

The oval brooch, encased in a delicate silver framework, had a muted pink background over which an ivory carving depicted a woman's profile with delicate features and an elaborate updo of hair.

I gasped. Everything about the pin was special. It went perfectly with the look Penny was going after. And should she wear her hair up with tendrils framing her face, she would certainly mimic the portrait. But none of that was what had me sucking air. It was a pink lady. And, moreover, our grandmothers had once fought over this item because each had believed it was intended for their own descendant. Visions of my recent discoveries crowded my thoughts. There had to be a connection between "dinky pal" scrambling to "pink lady" and this item. By the time my head cleared, Penny was obviously on her second round of questioning.

"You didn't answer me."

"Sorry. What did you say?"

"I asked if you liked it."

"It's gorgeous. And perfect for that dress."

"I know. It's what drew me to the color of this fabric."

Jinky stepped between us. "It's very old, isn't it?"

"Yes. I think so, anyway," Penny said. "It once belonged to the woman who owned Kat's new house. She was a friend of both of our *ammas*." Penny lowered her head, seemingly not wanting to bring up their disagreement.

Jinky fingered the brooch, but then pulled her hand away suddenly. "I don't know how you say it in English, but in Icelandic, my grandmother would call this a keep-safe."

"You mean a keepsake," I said.

"No. A keep-safe."

"What's the difference?" Penny asked.

I wasn't sure I wanted to know.

"It's possible to leave a personal item embedded with a message or intention of the deceased."

Penny looked at Jinky like she was headless, which was bizarrely prophetic, as I did want to rip Jinky's throat out.

"She was already known as a witch," Penny said, dropping the pin back in its box. "Now you're telling me she's a ghost, too." She placed the open box onto her dresser.

"It's really rather nice, when you think about it,"

Jinky said, "especially when you own a keep-safe from someone special. Like this ring of my mother's." She held her hand flat, showing a ruby-studded band she wore on her right ring finger.

I was confused. I'd seen her mother in Iceland; she was the not-so-friendly, gypsy-garbed vendor I'd met at the festival. She had been alive and kicking, last I'd seen her.

"But you just said they were items of the deceased," I said.

"That's right."

"But I met your mother, didn't I?"

"That was my stepmother: my evil stepmother, who insists I call her Mother even though I hate her and would rather travel halfway across the globe than live under the same roof with her."

"Oh," I said, collapsing onto Penny's bed. I'd known Jinky for weeks; she'd been instrumental in rescuing Jack from Brigid's clutches and we'd broken onto the site of a prehistoric settlement together, but, the truth was, I'd made very little effort to *really* get to know her. "I'm sorry; I didn't know. What happened to your real mom?"

"She died. In childbirth."

I must have flinched or popped my mouth open.

"Yes. With me."

Knowing what I knew about a soul's journey, the tragedy of an essence and vessel crossing paths like that stabbed me with sorrow. And I still hadn't said anything, but I felt like I needed a moment — and possibly a wall of cubbyholes — to sort through my mixed feelings for Jinky.

"That must have been tough," I said, fumbling.

"Yeah, well, not all paths are straightforward or without their climbs."

"Having an everyday connection to her must help," Penny said, schooling me with her superior diplomacy skills. "I lost my parents, too. I know it's hard."

Jinky gave Penny a long, contemplative look. "I still haven't read your runes, you know. I should do it now."

"We don't have time for that," I said. "We have to get going on these dresses."

"It won't take long," Jinky said, removing a pouch from her pocket. "A simple three-rune Norns cast is quick and easy." She bent down to her knees.

*Easy,* yeah, right. Nothing was ever *easy,* not lately, anyway.

"I don't know," Penny said. "It sounds kind of odd. We all know *norn* is the Icelandic word for 'witch.' Besides, the runes seem like the sort of thing —"

"We'd sell in the Sage Hand?" Jinky finished for her.

Penny colored. "Exactly."

"All the more reason for you to see that they're harmless."

"Do I have to do anything?" Penny still sounded

hesitant, but she, too, crouched down. I had no choice but to join them.

"Not a thing." From the pouch, Jinky first pulled a square of white fabric and spread it on the floor. "Which way is north?" she asked, glancing up to the window.

"Why?" Penny asked, but pointed to her right.

"When casting runes, it's best to face north toward the Norse gods," Jinky said.

"Gods?" Penny asked. "You're joking, right?"

"Maybe *gods* is one of those words that doesn't translate well," Jinky said. "I think of them as the supernatural custodians of this vast universe, not necessarily its creator. And it doesn't mean you worship them, only that you recognize them as oracles, acknowledge their energies, and receive their messages."

I waited a beat. Jinky didn't crack a smile.

"Of course she's joking," I said to Penny. "As if there really are celestial janitors out there."

"Custodians," Jinky said. "Not janitors."

I huffed. Some jokes just didn't translate.

Jinky held the pouch by its gathered top and shook. Next, she held the sack out to Penny. "Choose one and place it on the cloth."

Penny reached in and took a single stone and set it on the white square. Jinky had her do the same with two more, being careful that Penny placed it just as it was in her hand — upside down, in one case — until Penny had a line of three. Then, as if turning the page of a book, Jinky uprighted the third rune

"Now, concentrate on an issue," Jinky said to Penny.

"What kind of issue?" Penny asked.

"Something that is important to you."

Penny's mouth twitched to the side, and she went Bazooka pink: a dead giveaway to what she had conjured. Good thing she was destined for the straight and narrow; she would suck at professional poker, as well as espionage.

Jinky pointed to the first rune. It looked like a blocked capital *C,* but with the top and bottom lines bumped inward. "In a three-rune draw, we first consult Urdh, goddess of the past. Urdh calls to the rune Perthro, a symbol of mysteries, secret matters, and hidden things; it often indicates that things are not quite what they seem. It is known as the All-Mother rune because of its association with fertility and feminine mysteries. Its symbol in fact is a 'cup,' which some suggest is representative of the vagina."

I coughed. And not only because of her anatomical reference. On my vision quest, one of the women surrounding Frigg had carried a golden cup. Jinky stopped and, after slashing a look my way, studied Penny; neither spoke or moved. I finally cleared my throat.

"We next consult Verdandi, goddess of *what is,* or the present." Jinky pointed to the center stone, marked with an *X*. "Here we see Gebo. It is a balance symbol and refers to exchanges, contracts, and partnerships. Though it can refer to a group affiliation, it is often called the Lover's Kiss because it can mean that a relationship will move to a deeper level."

It was my turn to shoot Jinky a look. Was she seriously trying to mess with Penny's mind? Penny's crush on Marik was about as subtle as Borat, so Jinky had to know she was telling her exactly what she wanted to hear. Penny leaned forward as if getting into the reading.

"For the final stone that reveals *what shall be,* the future, we look to the goddess Skuld, who displays a very interesting rune, Othala, the rune of ancestral property. This rune represents inheritance and the discarding of the past in order to move forward. Sometimes Othala can symbolize a property or possession; other times it can mean a mental or spiritual heritage. Often it can be an omen of safety." Jinky trailed her hand across the bottom of the three stones. "So there you have it: feminine mystery, the Lover's Kiss, and an inheritance."

The latter had me thinking. I glanced over to the open jewelry box atop Penny's dresser. The brooch had been a matter of dispute between our grandmothers. Steel-faced Grim had won out — no surprise there; my *amma* had been a marshmallow by comparison. But now, seeing it in the form of a pink lady, I couldn't help but wonder: Was it rightfully mine? Were the runes intentionally prompting this question of inheritance? It was almost too much to take in. For now, the task at hand seemed a better use of my time.

"Does it say anything about the future of three dresses?" I asked, scrambling to a stand. "Because that's why we're here." I sorted through the pile on Penny's bed. "We'll need to rip out the side seams on Jinky's dress, and pin the hem on those silk pants. Plus our own dresses. I don't know why we're putzing around here."

Jinky gathered up the pieces to her intended outfit. "I'll do my own. Mrs. Cantwright will help me, I'm sure."

Mrs. Cantwright—Jinky's host mother, my new neighbor, and a gray-haired, doddering antiquity—had a hard time getting her clothes on straight. I didn't know how much help she could be at pinning and hemming.

"If you need any supplies, needles or thread or whatever, let me know," I said, collecting my own pile of loot.

There was a knock at Penny's door. It opened and old Grim stuck her head into the room. "I thought I heard voices." I was so used to seeing her in her usual grim-on-Grim attire that her current getup surprised me. She wore head-to-toe white and a volunteer badge I recognized from Pinewood General Hospital. Grim a good Samaritan? I just couldn't picture it.

"Amma, you haven't met my friend Jinky yet. She's an exchange student from Iceland."

*"Komdu sæl,"* Grim said to Jinky.

"Very well, thank you," Jinky replied with more respect than I could have mustered.

Grim gave me a squint. "Katla," she said, by way of greeting.

For the record, it was a name, not a salutation. "Hello, Fru Grimilla," I said dutifully.

"What's going on?" Grim asked.

"We bought our things for the dance this weekend," Penny replied.

Grim's eyes raked over the piles of clothing on the bed and in the arms of both me and Jinky. Her glare then strayed to the dresser top. "What on earth? Why is that out?"

"I was showing them," Penny said in a small voice. "It matches my dress. I was thinking of wearing it."

"It's much too valuable," Grim said, striding across the room. She lifted the velvet-covered box and snapped it shut. Pocketing it, she turned and harrumphed out of the room. Just before the door closed, our eyes met, *bucked* truly the more apt description. I may have even brayed ever so slightly; I had to bring my fist to my mouth in a mock cough.

As usual, Grim left me spiraling. Not only was the pin possibly mine, but it was valuable. What I valued was its link to information I required, but with it currently in Grim's gnarled knuckles, I doubted I'd see it again. If only as much could be said of Grim. At least I didn't run into her on my way from Penny's room to the front door. I was feeling mulish enough to kick.

# CHAPTER THIRTY

Walking into school on Monday morning was like tightroping across power lines. Every step buzzed with a palpable current, one that was, to my great relief, harmless.

"Let me guess," I said, joining Penny at the back of the shifting crowd. "The Homecoming ballots are being handed out."

"Yep," she replied.

She looked down at my attire, a belted blouse over jeans tucked into boots, and asked, "Why are you dressed?"

I laughed; it was a pretty strange question. "I forgot," I said, swiveling my head to take in the various interpretations of Jammies Day, the first in a full week of Homecoming dress-up assignments. Penny in her fleecy two-piece PJs was at least decent. There was a girl standing not far from us in a frilly baby-doll number who, I guessed, would be sent home to change.

"What's the word on the court?" I asked. "Who are the front-runners?"

"Abby for queen and John Gilbert for king, though I've heard talk of Marik, too."

"Marik?" My voice broke like some puberty-struck, thirteen-year-old boy. "But he's only been here a couple of weeks."

"People like him. He's different."

If only she knew just how different. I could see, though, as his date, this was a source of great satisfaction to her. I could also appreciate it as a shake-up to tradition. Most everyone around here had lived in Norse Falls their whole lives. The pecking order probably dated back to kindergarten and was probably decided over Red Rover and cuts in line rather than merit or character.

"So where is he?" I was curious about his Jammies Day garb and half expected giant bunny slippers to charge us at any moment.

"He's still not feeling all that great, according to Jinky."

"Weird," I said. It was. What ailed a merman?

At the front of the throng, I spotted Abby and

Shauna, dressed in matching knee-length white nighties, grasping their ballots like winning lottery tickets. Abby seemed to have rebounded from the Asking Fire scene. Rumor had it she was back together with Gabe, the basketball player she had thrown over in her brazen pursuit of Marik. Nor did there seem to be any lasting effects of the frenzy and ugliness that had affected the crowd on Saturday night. Still, I wasn't about to belt out a "Beat Pinewood" cheer or ask anyone for a light.

Janie, a girl Penny and I knew from Design, retreated from the press of bodies with a fistful of ballots. "Here," she said, handing us one each. "I grabbed a few extras." She paused for a moment and then prodded Penny with her elbow. "You and Marik, huh?"

"Yeah." Penny tucked a band of hair behind an ear. As they had been for some time now, her curls were sleek and serpentine, falling in cascades over her shoulders.

"Congrats and good luck," Janie said, thumbing the corner of her ballot.

Penny dipped her head and shoulders, revealing a peek of cleavage.

*Good luck?* As in Penny was a contender? A puff of pure, clean air filled my lungs. Penny was a contender?

Despite everything going on in my life, this kernel of possibility bumped itself to the top of my do-now list. And with the overwhelming sense of futility and frustration I was feeling in my quest to thwart Marik's mission and even my attempt to manipulate a placement for Jaelle, *this* felt like something actionable.

And why not Penny for Homecoming Queen? A year ago, I'd have conceded it as some kind of cruel Mean Girls' prank. But now, the Penny before me had serious potential. While the best of her qualities — intelligence, kindness, enthusiasm — were intact, other character traits had developed: confidence and poise. Not to mention that she was morphing into a stone-cold fox. With cleavage.

"When are these things due?" I asked Penny.

"By the end of the day."

"And when do they announce the court?"

"Tomorrow." Penny gave me a you're-losing-it look. I probably should have remembered the announcement of the court from last year; Jack had, after all, been one of the royals. In my defense, I had been a little busy, what with him going AWOL days before our first date and the whole see-a-raven-and-nearly-get-flattened-by-a-logging-truck incident. I did, at any rate, remember the Friday pep rally, the one at which — should I prove successful — Penny would be crowned this year's queen.

"Gotta go," I said, kicking up do-good dust and leaving our potential monarch looking puzzled.

In every class that day, I campaigned for Penny. "Wouldn't she and Marik make the cutest king and queen ever?" "Wouldn't it be nice to reward someone based on merit: like an editor of the paper or the chair of every committee, not to mention a whip-smart honor student?" "And isn't it refreshing that Penny is nice and pretty and totally not expecting it?"

I know I planted a seed in some people's minds and outright changed a few on the spot. But the best part of the whole thing, by far, was that people told me they had already voted for her. Guys and girls both. Were it only that this regime overthrow and underdog crusade represented the utmost of my challenges. Regardless, it was a distraction that carried me through to the final bell.

Leaving school that day, I was preoccupied by thoughts of how great it would be for something to finally go my way, when I almost plowed into my dad as he bounded up the front steps.

"What are you doing here?" I asked.

"Reporting to the lovely Sage Bryant for a chaperone meeting." My dad fingered the collar of his crisply laundered black-and-white checked shirt with rolled, contrasting paisley French cuffs. It was an awesome shirt that looked both new and expensive. I begrudged him neither and had always liked his sense of style, but he had clearly made an effort.

"Oh. Is this something I'm supposed to attend as well?" I asked.

"No, no. Chaperones only." My dad brushed a bit of lint from his black dress pants.

202

"Have fun, then," I said, watching him enter the building.

It was nice to casually throw around the word "fun," but something about the way he said "lovely" had me a little worried. Ms. Bryant was my teacher, and I depended on her for a good grade, especially if a design college was in my future. Though, with Marik and Safira and Brigid posing bigger-picture threats, it was yet another relief to worry about something else, something as trivial as transcripts, something with future significance, something with a future *period*.

# CHAPTER THIRTY-ONE

I didn't notice the eerily quiet house when I got home. With Faulkner to read for English and my dress to work on, I grabbed a PowerBar and a vitaminwater and headed up to my room. My mom, believing it was important for Leira to get fresh air and be exposed to external stimuli, often took her on afternoon outings. When it got to be dinnertime and there were still no sounds in the house, I got suspicious and checked my — oops — dead cell phone. I plugged it in and, once it had a little juice, discovered I had three texts from my mom, all of them telling me to call her ASAP. The last ASAP had been two hours ago. Oops again.

"Hey, Mom, what's up?"

"I don't want to alarm you, but it's Leira."

"Why? What happened?"

"We had to take her to the emergency room. She was running a fever."

"Is she OK?"

"They suspect an infection. Possibly pneumonia. The good news is that she's stable now."

"There's bad news?"

"They admitted her, and she's back on a ventilator. Her compromised lungs aren't quite getting the job done."

Of course it had to be lung related. It led me to fear that Leira — because of her special selkie ancestry — was never intended to have lungs. That her long-term prognosis on earth, even should I be successful in thwarting Marik, wasn't good.

"Should I come to the hospital?" I asked.

Even through the phone, I could hear her release of pent-up air. "I don't think so. It's late. There's nothing to be done here. I've even talked Stanley into going home; he has an early lecture. If she takes a turn for the worse, I'll have Stanley wake you. But if she's holding or improving, you should go to school, and then we'll see what's to be done tomorrow."

"I don't feel right carrying on if Leira is sick," I said.

Following a couple more rounds of my mom and me debating this, I finally agreed to stay put. I had spent enough time at the hospital over the summer to know that the night shift was long and tedious.

Immediately after hanging up with my mom, I phoned Jack. It was an entirely spontaneous response, as reflexive as covering a yawn.

"I'm coming over," he said, after hearing the latest.

"It's late," I said, sounding scarily like my mom. "Besides, you know the rule." It was a stupid one, but Jack wasn't allowed over unless my mom or Stanley were home.

"It's an emergency situation, though. Martial law, right?"

"I'm not sure that applies when the emergency's someone else's," I said.

"Well, then, we'll make it a covert op."

This disobedient side wasn't like him. I kind of liked it. And I *definitely* liked the burly quality to his voice. I went all tingly just thinking about how, in person, he'd follow that up.

About twenty minutes later, as I finished a plate of cheese and crackers, I got what I was secretly hoping for: the real Jack, husky voice and all.

"Did anyone see you?" I asked, looking both left and right down the street.

"No. And I parked a block away."

I pulled him inside quickly. Responding to my

urgency, he backed me up against the front door and kissed me. I knew I should be thinking about Leira and all that she was going through. I also knew that Stanley was due home anytime. But with Jack's mouth on mine and his strong hands raking through my hair, kneading my shoulders, and sliding down my back, every concern of mine spiraled away like water rushing down a whirlpool. And, yes, the tingles were back.

"Now tell me about Leira," he said after pulling away and straightening my shirt with a swift tug.

With the abrupt separation, the worries his kiss had temporarily dispelled returned. As I parted my lips, intending to update him on her medical condition, what spilled forth was, instead, a sob followed by a sheet of tears washing down my face.

"Hey, there. It's OK," he said, folding me into his arms.

We stood there for a long time while I struggled to get a handle on my emotions. I sensed the frailty of so many things at that moment: of Leira's hold on this world, of my own abilities, of the all-is-well façade I'd been faking since our return from Iceland, Greenland, and beyond.

"What can I do?" he asked.

"Nothing, but I'm glad you're here. It does help."

"I knew it."

"Knew what?"

"That you needed me. You put up a tough front. Anyone else would be fooled."

I gulped. Was he onto me? Did he know more than he was saying? If so, how much? Everything? I panicked momentarily but then thought of how Marik amused him. If he really knew, Marik would *not* amuse him. Just the opposite, in fact.

"But I can be tough, too," he continued. "And behind that front, I got your back. Remember that."

"I will," I replied.

Jack led me upstairs to my room, where we lay on my bed simply holding each other. Once I had calmed down and my nose was all snotted out and my face looked like it had been used as a punching bag, he, rather diplomatically, segued into lighter subjects: my affinity for purple décor, my fondness for feather boas, and my overuse—in his opinion—of throw pillows. I demonstrated their multi-functionality by smacking him upside the head with a beaded one, after which we tumbled into a ticklefest. And I was back. Restored. Reinvigorated. Reminded of our bond.

Shortly thereafter, I heard Stanley knocking about the kitchen. I decided—based on the volume of his bangs—that he was not in the mood for company, not mine and certainly not rule-breaking Jack's. We tiptoed down the front steps, avoiding the second-from-the-bottom creaker. I watched Jack slip out the front door as Stanley clattered pots and pans in the kitchen, presumably rustling himself up a late supper. Making my way back to my room, I pitied him. It must have been even more painful for him than it was for me, that Leira's first few months of life were so difficult.

# CHAPTER THIRTY-TWO

Leira did remain stable through the night. My mom put in a brief appearance the next morning to shower and change after Leira had finally fallen asleep, following a long and wakeful night.

I watched my mom as she waded from the coffee-pot to the table as if navigating something much heavier than air. She looked pale and thinner than I remembered and, with her hair screwed into a twist at the back of her head, I had a glimpse of how she'd look as an old woman. It was also a bad sign that she hadn't commented on my appearance. It was Crazy Hair Day and I currently sported two of the highest, boingiest pigtails possible.

They were pulled so tight the corners of my mouth were yanked upward, the Joker's grin, but my mom said nothing. It was unsettling, and I pushed my bowl of Raisin Bran to the side.

"I'm supposed to work at the store after school," I said. "Should I check if Ofelia could cover for me so I can come and see Leira?"

"There's not much to see. Even I just sit there helpless and useless. And we already rely on Ofelia for so much. I've talked with Afi more than once about hiring another part-timer. Given his age and own health concerns, I'd like to see him cut his hours to next to nothing, if not sell the store outright."

I clanked my spoon onto the table. It was true that Ofelia was essentially running the store. To ask her to pick up extra hours wasn't fair. It was, however, this most recent mention of selling the store that had me half-staffing my head. Norse Falls General Store was Afi's. And I knew that it was what got him up and going most days. Even though his "up and going" was getting more and more difficult. Somehow, I sensed it was important to help him hang on to the store for as long as possible.

"I'll keep my shift. If something does change, you'll let me know?"

"Yes, of course."

At school, I had a hard time shifting gears and getting my head back into the Homecoming mania that had invaded. But with the court announcement being posted first thing, I had to adjust quickly.

"Anyone we know?" I asked Penny as she ducked through the crowd on her return from the bulletin board. Hope elevated my voice in a childish lilt.

"Marik," she said, rolling a curl between her thumb and index finger. Her crazy hair was a mass of ringlets. With her color and volume, the effect was like a cross between Little Orphan Annie and Medusa. "And me."

I grabbed her by the shoulders and squealed like a blue-ribbon sow. Heads turned in our direction, but I didn't care. Penny was on the Homecoming court; good things *did* happen to good people. "Woo-hoo. You made court!"

"And Marik, too."

"So where is he, anyway? I haven't seen him. Is he still sick?" I asked.

"Yeah. But nothing serious, according to Jinky."

A part of me was concerned by his two-day absence. Another part had enjoyed the reprieve. With the news that he was on the mend, I decided to savor another Marik-free school day.

I noticed Abby and Shauna giving each other congratulatory hugs as well, their matching Marge Simpson beehives colliding like foamy heads of beer; I was so happy I allowed them their celebration.

Jinky walked up. I had no idea if her spiked hairstyle

had anything to do with Homecoming, but it certainly made a point, or came to one, rather.

"Congratulations," she said to Penny.

"Thanks."

"Do you have anything like this in Iceland?" Penny asked.

"No," Jinky said. "No American football. No silly popularity contests. And no mock royalty."

No mistaking what she thought of the whole thing.

"How're your dresses coming along?" Penny asked us.

I groaned my not-so-good response.

Jinky, to my surprise, said, "All done."

"So not fair," I said. "I've got a shift at my grandfather's store tonight, and my baby sister's back in the hospital with pneumonia. There aren't enough hours between now and Saturday."

"Maybe I could help out. Is your grandfather hiring?" Jinky asked. "I'm looking for a job."

"Oh. Well. As a matter of fact," I said, "he just may be." Wheels were grinding in my head; I heard the gear shifts and even smelled something burning. "Why don't you head over there with me after school? I'm pretty sure my *afi* will be there; you could meet him."

"Sounds OK," Jinky said. "I'll meet you at your locker."

As Jinky strolled off, I reflected on my evolving

opinion of her. She took her own mystical side seriously. You gotta respect that. And though Marik and I were both cagey about what was going on, she continued to act as a medium for us to the spirit world. And after an aloof start, she was making a serious effort to blend: the paper, a mystery date to Homecoming, and now maybe a job. Change was good. I liked change. It gave me hope that it was possible in all things.

After school, Jinky was waiting for me at my locker. I texted my mom asking for an update on Leira. "Stable" was her brief but satisfying response. I therefore relaxed a little and enjoyed the glorious crisp fall day and walk to downtown. These trees were just beginning their fall reveal, and bursts of canary yellow and sumac red flapped overhead. Jinky was kind of chatty, talking about a motorcycle she wanted to buy. So Jinky hadn't done a complete personality flop; some character traits of hers — like her hell-on-wheels need for speed, for instance — were intact.

"What's the deal with Marik?" I asked.

"Well, you know he only shares what he wants to." Jinky said this in a way that implied I did the same. I did, of course.

"But is he really sick?"

Jinky shrugged her shoulders. "If I knew, I'd tell you."

I believed her. It didn't provide me any more information on Marik, but it was a nice moment between us.

At the store, both Afi and Ofelia were behind the counter. If I remembered correctly, it had been Ofelia's day off. Her presence had me worried; it meant Afi had needed backup.

"What's new?" I asked.

"York, Guinea, and Zealand," Afi said.

For the record, I had intentionally walked into one of his snappy comebacks. It was a gauge as to his state of mind. Too-beat-to-banter would have been a bad omen.

I introduced Jinky to Ofelia and Afi, reminding him that he'd met her at the fair in Iceland.

"If you're looking for someone to pick up a few hours here at the store, Jinky's interested in an after-school job."

Afi grunted, probably sensing it was a reflection of his age and health.

"Can she work legally as an exchange student?" Afi asked.

Even I hadn't thought about that. For a guy who still operated with an old-fashioned cash register and a rotary phone, he was surprisingly up-to-date on laws and regulations.

"As long as the job is registered through the school's

BVP, Business and Vocational Program, it will be considered an on-campus job and permitted under my F-1 student visa."

Now it was Jinky's turn to surprise me. The girl could read runes, drive a Harley, stoke a sacred fire, and speak legalese. And BVP? I'd never even heard of it, never mind be able to employ it as a loophole.

Ofelia said something in Icelandic to Jinky. She replied; it was long and, with the guttural Germanic roots of the language, sounded strong and confident. Afi joined in, adding his own string of gargled spluttering. I watched their back-and-forth conversation with a mounting annoyance and a growing stiffness in my neck. Without the benefit of comprehending the words, I was left to translate their body language. Ofelia, I could tell, was highly curious of Jinky, and I sensed — from the fold in Ofelia's brow — that she was actively running one of her scanner operations.

Immediately thereafter, Ofelia urged Afi into his jacket and proclaimed that he'd been on his feet for long enough. After they left, Jinky said, "I start training tomorrow."

"That's it?" I asked, feeling like I'd just relived a scene straight out of *Lost in Translation*. "You guys talked for a long time. Something had to have been edited."

"Ofelia told your *afi* that you had enough on your plate without thinking you had to keep the store going on his behalf. And your *afi* wants your mom to focus on Leira and stop worrying about him and leave him alone about selling the store. And then Ofelia added that you had to get your dress done by Saturday and study for your English test on Friday."

That last part had my heart hammering. Had I mentioned my complete and thorough hatred of Faulkner to Ofelia? To anyone?

"I think I'm sorry I asked," I said.

"I liked them both," Jinky said. "I think I'll fit in just fine around here. Ofelia, in particular, is going to be fun."

With this, Jinky tapped her head. I had no idea what to think of this, but worried about the kind of *fun* a shaman—even one in training—and a mind reader could have.

# CHAPTER THIRTY-THREE

It was kind of nice after school on Thursday when I didn't have a shift at the store. I was able to visit Leira at the hospital, where she had been taken off the ventilator but still wasn't "out of the woods." I also had time to finish up my dress. Running the sewing machine over the last stretch of hem, I allowed myself to get excited about the dance. I'd be with Jack, dressed up, and at a special event. Win, win, win. And with any luck, I'd be watching Penny enjoy her evening as Homecoming Queen and as Marik's date.

The thought of Marik did give me some pause. He had been back at school today—having been absent yet again yesterday—but uncharacteristically quiet. He'd arrived late to Design and had sat with Mean Dean in the corner. The two of them had passed Mean Dean's *Manga Club* between them. At the end of class, I had noticed Mean Dean press the magazine into Marik's hands, a keep-it gesture. Marik had taken it almost reverentially, and Mean Dean's reaction had been one of pure satisfaction. Whatever Marik's ailment or absence had been — or was — he still had that *way* with others.

I pulled the dress from under the sewing machine's arm and cut the threads. In addition to Marik, I was bothered by the lack of another Stork dream; nearly a month had now passed since that last one. I was keenly aware of the narrow window of opportunity between a woman's physical state and an undecided soul's bestowment. The lapse seemed like a deal breaker. Jaelle would be on an entirely new menstrual cycle, after all.

This bummed me out, and I set the dress down and dropped my head into my hands. As soon as my fingers touched my scalp, it started to tingle: the summons to a Stork meeting. The timing seemed bizarre. Too bizarre. And I wasn't such a big believer in coincidence anymore.

An hour or so later, I took my Robin's chair at the Stork-council table. After the usual start-up protocol, Hulda announced that, with a soul to place, she herself had called the meeting. She described an entirely typical situation, a single essence — a sweet and gentle girl — for which three average-sounding women were presented as potential vessels. It was all very SOP, so textbook, in fact, that there was almost no necessity to think. Hulda recommended on behalf of the first-time mother, and we all voted in favor of this selection.

Though I had no doubt our gathering was a bona fide placement and that an undecided soul *had* turned to Hulda for guidance, I was also buzzing with a sensation of interconnectedness. If my wondrous experience as a Stork had taught me anything, it was that "random" simply wasn't.

The patience lesson that Hulda was so keen for me to learn, I was still working on. The moment the others filed out following Hulda's "peace be," I was tugging at her scratchy gray cardigan.

"Do you have a minute?"

"Of course, child. What is it?"

"Recently I had what I can only describe as . . . a partial Stork dream. . . . No vessels presented themselves."

I hesitated, not sure if I should mention the anomaly of two physically distinct souls or my intention to steer one of them to Jaelle.

"Ah," Hulda said, breaking my pause. "I'm impressed."

"Impressed?"

"Yes. This is a clear sign of your practicing patience."

"It is?"

"Of course. Something about the presenting soul is hesitant. You know by now it's only the undecided who turn to us for counsel."

"Yeah. Sure."

"This one possibly more so than the rest."

*These two,* I almost corrected, but I didn't want to interrupt.

"By not pressuring the soul, by not urging it to complete the dream cycle, you show an acceptance of the fullness of time," Hulda continued.

"Except," I just had to interject here, "I can't shake the feeling that the delay signaled a . . . termination of sorts."

"Do not worry yourself about such things. If meant to be, the bestowment will continue."

"But a full month has passed, you know, a menstrual cycle."

"Again, an attunement of life's natural rhythms. The fullness of time. And *menses* is from the Latin *mēnsis,* meaning 'month.' Many Native Americans refer to a woman as 'on her moon.' I prefer this imagery. It evokes the communion of life's cycles: the waning and waxing, the ebb and flow. When respected, such rhythms are a gift."

*Ho, boy.* School was in session. And, as usual, it was a lot to process. I had no idea if we were still talking

221

about a placement. It all could apply to the unfolding of events between me, Safira, and Leira. And with Hulda's mention of "Native American," my heart had somersaulted. Sure, she often paid tribute to their culture and beliefs — respecting the ancestry of her adopted home — but having so recently snuck onto consecrated land and spirit-walked, I was a little wigged out. Because random simply wasn't.

"There's another thing that has seemed a little coincidental to me lately: our house was once owned by someone called the Bleika Norn, the Pink Witch. Did you know her?"

"Yes."

"It sounds to me — given her association with my *amma,* Fru Grimilla, and now you — like she might have been a Stork. Plus, she was known as a healer."

Hulda stared at me. Possibly because I hadn't really asked a question. It also occurred to me that she had to be careful about just how much she divulged. The Storks were skittish with their secrets. I tried another approach. "There's a cameo that was once hers. Was it, as my *amma* believed, rightfully mine?"

"That is to be seen."

An interesting response that went with the *patience* she preached. It was all well and good for her, but I had a bit of a *situation* on my hands. And the *patience* I'd been practicing wasn't cutting it. "Does the Bleika Norn have any connection to Bleik, the Norn of Childbirth, one of Frigg's ten maidens?"

"The goddess Frigg? Of what relevance is the goddess Frigg? And ten maidens? Do you not mean nine?"

"Oh, you're right. Nine. I don't know why I said ten." It seemed such a silly error. I mean, I'd been there myself and counted them so carefully.

Hulda cocked her head and studied me closely. *Uh-oh.*

"It is curious that you should mention ten. There was another, Idunn, the Goddess of Eternal Youth and keeper of the golden apples of fertility. In her naïveté and playfulness, she erred, though, thinking Loki— the wicked trickster—joined in her games. Instead, he made off with the precious apples. To recover them for the gods, Odin had to battle the giant Thiazi. As punishment, the goddess Frigg confiscated Idunn's apples and expelled her from Asgard."

I wasn't sure where Hulda was going with this one. I myself had found mention of Idunn in my own research. It seemed important, but I always got a little nervous around the topic of "expelled" members. I continued to test the limits of my gift.

"Mostly I was interested in the word *norn*. It seems to keep popping up is all." Even Jinky's rune reading had referenced the word.

"*Norn* is Old Norse for 'protective goddess or spirit'

and was even once used to describe mortal women with magical knowledge. And, yes, white witches such as ourselves have been described as norns."

I took this as confirmation that the Bleika Norn had been a Stork. Leave it to Hulda to make me go around the block an extra time or two. And, as usual, she'd given me plenty to think about. "I've probably overstayed my welcome by now." I stood and pushed my chair back. "And now I know to be patient regarding the completion of that Stork dream."

"I trust you will," Hulda said with a bow of her head.

I left with my head spun tight. It was, as ever, vintage Hulda. I did, at any rate, have renewed hope on Jaelle's behalf. Hulda had said: "If meant to be, the bestowment would continue." And I meant it to be, all right.

# CHAPTER THIRTY-FOUR

School that Friday was one of those occasions when academics—and sanity, for that matter—were no match for the firebomb that was Homecoming mania. Even with another Hulda powwow raiding my thoughts like marauders, I, too, was swept along by school spirit.

The big event was the third-period pep rally at which the queen and king were named. I took my seat in the bleachers, finding a third-row spot next to Jinky.

We all suffered through the mandatory speeches and announcements. I noticed that any mention of a merge with Pinewood was clearly off topic; chaperones had witnessed the scene at the Asking Fire. Point of fact, sportsmanship, comportment, and character were the theme of both the principal's and the coach's talks. The latter managed to convey the importance of both appropriate conduct *and* a win. I personally couldn't have cared less about who won that night's football game. Queen, on the other hand . . .

When the rally did get around to its true purpose, I was so nervous my legs were stamping at the floorboards of the stands like tap shoes on a tin roof. Jinky gave me a look, but she didn't have me fooled. She'd been chewing at her thumbnail since I plopped down next to her.

The ten chosen blue bloods were lined up on the track ringing the football field. The king was announced first. The miked principal announced John Gilbert's name, placed a crown on his head, and thrust a scepter into his hand. Marik, as far as I could tell, had little or no reaction. Instead, he stood stiffly in place in the horseshoe formation.

Next, the principal, bearing two more royal instruments, approached the line of girls. The crowd was so loud that I couldn't hear the name as it was announced. I held my breath but almost hyperventilated in disbelief when the tiara was planted atop Abby's head. She had to hold on to it to keep it from tumbling as she was team-hugged by the other female members of her court. From the bleachers, I could see tears glistening her face.

"What a rip," I said, triggering a turn and a once-over from a known consort of Abby's.

"That sucks," Jinky said, earning her own disapproving glare.

Back inside, I found Penny at her locker and gave her a big consolation embrace.

"Dang it all," I said. "I so wanted you to be queen."

Penny rolled her eyes. "I never expected to win. Quite frankly, it's a small miracle I made court. A year ago I didn't stand a chance. And without a certain someone championing me and running a little PR operation, I wouldn't have."

"Sure you would have," I said. "Tons of people told me they had already voted for you. And if not you, who else? There's not another girl in this school who deserves to make court in your place."

Penny closed her locker and gave a furtive look to her left and right. "I happen to know, via a very good source, the identity of the next in line, and she would have been an excellent choice."

"Who?" I asked.

"You." Penny nudged me so hard with her shoulder that I crashed into the bank of lockers with a loud clang.

"Not funny," I said, rubbing my shoulder.

"I'm not joking."

"Well, then, I'm doubly glad I swayed a few votes in your favor, because I'm firmly New World and pro-democracy. Remember?" *And not too keen on queens these days, either.*

227

Penny laughed. "You arrived last year talking an overthrow. How could I forget?"

I was mulling over the word *overthrow* as Marik walked up — hobbled over, more like, actually.

"Are you OK?" I asked. He was pale and his forehead was tight and shiny.

"Still recuperating," Penny said, biting her lips back. "I've tried to get him to see a doctor, or at least the school nurse."

"I'm fine," Marik said quickly. "It's just a small pain in my side."

I watched him clutch at his waist, a gesture I'd noticed before. He definitely didn't look well, and who knows what a side pain could indicate? A burst appendix came to mind, but then I thought — blinking with the enormity of it — did Marik even have an appendix? Could he go to a doctor? What would they find? Just what did a merman have for organs and innards?

"But the dance is tomorrow," Penny said. "And the big game tonight. You should at least go home and rest."

Marik shook off the idea, leaving the two of us with his "Don't worry about me. I finish what I start."

While this cheered Penny measurably, it jarred me to the core. And it was my turn to feel a sharp pain.

# CHAPTER THIRTY-FIVE

I way preferred having Jack in the stands with me during a football game than watching him play, even though he had been a fine specimen to behold. I could tell by the way his body shifted with every play that he missed the sport. I was happy, anyway, and snuggled in close to him, risking the occasional elbow he threw when reacting to the action down on the field.

Penny was a nervous ninny the entire first half watching for Marik, who was late. Jinky — off taking photos — had reported earlier that he was "on his way."

When it was time for the members of the court to assemble pre-halftime, Penny started down the bleachers with a nervous backward glance in my direction.

"He'll show," I called down to her. "He said so."

Just as the court began their procession onto the field, I caught sight of Marik hotfooting it to catch up with them. Had I not known he was razor-edge close to missing the whole show, I wouldn't have noticed anything amiss. And if he still wasn't feeling well, he sure didn't show it. He carried out his escort duties with grace and ease as he smiled and waved pleasantly when his own name was called. He got a big cheer from the crowd, as big as John's, I'd have guessed.

Our team, contrary to the vitriol shouted at the Asking Fire, did not destroy Pinewood. Sadly, it was the reverse. With a twenty-one to three victory, Pinewood high-stepped it off the field while our Falcons hangdogged their way to the locker room.

Postgame, while we lingered in the commons area near the concessions, Jack got pulled into a Homecoming photo of past players. The moment he headed off to the field, Marik appeared at my side.

"May I talk to you?" he asked.

"Sure," I replied.

"In private." He grimaced as he said this.

I led the way to the side of the snack stand. Behind me, I could hear Marik's labored breathing.

"What's going on, Marik? Are you OK?"

"No."

"What do you mean, no?"

"I'm not well," he said, grabbing at his front below his ribs. "I'm in pain and feeling weak."

"What do you think it is? Can you see someone for it? You know, a doctor?"

"I don't need to."

"What? Why?"

"Because I know what it is. Something happened at the Asking Fire."

"Yes. I know. A presence invaded. Thank God for the storm, or else—"

"No," Marik interrupted. "The storm is what happened." With this, he winced.

"You're confused," I said. "The storm chased the evil away."

"The evil," Marik said, "was too distant and too crude to affect me. The rain, the cold, however, its icy core . . ." Marik closed his eyes as if the memory was too much. "I knew of your mission to Brigid's Niflheim and what, or who, rather, you sought to recover."

"Jack," I said plainly.

"Our mistake was to underestimate his effect."

"I don't understand."

"I am water." Marik dropped his head. "Jack freezes water. We are not a good combination. His recent . . . display . . . has been most detrimental."

"What do you mean?"

"I am not of this world. I was never meant to be here

permanently. This incident has impacted my viability. I am, I fear, out of time."

When the realization of what his being out of time meant for me, for Leira, I gasped.

"But if you have to go . . . ?" I asked.

"Then my mission is coming to an end." With this pronouncement, Marik doubled over as if clubbed by a sudden spasm of pain.

In a weakened state, he braced his right arm on the wall, reaching over me to do so. In reaction, I reached up with both arms to support him, my fear being that he'd collapse to the ground without assistance.

"What's going on?" Jack asked, stepping around the corner of the concessions hut.

A warning look glinted in Marik's eyes; with this brief prompt, I was reminded of the gravity of our pact.

"Nothing," I said. "Marik's not feeling so great."

"But why are you back here?" Jack's voice registered mistrust.

"I followed him when he didn't look well."

Jack gazed from me to Marik and back to me. Marik, in the meantime, recovered enough to stretch to his full height.

"I. Am. Fine," Marik said, passing us and heading back toward where we'd left the others.

Watching him go, I shuddered.

"What's wrong? You look upset," Jack said. He took my arm at the elbow.

"It's nothing," I said, pulling away gently.

"You are. You're upset. Did he do something to you? Say something to you?"

"No, of course not."

"There's something. I know there is." He held me by the shoulders.

"I was worried for him; that's all. He was late tonight, and Penny's counting on him for the dance." I pulled myself together, drawing on the pressure building in my chest and directing it toward the bluff I was presenting for Jack. "I just want to make sure he knows how important tomorrow is to Penny, that he doesn't bail on her."

Jack looked as deeply into my eyes as he ever had, searching, penetrating. I steeled myself against his figuring it all out. He could. I knew he could. He was so confoundingly close to splitting me open. But he didn't. Instead, he took my hand gently and pulled me toward the commons. Marik, I noticed, was gone. When the first moment presented itself, I excused myself for the bathroom.

En route, I found Jinky talking to Shauna —*huh?*— and pulled her aside.

"Are you up for another field trip tonight?" I asked.

Jinky looked side to side, making sure we were out of earshot. "Does it have to be tonight?"

"Yes."

"When?" she asked with a small sigh of disappointment.

I told her where to be and when and then took my fake trip to the restroom. *Rest. Ha.* Not likely anytime soon.

# CHAPTER THIRTY-SIX

Late that same night, Jinky and I beat a quick path to Alpenstock and its sweat lodge. She wanted no assistance with the sacred fire, so I, again, sat back and observed her. She was cool and efficient in all things. I'd have called it dispassionate, once upon a time. I now saw her as confident. And focused. And hardly without passion. She was out here in the middle of the night assisting me, though I still had never fully explained why. She deserved her shaman wings, all right.

Once inside the small space, I gave myself freely to the ceremony and transition. Again, upon passage, I felt myself dissolve as if into smoke.

\* \* \*

A whinny roused me from slumber. My lids parted slowly, reluctantly. Grasses tickled my cheek and nose. I stifled a sneeze as I sat up with a cottony head and unwieldy limbs. Above me, upon a tree limb, the lark sang: *Tee, tee, hoo. Tee, tee, hoo.*

When the song gave way to voices, I stood, crouching behind the tallest of nearby reeds.

Frigg and most of her maidens were still gathered with only a few noticeable changes. The freckled tomboy held the reins of a horse, the white-blond identical twins were no longer present, but two swans circled the glassy waters beneath a giant weeping tree.

For a better view, I stepped forward, crunching a branch underfoot. I gasped, thinking I'd surely alerted them to my presence, but, as before, they took no notice of me.

"Hurry, my maidens, for evil threatens," Frigg urged. "One queen is consumed by rage, while the other grows desperate and restless. Should they conspire, it would be catastrophic. Ragnarök, I fear."

The women reacted with cries of alarm.

"We prepare," Frigg said, silencing their outburst. "Bleik, Norn of Childbirth, and Eyra, Norn of Healing, have you my magical aliments, kept in another's stead?"

At the mention of "another's stead," the lark startled, flying off with an agitated *kerr, kerr, kerr.* Something about the bird's vacant post caught my eye. There, wedged between two limbs, was the pretty young girl's upside-down basket.

The two with similar dark features—the one who held a golden bowl and the other who held a mortar and pestle—stepped forward. "Yes, Goddess Frigg," they answered as one.

They handed items to Frigg, but from my position I could not make them out. Frigg took it quickly and dropped it into the pocket of her voluminous skirt.

"And Helin,. Maiden of Protection, do you and Orbotha, Chooser of the Dead, stand ready?"

"We do," answered the sword bearer and the shroud wearer.

"Then Saga, Maiden of Poetry, recount our epic preparations. Already Blith and Frith, my Swan Maidens, swim in the wells of fate. Only Nyah, my Carrier of Messages, remains."

Nyah opened her pouch. From the fold of her skirt, Frigg removed objects and carefully placed them in Nyah's bag.

I stepped closer, hoping to see what it was that Nyah received, but I only caught her folding down the large flap and buckling its closure. With the satchel stored across her chest, Nyah swung atop the horse. Once secure in the saddle, the horse took two or three thundering strides, vaulted over the water, and was, astoundingly, airborne. With a great flap of wings, one of the swans also lifted into the air and fell behind Nyah's horse as if a contrail to her flight.

# CHAPTER THIRTY-SEVEN

The start of Homecoming Saturday was brutal. I slept in but still felt like I had left a particle or two—brain matter, for sure—back at Alpenstock. Or would it be Asgard?

On rubbery legs, I limped over to my desk. It couldn't be good that Frigg—queen of Asgard—was panicking. With the nearest pen and scrap of paper, I scribbled down the names she had called out. When I got to Bleik, Norn of Childbirth, my hand cramped and I had to set the pen down. What had she and Eyra given to Frigg? And what was with the lark calling my attention to the empty basket, which could only have been Idunn's? Naïve Idunn, who had wanted to play games with the wicked Loki but ended up stripped of her magical apples and expelled from Asgard. Had she been there? If so, what was she trying to tell me? And one of the blonds had shape-shifted into a swan and followed the messenger. It made for an interesting convoy and for some wild speculations on my part, but nothing I could prove or act on. And I'd about had it with patience.

Downstairs, my mom had left a message stating that she and Stanley were at the hospital but would be home in time for pre-dance photos. With the house to myself for the entire day, I holed up in my room, writing notes regarding every piece of advice I'd received from Hulda, what I knew of the other worlds and their portals, what was bequeathed to me by my *amma* — her lullaby, for instance, and the cameo — and both vision quests and their potential meaning. Those, I felt, were the most important. More than once I thought about reaching out for help: Hulda, Ofelia, Jinky, Jack. Above all Jack. I was ready to. And ready to admit that I was unequal to this challenge, unworthy of my gifts, and responsible for so much that was amiss: Leira's not-meant-for-this-world frailty, the presence of a merman among us, and the looming threat of Brigid's domination scheme.

At the end of this exercise, I'd filled a good portion of a composition book, my hand was cramped, and I had come to only one conclusion. If the goddess Frigg was rallying her maidens against a threatening "evil," I was in — we all were in — seriously deep trouble. Trouble it was up to me, and me alone, to fix.

In the late afternoon, I turned my attention to the dance. Plenty of girls, I knew, had spent the day at the salon getting pampered. I seriously gave my hair a long look before deciding I could not get away without washing it.

As I was putting an iron to the last of a few curls, my mom called out, "Knock, knock," as she ascended the last few steps to my attic space.

After filling me in on Leira's holding-stable condition, she fussed over my dress and said all the things a mother is supposed to. And, in spite of the overall funk I was in and entitled to, I did like the way my dress had turned out. What was once a silvery chain-mail jacket was now a scoop-necked bodice that shimmered like glass. And the gauzy, light putty-colored skirt had its own gossamer qualities.

"It's gorgeous," my mom said. She lifted one of the skirt's layers and then stood back and watched it drop into place. "Your creations always amaze me. A talent from your father's side of the family, I have to admit."

I'd inherited enough from my mom's side, with both the Stork and selkie lineage dropping from her branches of the family tree. Besides, there had never been any question where my style gene came from. My mom had no less than four pairs of Birkenstocks, while the clerks at the Coach store at Santa Monica Place knew my grandmother by name. No need to consult the Human Genome Project on this DNA sequence.

"Thank you. And it didn't even cost that much." I knew that feature of the dress would impress my number-crunching mom.

We heard the old-fashioned *dong* of the front doorbell.

"That must be Jack," my mom said, springing to action. "Give it a minute or two and then make your entrance."

So maybe I'd sold my mom short on the vogue gene; the ability to premeditate an entrance required some innate understanding of style.

I did give it a few minutes, but not many. I had a sudden onset of restless body syndrome that produced in me an irrepressible urge to get the evening under way — "over with" being the sentiment I couldn't quite admit to at the time.

Jack held up his side of the requisite girl-enters-and-boy-goes-gummy equation. Another thing to add to the growing list of things for which I could count on him.

"You look beautiful," he said, coloring. He was always a little different, more reserved, in front of the parental units.

My mom and Stanley did their best to get the obligatory photos quickly so that we could be on our way. My mom did want a few snapped in front of the house. We didn't have too many of it in its still-pink capacity, and she thought it would be fun "in the future" to remember it that way. Personally, I thought it would be fun to have a future at all, but I didn't bring that up while we were posing for posterity.

# CHAPTER THIRTY-EIGHT

Until I stepped into the transformed gym that evening, I wasn't sure I had ever fully registered the dance's "Starry, Starry Night" theme. The celestial decor created an alternate world. As if I needed another of those! But, once again, I had to hand it to the decorations committee for an above-and-beyond effort. A thousand glittery stars and orbs hung from the ceiling. Wall art consisted of backlit dark canvases depicting the various constellations: Orion, the hunter; Canis Major, his hunting dog; Aquarius, the water bearer; Pegasus, the winged horse; and many more.

While the event was fresh and we were settling into the occasion, Jack and I did the auto pilot routine. I talked dresses and hair with the girls I knew and liked, a much larger and still-growing group compared to the year before.

Penny looked radiant in her pink. Her loose updo held an array of shimmery star pins, which looked gorgeous against her red locks. I was more than a little surprised, and oddly miffed, to see the cameo—the pink lady?—at her throat. It looked lovely and belonged with the dress, but I still felt peevishly proprietary about the piece. I only hoped that Penny's procurement of it had been an act of defiance. *That* would, at the minimum, be a mitigating factor.

Jinky looked great, too. Her long, black mandarin-style tunic was exotic among the pastels and brights. And with her full complement of nose and brow rings, as well as her dramatically penciled eyes, she was striking while fully retaining her bad-girl image. I kept looking around for her date, but she seemed to be hanging only with Shauna and a couple of her track friends until it hit me like a boot to the face. Shauna. How had I not seen that one coming?

Jack, over in guy world, talked football and lamented the stuffy shirts and ties. For that first part of the evening, our two separate spheres were like a moving Venn diagram, intersecting at points, veering off for a while without a single point of contact, until eventually merging.

The first few songs played by the DJ had been

top-forty and lame. At last he slowed it down, and I immediately tugged on Jack's arm. For all his protests about not liking to dance, the guy definitely wasn't opposed to a little rubbing of bodies and long, hot kisses. And nothing like moving to the center of a mash-up of couples to avoid notice. At moments like these, with Jack's body fitting into every contour of my own, I was strengthened by our bond and practically brought to my knees by his strong hands around my waist and the intensity of his gaze.

When the tempo picked back up, we returned to our corner, where I was surprised to see Penny standing alone.

"Where'd Marik go?" I asked Penny.

I'd only had one brief look at him earlier — kitted out in all black — before he hurried away from our group with his head down.

"That's the question of the day." Penny searched the room, pinching her brows together as she did so. At that moment Beyoncé's "All the Single Ladies" started up.

"Come on," I said, dragging her toward the dance floor. "We'll show the guy what he's missing."

One of the best things about Penny was that, given the opportunity, she could be over-the-top, girly-girl silly. We worked that song, *oh-oh*ing and ring-finger wagging, until finally even Jinky succumbed and joined in for some booty-shaking. I noticed Jack up against the wall with his arms crossed and a bemused expression skewing his mouth to the side. I'd hear about the display, suffer a comment or two, but he had enjoyed the show. His foot may have even tapped to the beat.

We returned to our group, and, to my surprise, Marik was still nowhere to be found. He and Penny were due to take part in the pageantry that was about to start.

"Would the members of this year's Homecoming court please assemble behind the stage?" the DJ said over the microphone. His announcement produced another anxious swiping left-to-right glance from Penny.

"Go. I'll send him to the stage if he shows up here," I said, giving her the gentlest of nudges in that direction.

Jack and I got into a conversation about couples matching their Homecoming attire. He was adamantly opposed; I was slightly more accepting, provided hot pink was removed from the men's side of the equation.

A stocky guy looking miserable in a fuchsia-satin bow tie trudged past. I ducked behind Jack's back to hide my fit of giggles.

While sheltered by Jack and admiring—as if I had never seen them before, had never run my hand across their sinewy blades—his broad shoulders, something went *thwomp* against the door behind me. We were standing near an exit. They were your standard industrial-purpose metal doors. Jack and I turned, inspecting the area, but as the sound had come from outside, we ignored it.

Besides, at that moment, something else caught my attention. Across the room, a figure darted in and out of the crowd. Only Marik had that odd combination of bulk and lightness of being.

"Would Marik Galdursson please report to the stage?" the DJ announced. The timing was uncanny.

I watched for Marik, and again saw him dodging between packs of kids, but he was moving away from the stage and out of the gym entirely.

"I have to go to the bathroom," I said to Jack. Having struck up a conversation with one of his football buddies from last year's team, he waved me off distractedly.

I stepped out of the gym and into the long hallway that connected it to the school. I heard another *thump* from outside, but this one sounded like something hitting the roof. I barely registered it, though, as I spied Marik rounding a corner ahead of me.

"Marik!" I called out.

He turned, looked at me, and then continued, picking up his pace, even.

"Marik!" I yelled louder, because when someone is clearly running away from you, that second shout-out makes all the difference.

He was heading toward the main building, away

from the field house. I hiked up my gauzy skirt, so not designed for a chase scene, and took off after him.

He was wickedly fast for someone who was new to legs. Nor did it help that I had four-inch backless sandals on.

I'd never have caught up with him if he hadn't suddenly doubled over, presumably in pain.

"What's wrong?" I asked, coming to an arm-flailing stop at his side. "Didn't you hear me? Plus, they're calling for you up onstage."

"It doesn't matter," Marik said, his eyes focused on the floor. "None of that matters; the dance is over."

"No, it's not," I said. "What are you talking about? It only just started."

Again, something smacked against the building, a window this time.

"Do you hear it?" Marik said, groaning to a stand. "It's wrong. Very wrong. And have you not felt the darkness arriving?"

I looked up to the window at the very end of the corridor. It did appear particularly gloomy for early evening. The sky, in fact, had a purplish quality to it.

"What is it?" I asked.

Marik clutched at his chest. "A presence. And it's close, very, very close."

A presence? I thought immediately of the scene at the Asking Fire.

Again, something, a muffled *whomp,* crashed against the building.

And then all hell broke loose. From the hallway outside the gym, I heard a shriek. Marik muttered some foreign expletive-sounding remark and began jogging in that direction.

Wising up, I slipped my sandals off and started after him. In the wide hallway outside the gym, a door to the outside had been propped open and kids were streaming out. Some were screaming, and some held their arms up, shielding their faces. Marik and I followed them into the parking lot, where littered on the ground were lifeless dark blobs. I couldn't quite make out what they were until something dropped from the sky just a few feet from where Marik and I stood. A bird. A dead bird.

I felt my throat constrict. My breath came in rasping, painful drags. Another bird landed behind me. Its wings crumpled awkwardly and its beak open as if in mid-caw.

And now the presence that Marik had felt overtook me. Something icy-cold descended, invisible, soundless, and scentless. I felt its weight, like a material precipitation, but then it became vaporous and expansive, lodging in my throat and lungs. Gasping for air, I noticed Marik, too, was suffering.

Birds. Blackbirds. Crows. Jays. Robins. And more. No other symbol, no other message could be more targeted at me.

More kids were exiting the gym and joining us in the parking lot for this aerial and funereal display. As they coursed among us, shouting, pointing, and stepping among the dark carcasses, more birds dropped from the sky. A panic ensued. People were knocked to the ground in the frantic rush to avoid the falling birds. And again, the faces in the crowd became ugly and distorted. Some pointed and laughed with a menacing snarl at the lifeless winged creatures. Others scurried about with vacant, zombified expressions, while a few became hostile. I noticed two simultaneous shoving matches break out. One was between two girls.

With the dark energy still lodging over the area, I myself was slowed by its density and felt an overall torpor that had me struggling as if in water or even quicksand.

As the volume of birds dropping increased, so did the pandemonium. From far above, desperate squawks and screeches filled the air. Their pitiful cries of distress were all the more woeful given the increasing number of birds tumbling with horrific *thwacks* all around us.

One girl was hit dead-on by a rather large blackbird, its extended wings folding over her like a curtain. Her scream was frantic and hysterical as the bird's broken wings became entangled in the straps and sashes of her dress's layers.

What possessed the crowd — myself included — to

251

remain outdoors was as inexplicable as the event itself. Girls continued to scream and cry, boys hollered for their dates and friends, and another fight erupted. Some kids ran, knocking others out of the way, to take shelter under the trees dotting the parking lots and the awnings of the exits facing that side of the building, but many stayed as if they, too, were held outside by an invisible force. In the ensuing panic, Marik and I became separated.

Wandering aimlessly among the mayhem, I eventually became aware of a few teachers and chaperones barking orders to return to the building. Their authoritative tones dragged me out of my stupor. So much had transpired in such a short time frame—the physical effects of the dark energy, the havoc of the crowd's reaction, and the realization of its symbolism—that I hadn't had a chance to wonder about, never mind look for, Jack.

In my defense, the huddle of bodies was so thick and their movements so frantic that it would have been a tough chore to find him. Now, with the crowd herding back toward the school, I looked for him, scanning my eyes left and right.

"Everyone back inside, now," Principal Henrich shouted, directing traffic with wide arm movements. In the distance, I heard the blare of sirens, authorities having been alerted to the situation. And still the *plonk* of dead birds continued to rain down.

With another sweep of the crowd, I caught sight of

Marik frantically waving to me. He was at the corner of the building some twenty or so feet away from me, but the shifting pulse of kids still milling about obscured him at intervals.

When the crowd parted again, I got another look at Marik. His full-arm pumping wave was a plea for me to follow him.

While birds continued to drop all around, the principal had now organized the teachers and chaperones to usher everyone back into the building. They corralled kids into a funnel-shaped formation. With two cop cars already pulled up to the fire lane, it seemed an official get-inside directive.

I looked again at the crowd issuing back into the gym. One of the cops had stepped out of his car. He shielded his head from the aviary bombs and jogged to assist the staff with an orderly procession toward shelter. Finally, there in the midst of the throng entering the building, I caught sight of Jack. Our eyes locked, and he sent me his own waving come-here message.

I took a step in that direction while quickly, with a flick of my eyes, relocating Marik, or where he had previously been. I saw only the flash of a dark suit darting around the building's corner and out of view. Turning, I signaled a go-without-me wave to Jack. He looked at me with an expression I couldn't quite place until his entire body stiffened and turned to face the spot where Marik had been. Someone else standing beside Jack came into focus at that moment, too. Penny. She looked at me, confused. Without thinking, I hiked my skirt up and took off, following Marik. Immediately, my heart cramped with the decision. In that fleeting moment, Jack's face had registered a thousand emotions: surprise, alarm, fear, and hurt. That last one cut me to the quick, but, still, I pounded after Marik.

Already, I was defending my actions. It would do no good for me to be sequestered inside. No matter the danger or consequences, I needed to know what was going on.

It was no easy feat dodging falling birds, even though the aerial pelting had lessened considerably. And the icy presence I had intuited — it, too, was diminished. I lost sight of Marik and ran without destination, following a hunch and heading toward the baseball diamond. In the dugout, I found Marik sprawled, as if spent, across the crude wooden bench.

I collapsed next to him. It was the first moment I'd had, away from the hysteria, to truly process the situation. With pinpoint accuracy, it hit me like a guided missile. Straight to the heart. With the *whack* of another dead bird hitting the flimsy roof above us, I drew my legs up under my skirt and huddled into a knot of pain. In this moment of stillness, I heard every bird's thud to the ground replayed, only double-time, so that the pounding became a constant beat. The visuals to this track were the grotesque faces of my classmates and, finally, Jack's clouding over with disbelief and hurt. He had seen Marik, of course. Why else would he have stared in that direction?

"I'm not sure what it was," Marik said, breaking the silence, "but it's retreating."

"I know," I said.

"You know what it was, or you know that it's going?" Marik pulled his arms across his chest. He looked bigger and more imposing than ever.

I took a long time to answer him, trying to steady my breath, to wait out my thundering heart. "Both," I said placing my feet on the ground.

"Not Jack," he said.

"Definitely not Jack," I replied.

"Brigid of Niflheim, then?" he asked, a note of sadness in the question.

"Yes. What was here tonight was evil to its core."

"Not in person, though," he said. "That's an important distinction."

Then, to my utter amazement, Marik popped to a stand and hopped up onto the dugout bench. Though it obviously exerted him, he bobbed up and down with an entirely inappropriate giddiness; he hugged his arms to his sides, smiling and even laughing. Tears welled in his eyes.

"What is wrong with you?" I asked, scooting away from his madness.

"You wouldn't understand," he said, turning his beaming face to the field and the carcasses littering the infield and outfield with dark spots. "You don't know what it's like to live without unpredictability, without volatility. And you don't understand that to have it—even in its darkest permutation—is like a window of blue sky after an eternity of blank walls."

"I'll take the blank walls over what we just went through, thank you very much."

"You think you would." Marik jumped down and came to a stand in front of me. "But you wouldn't. You must have seen a few of the beings in Niflheim, witnessed their shrunken forms, their vacant faces. It's much the same for Vatnheim, but here"—he stretched his arms out wide, turning—"on mercurial Midgard, every moment is full of glorious, unbridled passion and the thrill of the unknown."

"What if the unknown turns out to be a tragedy of the worst kind of personal misfortune there is?" I asked.

Marik turned back to face me. "You think I don't understand personal tragedy?" He clutched at his chest. "I'm out of time, remember?"

Something about his intonation when saying "out of time" was different. Its meaning was altered, deeper.

"Out of time how, exactly?"

"Months ago, when I was sent through to broker the original deal, the portals were vulnerable. What we've witnessed is an impressive display, one that would require great magic, but that ultimately demonstrates her limitations. The portals hold, as they had for centuries. Anyway, I knew the risk when accepting the assignment."

"You don't mean . . . ?"

He nodded his head slowly. "The portals hold. There is no return."

"But I thought you were, like, immortal or something." I could hear the fear in my squawky voice.

"Our lives are very long — by your standards, especially — but, like most things, we expire."

I stood and paced a few steps away from him, thinking. It made sense, I supposed, given Safira's quest for an heir. But another point didn't.

"I don't get it. Someone once told me you were soulless."

"We are. And a trade-off, perhaps. Though we enjoy longevity, we do not have a reincarnate spirit form as you do. The best English words to describe the difference is that we have an animus while you have a soul."

Animus? It sounded primitive.

"So when you . . . die . . . ?" My pacing brought me round-trip.

"It's permanent."

"But why would Safira sacrifice one of her own people?"

"To gain something much dearer to her: an heir."

Thoughts twisted through my brain until they became directional, wringing like a rag mop. "But if you're not returning—if that was always a risk—how are you to take Leira back?"

"I was never to *take* Leira back."

"I don't understand."

"Leira is prophesied to die soon. In spirit form, with your assistance, she will transition."

"What?" I punched my fists down on my hips. "This was never made clear to me." The full impact of this pronouncement rocked me to my core.

Leira would die. My mom and Stanley would hold her lifeless body. There'd be a funeral and the kind of grief that altered lives, after which I'd be expected to arrange her passage to Vatnheim. It was unthinkable.

"I won't do it," I said, rounding on him.

"I am only the messenger." Marik lifted his hands, a double stop-sign gesture.

I snapped; I heard it, a popping sound like cracked

knuckles. *I won't do it,* I repeated to myself, but then realized it meant nothing if merely internalized. I spun and grabbed him by both shoulders, enunciating, my voice rising with every word, "I won't do it. I defy Queen Safira. I break the pact."

"It's not so easy," Marik said, plying my fingers off him. "Do you not remember that the pact is charmed with magic, that a powerful spell connects the essentials of the agreement?"

"I don't care." My voice increased in volume. "And besides, what does that even mean?"

"Without a change to one of the three essentials — Leira's soul, your ability, and my animus — the pact holds as far as Queen Safira is concerned. As long as she senses those three are intact, she remains patient."

"And were one of those *essentials* to change in nature?" I hated even using Safira's terminology for the heinous agreement.

"I can only guess." Marik stumbled backward a step. His eyes grew round, and his face blanched.

"Well, what?" "Queen Safira would seek vengeance. And without an heir — with the failure of what she claimed was her last hope — there's no telling what she would do."

"I'll take my chances."

Marik walked the length of the dugout; his arms

were pulled close into his body and his awkward lunges forward were so different from his usual smooth glides. "But you take chances with everything. Everything! Don't you see?"

"Yes, I'm taking chances. Who wouldn't to save a sister? As if I could watch her die. As if I could send her to Vatnheim. You yourself described shrunken forms and vacant faces. Even you prefer it here; you said as much."

Marik hung his head as if it were too heavy to hold upright. "Do you not understand? Life, all life, is a precarious balance. If one realm fails, all fail. And if a personal sacrifice is for the greater good . . ."

That last bit was a wrench to the heart. Marik, whose animus would go out like a light, still cherished everyone and *everything* enough to vie for life's continuation.

"It just can't be Leira," I said, choking up.

"While the three essentials hold, there is still hope, Katla. Believe this." His skin had gone clammy and pale, and he clutched at his side in pain. "But Jack, I know now, is poison to me. With every moment in his presence, my life force drains. He alone could ruin everything. You must keep him away from me at all costs. Can you agree to this much?"

"I . . . I guess."

"I trust you in this," Marik said, backing a few steps before turning and running off slowly and stiffly, as if in great pain.

With his departure, I was gusted back to the scene at hand. The sensory affront of the immediate situation flooded me, and I lifted my tear-filled eyes back to the school. A cacophony of sights and sounds overwhelmed me. More emergency vehicles had arrived; their flashing lights and blaring sirens hurt my eyes and ears. I was aware also of voices, many more voices than before. A line of arriving vehicles bearing, no doubt, anxious parents made their way into the parking lot. In the distance I could see a news truck pulled up onto a curb, with workers scurrying about with cords and cameras. I knew I should find Jack. I owed him an explanation and an apology at the very least. Others would be worried about me as well. For all I knew, my mom's car was among the procession pulling into the parking lot. But it was all too much to handle. What could I possibly say? How would I explain my absence to Jack? How could I bear distracting my mom and Stanley, diverting them from Leira's side when she had, according to Marik, little time left? That last thought had me welling with tears as I sprinted over third base and across left field to the line of trees behind the school.

# CHAPTER THIRTY-NINE

I hid in the stand of woods behind Norse Falls High for what felt like a very long time. Reliving the chain of events since last spring, I crouched under a tree. I was frightened and sad and exhausted and, above all, ashamed. Had I anywhere to go, I'd have set out for it immediately. California crossed my mind more than once.

What exactly did Marik mean that Safira would seek vengeance? Did he know that Brigid sought her cooperation in unleashing Ragnarök? I already had one queen after me; was a second a mere doubling, or was it an exponential increase? Would Safira truly be led into such an evil and irrevocable act? On more earthly matters:

Leira was gravely ill, destined to die, were Marik to be believed. And what of his own dilemma? How much longer did he have? And how would I keep Jack away from him?

In this state of limbo, alone and without my purse or phone, both of which I'd left at the dance, I felt disconnected from the world—all worlds. It was, finally, the memory of Leira's helpless mewl that got me to my feet.

With our new house in Norse Falls proper, it didn't take me too long to make the walk-of-shame home, my sandals dangling from my heavy-as-my-heart arms and the hem of my dress frayed and covered in mud and bird guts, for all I knew. Just as I rounded the corner to our street, a familiar green truck pulled up alongside me.

*Crap.*

The door flung open, and Jack came running toward me, wrestling me into a shoulder-dislocating hug. "I was so worried. Where the hell have you been?"

"Walking." Feeling unworthy, I wriggled out of his hold.

"But where did you go?"

"I just . . . It was the birds. I freaked and had to get away from there."

"And Marik?"

"What about him?"

"You followed him."

"Yes, but—"

"Why would you do that? You saw me, right?"

"I did, but just don't ask."

"Don't ask. Why not?"

Then it occurred to me: I needed a way to keep the two apart. And the way Marik had girls in heat was like something straight out of *National Geographic*. Why not me? We did spend a lot of time together; we were project partners and neighbors.

"Because . . ." I intentionally trailed off.

"Is there something going on?" The lines around Jack's eyes creased. More shock. More confusion. More hurt.

"It's complicated," I said. It wasn't an affirmation or a denial, but damning all the same.

"What's that supposed to mean?"

"That it's not . . . easy to explain."

"I don't believe you."

"I just need some time," I said. It was true. All of it was true, but the damage I was doing was so swift, Jack reeled as if physically injured.

"What the hell are you saying?"

"I need a break."

His face went red. Anger this time. It, the least rational of emotions, was the one I intended to exploit. He finally held up his right hand in a wait-there gesture and stepped over to his truck. He returned a moment later and pressed my purse and cell phone into my hands.

"These are yours," he said, and turned back to his car.

I didn't reply. I didn't trust myself not to take it all back. To cave and tell him everything. Watching him drive away was horrible. He wouldn't look at me. His eyes, hard and cold, were fixed straight ahead. When his tires squealed taking the corner, I knew it was because he couldn't get away fast enough. I had the "break" I asked for but didn't want.

Coming in the back way, I found my mom at the kitchen table with the home phone and a cup of coffee in front of her.

"Kat. Oh, my God, Kat. Where have you been?" She jumped to a stand.

"I walked home," I said, hanging my head.

"But what took you so long? You've got everyone worried about you. Stanley, your dad, and Jack are all out driving, looking for you."

"I got confused. Went the wrong way. Had to double back. It was stupid, I know. But that scene at the school was just so . . . crazy . . . I don't know. I probably don't even make much sense."

My mom came forward and hugged me. "You're all right. That's all that matters." She released me. "And what a thing to go through. Especially after last year's barn fire. I swear that school should suspend all future Homecoming dances. It's all over the news, of course. They're saying that mass bird die-offs like that are rare, but not unheard of. But to shower down on a group of kids all dressed up. It must have been awful."

I lifted my shoulders in the wimpiest of shrugs.

My mom pulled her hand to her temple. "I better let the others know. They'll be so relieved."

I overheard her conversations with Stanley and my dad. They were brief but upbeat. She then held the phone out to me. "Do you want to call Jack yourself? The poor guy. When I spoke with him earlier, he was beside himself."

"He found me a few minutes ago on our street. I got my purse and phone back from him"—I lifted both for my mom to see—"so we're good." We weren't, of course. But my mom probably figured the panic at the school was the source of my sad eyes and faltering voice.

"Can I get you anything? You look shaken."

"Just tired. I'm heading up." The stairs to the attic seemed steeper than usual. That or my legs were as heavy as my conscience.

Moments later I stepped out of my dress and let it float down in a shimmery ring. In a camisole and my undies, I crawled under the covers, too weary to even produce tears.

I had a hard time falling asleep. Though the forecasters hadn't called for it, a storm blew up. I, of course, knew its source. Jack. Another thing to feel all-over awful about. Rain pelted my windows in crashing waves, and the wind battered the house, rattling the panes and yelping like something wounded. He hadn't used his own powers here on Midgard since last Christmas's snowstorm, but now two Saturdays in a row . . . I wondered where he was and what he was doing. Was he curled up on his bed like me? Or at the window watching his handiwork? Or, worse still, doing everything in his power to control the outburst, but failing? Just thinking of that scenario was a stake to the heart.

Marik came to mind, too. How was this storm affecting him? His animus was already frail. Without him, an essential, the pact would be broken. Safira—and willing accomplice Brigid—would seek vengeance. Even the goddess Frigg was worried about the treachery their conspiracy would unleash. If there was an occasion for Hulda's patience-above-all mantra, I felt it was now. There was yet one small glitch in my developing scheme.

In pain and with frustration, I pulled my pillow over my head to muffle my sobs.

# CHAPTER FORTY

I wake cold, alone, and on a beach. To my right are thick woods and to the left an expanse of rolling waves. Above me, the sun breaks over the treetops; it is the dawn of a new day. I sit up, taking in the rest of the scene. At the edge of the trees and sitting on a fallen log, I spy a lone figure with its back to me. The ebony hair and the shape of her outline look familiar. I stand and hurry over the sand; small shells jab at my bare feet.

As I draw near, I shout, "Jaelle, it's me, Kat!"

She rocks back and forth with her arms wrapped around her knees and her white nightgown billowing in the breeze. She doesn't turn or make any indication she hears me.

"Jaelle, can you hear me?" I continue.

It's no use, I soon realize. She's in a trancelike state.

A bleat alerts me to something at one end of the fallen log. I jog a few steps to find the baby girl atop a bed of kelp. She stretches, gurgling, but shows no sign of distress or discomfort, but she can't stay here. I stoop, readying to pick her up when a head pops up from the other end of the log. It's the boy. He waves shyly and sits on the end of the log, staring. I can't tell if he's looking out to the water or gazing upon Jaelle. When I take a step to investigate, I'm suddenly losing purchase with the sand around me. It's caving, sucking all of us down with it.

# CHAPTER FORTY-ONE

Because my life didn't suck enough, when I awoke on Sunday I had another Stork dream to contend with. This one at least felt like a move in the right direction. Jaelle. Finally, she put in an appearance. Unfortunately, there was a hitch, a big one: there should have been at least two other potential mothers present. With only Jaelle, it felt like inadequate information. And, of course, the two separate, non-twinlike essences seemed a problem, too. And it was short. Too short, I feared.

I made a conscious effort to ignore these anomalies, shelve them. Burrowing under the covers, I wished that it had all been a dream. Everything. Beginning with our move from California to Minnesota. Had we never come to Norse Falls, I'd be blissfully ignorant of my gift—and have a much better tan. But there'd be no Jack. Even though the thought of him made me hurt at a molecular level, I couldn't imagine a life without him.

I rolled over and snatched my phone off my nightstand. Penny had left me a *what happened 2 U?* text, but that was it. What did I expect? I'd asked Jack for a "break," after all.

I showered and arrived wet-headed downstairs, where I found Stanley on his laptop and my mom unloading the circa-1977 dishwasher.

"Good morning." My mom eyed me nervously.

I grunted a response.

"How do you feel? Did you sleep well?" she asked.

I collapsed onto a chair, which I figured was reply enough.

"We were just talking about last night," Stanley said. His voice was chipper; he was obviously clueless as to my mom's concern and my slump. "Though nothing's been released to the press yet, some findings are coming in." He lowered his computer screen. "Some of the birds were brought to Walden for a necropsy. The findings are interesting, to say the least."

"Why?" my mom asked.

"Preliminary evidence suggests they suffered from a sudden plunge in body temperature, but that would have meant they were flying at altitudes they couldn't sustain."

"You're ruling out another possibility," my smart mom said. "A cold air mass could have descended to them."

I could tell by the way Stanley's forehead folded into pleats that he rejected this theory. "Anything cold enough to drop birds from the sky would have been felt on the ground. We'd have had record lows last night."

I looked out the window. The sky was a dingy aluminum; drops spattered the pane. Though I wondered at the origin of this particular weather system, it didn't look particularly cold outside.

My mom closed an upper cupboard on a tidy row of mugs. "It was an ugly mess and unfortunate; that's a fact we can all agree on."

My mom looked at her watch. "Are you about ready?" she said to Stanley. "I don't want Leira to wake up alone."

The phone rang, and we all turned our heads in unison.

"Hello," my mom said into the receiver. "We were just on our way." She paused, listening. "We'll be there as soon as we can. Thank you for calling." She hung up and brought the heel of her palm to her forehead.

"What is it?" Stanley asked, standing.

"Leira's fever has spiked again. They want to discuss a different antibiotic. We need to go now."

"I'm coming with you," I said, pushing away from the table.

The lobby of Pinewood General was becoming all too familiar. This fact was confirmed when the nurses didn't ask us to sign in or check for our visitors' badges. We could probably have used the staff elevators without turning too many heads.

Leira's doctor met us in the hallway, where he quickly updated us on her relapse and treatment options. Not one minute after my mom and Stanley agreed to a new round of IV-delivered antibiotics, her cell phone rang. The conversation was brief but tense.

"That was Ofelia," my mom said, dropping her phone back into her purse. "She's down in the emergency room with Afi. He collapsed at the store."

I pressed my eyes shut at the sight of my mom wiping back tears and Stanley rubbing her shoulder.

"You go," he said. "Take Kat with you. I'll stay with Leira."

My mom and I didn't even speak as we made our way down to the emergency room, no directions required. I was too stunned and overwhelmed to work up the saliva necessary to form words. My mom, I could tell, was busy keeping her emotions in check. The occasional wipe of her wet cheeks confirmed this.

We found Ofelia in the waiting room.

"What is it?" my mom asked.

"They think it's his lungs," Ofelia replied. "The doctor's waiting to speak with you."

My mom hurried off after a woman in a white lab coat. I started to follow her, but Ofelia tugged on my arm.

"A word, if I may," she said, and looked around to make sure no one was close enough to overhear.

I sat down next to her. "OK."

"How's Leira?" she asked.

"Not good. And now Afi."

"I'm sorry," she said. "And on top of last night."

I clutched at the arms of the vinyl-padded chair. "A rough weekend."

"I wonder if the council should confer," Ofelia said, tucking an AWOL wisp of hair back into her loose twist.

"We will. Tonight."

"Oh," she said. "With everything else going on, you have a bestowment, too?"

I nodded my head. Before that moment I hadn't decided yet just what to do about last night's dream. With Jaelle as the only vessel and with multiple souls, the entire equation was backward. But if I'd learned anything at all in the past twenty-four hours, it was that life was unpredictable. And with everything else hanging by a frayed thread, what difference would a slightly unorthodox bestowment make? In for a penny, in for a pounding.

My mom returned from her consultation. "His lungs have filled with fluid; it's called a pulmonary edema and is likely due to an infection," she said. "They're going to admit him and administer an intravenous diuretic and antibiotics if they find an infection. He's on oxygen, too." My mom pulled her hair back nervously. "Can you believe we've got two of them on breathing machines? What are the odds of that?"

Personally, I could believe it. Because the odds of a family with mercreature genes having lung problems had to be pretty high. Not that I'd be opening my fish mouth with any such news.

"Thank you again, Ofelia," my mom continued. "You've been such a help with my father. What did we take you away from? Did you have to close the store?"

"Don't worry. The new girl, Kat's friend Jinky, was able to help out. She's been such a godsend already."

Even I had to admit that Jinky was a huge help. But godsend? That had to have been a first for her.

I spent the rest of the day migrating between Leira and Afi. Both were too sick to appreciate the bedside vigil, so later in the afternoon I took Ofelia up on her offer of a ride home. I waved her away from the curb, promising to give my sister Storks plenty of notice for our council meeting that night. I would. As if I needed Grim to show up all grinchy.

The house felt empty. I picked up my phone about

a dozen times to call Jack; he deserved to know about Leira and Afi, but I couldn't risk him coming here to console me. Marik had been clear about Jack's effect on him. Without knowing how close was too close, I couldn't have them on the same street. Besides, it was best, for now, to perpetuate our "break."

I did phone Penny. At first she was chilly with me, asking why I took off. She didn't ask about Marik directly, but her tone implied confusion. The conversation was quick; she was obviously going to make me work to make amends. She did, at least, update me on the bird situation. All kinds of theories were floating around, everything from a prank by Pinewood to insecticide poisoning to a high-altitude lightning strike, the day's continued showers probably lending credence to the latter. Stanley's cold-air-mass explanation had obviously not been released yet or had been dismissed.

I also finally got a hold of my dad, who was surprisingly tight-lipped about where he'd been all day and why he had never returned my messages. I could hear him jangling keys and huffing about, and it was nice to know that he was on his way to visit Afi, allowing my mom and Stanley to focus on Leira. Say what you will about the guy — he'd made his mistakes — but he came through when you needed him. That said a lot about a person. I just wished as much could be said about me.

# CHAPTER FORTY-TWO

Later that evening, I unlocked the back door and sat waiting in my second chair, the Robin's chair. From the waist up, I made a concerted effort to appear calm and cool, while under the table my knees were jingling like loose change.

Ofelia was the first to show up. The rest tumbled in behind her while I sat at my place with my hands grasping the table so as not to fall into the growing pit in my stomach.

Grim and Hulda were the last two to arrive; both wore an air of solemnity.

Hulda got right down to business, calling for roll, at which we were all accounted for.

"Before we proceed," Hulda said, rising from her chair, "let me assure my sister Storks that an account of last night's incident has been dispatched to the World Council."

This was a group that took its bird-watching seriously, and, much like lifting the cover on a manhole, a rush of steam in the form of remarks and exclamations shot forth. I overheard more than one mention of Dorit, our expelled member, as well as a hushed "enemy *still* in our midst" response. That one, I feared, was eerily on the mark.

"Order, please." Hulda calmed the room with fanning hands. "Let us not panic. We have no proof of a sinister connection to the occurrence." Her eyes raked over me as she said this, and I'm sure I went blotchy; I didn't even color well under pressure. "Now, who has initiated tonight's meeting?"

"I've been contacted"—I began in the way we always did, but I knew that what followed would be a major divergence. I squeezed my eyes shut briefly, bracing myself—"by two separate and distinct essences. . . . I know it's highly unusual."

"Unusual?" Hulda's head angled to the side.

"Twins, and other multiples, are not unknown to us," Grim interjected. "You yourself were present when Fru Svana placed twin girls."

"Except," I said, "there is only one vessel, someone

who is known to me, someone whose desire for a child is known to me, someone whom I want very much to help."

"What are you saying, child?" Hulda asked. "It almost sounds as if you're describing a situation in which you have two souls vying for a mother you've selected. A situation you've orchestrated on behalf of the mother—"

"That's impossible," Grim cut in. "It's quite the reverse of our purpose. The focus is always on the hovering soul. More importantly, such powers are beyond . . ." Here Grim stopped herself as if unwilling to suggest I was capable of anything special.

"Sisters, please," Hulda said, "hold your comments."

And, yes, it did gratify me that it had been one "sister" in particular who was being shushed. If I was going rogue, I wasn't opposed to having Grim's bitter pucker as my parting glance.

I stood and turned to Hulda. "Indeed, Fru Hulda, I believe this to be the case. I realize that it's not standard practice, but, yes, on behalf of a predetermined mother, multiple essences presented themselves."

Hulda sat back in her chair and flopped her arms over its sides. Many moments passed.

I remained standing, not knowing whether to continue or wait for her to comment. And my sister Storks— generally quick to fly into squawks of alarm—took me in with stretched lips and bulging eyes. I finally decided to take my seat. I sensed it was best to keep a low profile and preserve my strength.

"This is quite unprecedented," Hulda said finally. "Never have I heard of such a thing. Not here. Nor at my many visits to the World Council." Again, she went ashen. I didn't know what to do. "You best continue," she said. "I feel quite certain that we will not know how to proceed until all the information is known to us."

"But Fru Hulda, this is clearly an act of willful defiance," Grim said. "Would you have us encourage such behavior?"

Hulda, when turning to Grim, looked tired, the gray of her woolen cardigan the same shade as her neck and face. "Fru Grimilla, I have asked our sister Stork Katla to continue. Would you defy my authority?"

Grim's head snapped back so far I heard the ping. It sounded like a bullet dropping into a chamber.

All eyes swiveled back to me. How did I never learn with Grim? Her hatred of me was now so complete I could read the fill line at the top of her brow scrunch. But I supposed the bigger question was how did I never learn, period.

"The mother is confident and assertive." I wasn't about to use Grim's choice words of "gung ho and brassy" to describe Jaelle, nor did I have to. Her slitted eyes conveyed her comprehension. "And the souls, as I described earlier, are separate and distinct. I well remem-

280

ber Fru Svana's placement of twins; those essences presented together and remained united during all dream sequences." I looked off to the sconces lighting the room. They flared as if censuring me, too. "The two even present as different ages—"

"How so?" Hulda cut in, biting back her lips as if reproaching herself for interrupting.

"One is a baby girl, frightened and helpless. One is a boy, two or possibly three years of age, brave and inquisitive."

I paused, sensing a shock-and-awe reaction to my announcement. Not a one of them moved. Even the walls seemed to close in, as if leaning in to hear better.

"I recommend number one, the baby girl," I continued. "A preference for a girl is known to me." I looked around the room, realizing they were all gaping at me like my head was on backward. I touched my nose just to be sure. They were all still staring. "Should I go ahead with the vote now?"

Hulda stood, pushing her chair back. It scraped across the slab concrete floor. "It occurs to me that, per Stork protocol, once multiple candidates have been presented, a vote must follow."

Stork protocol? A memo I never got.

"Fru Hulda, this refers to multiple maternal or *vessel* candidates," Grim added.

"I believe," Hulda said, "you'll find the wording to

be nonspecific. Fru Birta, if you would be so kind as to check."

I'd never really pondered the thickness of Birta's book before, even after we'd had to replace it after the infamous vandalism incident — by Brigid, no less — to our meeting space. It would appear, however, the way Birta now ran her finger over pages and columns, that it was a reference tome, as well as an attendance log.

"Fru Hulda is correct," Birta said, removing her round, wire spectacles. "The wording simply states 'When a minimum of two candidates have been presented, a vote must forthwith proceed."

Hulda looked at me expectantly. I took it as a "Carry on" directive.

I raised a single shaky digit. "Who votes with me for essence one, the gentle baby girl?"

Half the room raised their index finger.

"And who votes for essence number two, the brave young boy?" I had made my choice clear as well as stated the mother's preference for a girl. It was no surprise, then, that Grim pumped her bony arm into the air, raising two fingers and leading a rebellion that was quickly joined by the other half of the room, Hulda — to my complete and utter shame — included.

I had a hard time perceiving what happened next. My vision had gone all wavy.

"A tie," Hulda said, stroking her chin. "Fru Birta, would you please read protocol regarding a tie?"

"We all know what to do in the case of a tie," Grim added, her voice struggling to tamp down her irritation.

"Fru Birta, please," Hulda said, overruling Grim's interruption.

Fru Birta trailed a bony digit along the bottom of a page. She'd always been a bit of a mumbler, but the voice she used as she scanned the text was positively crumbling. I had to strain, leaning forward in my seat, to hear her. She murmured bits of phrasing and then skipped ahead as she searched for the relevant clause. Though her articulation was grainy, like an old phonograph, I made out that she was under the section heading "Extenuating Circumstances," from which she read: "'Overlapping jurisdictions, unforeseen physical conditions and limitations, and autonomous bestowments,' as if we'd want to put any more ideas in Katla's head."

I hardly knew what to make of the last comment. It wasn't like Birta to be so outspoken.

Finally, she perked up and said, loud and clear, with her lips actually moving this time, "'In the event of a tie vote between two potential *vessels*—'"

"Stop there," Hulda broke in. "In this case, the book clearly specifies 'potential vessels.' Thus procedural instructions regarding a tie do not apply in the case at hand, one where we're deciding between potential *essences*."

"But what does that mean?" I asked, scooting forward in my seat.

"It means," Hulda said, sadness apparent in her voice, "that we are without precedent."

OK, but that didn't answer my question.

"So what do we do?" I asked, a more direct question this time.

Hulda folded her hands in front of her. "Sister Katla, you have presented us with a very difficult situation. One that, in disservice to all involved parties, leaves us at an impasse."

"What do you mean by an impasse?" I asked.

Hulda shook her head slowly from side to side, taking a long time to answer.

In the interim, I pondered the term *impasse,* as in obstruction or roadblock, nothing that a little elbow grease — and possibly a stick of dynamite — couldn't surmount.

"I shall take the matter to the World Council. This, in combination with the events of last night, merits further consideration."

Before I could react or object, Hulda had issued her customary "peace be," the meeting was adjourned, and my sister Storks were filing out past me with looks ranging from pity to fear to outright contempt.

I didn't mean to stay after, necessarily, but half my body was paralyzed by shock and the other half by plain old embarrassment. Hulda had voted against me. Forget Dickens, it hurt like Faulkner. And Jaelle's bestowment was on hold. This couldn't be good, either.

Finally, only Fru Hulda and I remained.

"I'm sorry," I said.

She didn't respond. Ouch.

I dropped my chin to my chest. "You're disappointed in me, aren't you?"

"Yes. You take on too much."

Ouch again.

"You should know, however, Katla, that when you came to us one year ago, I knew it was a sign of change. Your age, your impulsiveness, your unwitting but lodestone or magnetite quality of attracting other powerful beings, all combined to portend transformation of our ways. All of this I suspected and resigned myself to, but I wonder now . . ." Here she laid her hands flat against the smooth surface of the wooden table, seemingly studying the fretwork of veins on the backs of her hands. "I wonder at your recklessness, your disregard for advice and counsel, your willful independence." She paused, looking long and hard at me. "I don't suppose you have anything more to tell me about recent events or your sudden interest in Norse legends."

Tears stung at my eyes. How did I tease out the

stuff that she could help with from the stuff that would endanger her, that would endanger other loved ones? And, finally, how did I even begin to describe the plan taking shape in my head? I simply couldn't. Nor did I ever want her to think she missed an opportunity. "No," I said; my throat was dry and my words raspy.

"I didn't think so." Hulda stood. She looked weary and sad. "Katla, should the World Council move to discipline you, I would have very little in the way of mitigating information."

"I understand," I said, my voice actually cracking now.

I don't recall Hulda exiting the room. I only remember finding myself, some minutes later, alone in my grandfather's back room. It had reverted to its utilitarian purpose, and I sat in a simple folding chair. Gone was my Robin's chair. Gone was our massive oval table. Gone were the candles and sconces. Gone were my sister Storks.

I'd known I was on my own since the moment Marik had delivered his message, but now, having alienated both Jack and Hulda, I felt frightened and lonely and glum. And what did I have to look forward to? Possible disciplinary action. Man, I really knew how to screw things up royally. *Royally, ha.* As if I needed a pedigree to go with the doghouse I was in.

# CHAPTER FORTY-THREE

I had every intention of going to school on Monday morning, in spite of my lack of sleep and rock-bottom mood. My decision to walk that day and stop at Starbucks were supposed to be the jolts I needed to get my head back among the living. By now, the baristas and I were on friendly terms. They knew my usual, and I knew their names. It was a pleasant, if a little superficial, relationship. I was surprised, then, when Norah, even while smiling, muttered, "Must have been a rough night," as she handed me my change. I know my face soured in reaction; I felt my mouth push into a crimp. She had the brass to smile, turn, and address the next customer in line.

I *had* had a rough night. Rough week. Rough year.

But I hardly needed passing acquaintances pointing out my tangled ponytail and swollen eyes. It must have been a Monday-morning thing, because people, in general, were acting batty. I thought the guy standing next to me waiting for his beverage was on the phone; at first he was listing off the day's commitments: "Meeting at ten, lunch with Joe at twelve, report due by three." He wasn't, though; he was seemingly standing there reading aloud his appointment book for us all to hear. Things got odder still when he observed with a double blink and a throaty "Well, good morning, girls" that barista Monica was sporting a too-tight T-shirt. Odd that she didn't react to his comment. She didn't seem the type to take that kind of ogling from anyone. More Monday weirdness, I supposed.

I took my drink from high-beam Monica and exited the shop. I was in a bit of a fog; the people in Starbucks adding to my morning dementia, paranoia, even, because I had the weird sensation that someone was following me. I was halfway down the block before realizing I was headed in the wrong direction. I should have turned around; there was still time to make it to first period on time, but I didn't. I kept on going, eventually ending up at the old train tracks behind Afi's store.

The line had been abandoned years ago, and the rails were pulled up in sections with weeds and grass reclaiming the land. With the woods to one side and the backs of the downtown shops to the other, it was a good spot for a private walk and afforded plenty of space to think. The area reminded me of Jacob, the soul I'd reunited with his original mother. It had been here that I'd felt his presence strongest, here that we came to an understanding. This brought me around to thinking of Jaelle, and I tossed my head in annoyance. An impasse was an unwelcome delay, if not a complete breakdown. It was not what I had expected. And with the possibility of disciplinary action coming my way, who knew what that would do for Jaelle's cause?

Rounding a bend and coming to the huge fallen log where I'd once read to Jacob, I heard footsteps behind me. Turning, I was more than a little surprised to see Marik heading my way.

I wasn't in the mood to see anyone. Him especially.

"Are you following me?" I asked, noting his school backpack slung over his shoulder.

"Yes."

"Why?"

"You seemed lost."

"Trust me, I know my way around here by now."

"Not land lost," Marik said, coming to a stand beside me. I noticed that he limped and held one hand to his side gingerly. "Lost in spirit. Empty. Hurting. I thought maybe I could help. I've decided, in fact, that I want to help."

I brought a fist to my mouth, trying—but failing—to fight back emotions. Marik, who pretty much had an expiration date stamped on his forehead, was reaching out to me.

"Why would you want to help me? I've screwed up in every possible way and hurt some really good people in the process. You said it yourself on Saturday. And I'm scared and confused." I collapsed onto the log, splaying my legs in a wide V in front of me.

"Because what you pledged on Saturday was brave. If unwise, at least it was for all the right reasons. I admire that."

"You do?"

"Yes."

"But you implied it was selfish. And probably pointless."

"It may be pointless. She will do anything—anything—to procure an heir. Leira, she felt, was her last hope. I fear her reaction will be reckless, disastrous even."

"You're worried she'll join forces with Brigid of Niflheim."

He dropped onto the log next to me. "I don't like to think about it."

"Because together . . . ?"

He shuddered in reaction.

"Marik, what if I told you I was working on a substitute for Leira?"

"What? Who?"

"I can't say. Not yet, anyway."

He kicked a toe into a scruff of weeds. "She'll accept no second-rate substitute. Lineage and birthright and prophecy are critical."

So that last one would be a bit tricky. But it was *my* prophecy, after all, and a fabrication to begin with. The crazy thing was this wasn't the biggest of my obstacles. What I had ahead of me was a logistical puzzle the size and scope of Kennedy's man-on-the-moon mission. At least he had a team of scientists. All I had was a failing merman.

"Then I'll have to make sure my substitute's a good one."

He dug a look so deep into my eyes I had to blink him away.

"And you won't get in my way?" I continued.

"Not if you keep Jack out of mine." His voice went gruff just mentioning Jack's name. "That storm Saturday night almost killed me."

"He's hurt," I said.

"He's reckless," Marik replied.

I'd always been his undoing.

"We're taking a break," I said, hanging my hands

between my knees. "There shouldn't be any more of his . . . displays."

"Good." He exhaled with relief.

But nothing was good. Not for any of us.

"Come," Marik said, holding out his hand to me.

"Where?"

"School."

"School? You've got to be kidding." My hand stayed put.

"Our project is due this week. We have to finish it. Ms. Bryant is allowing class time all week to work on it."

"You think I care about a Design project with everything else going on?"

"I think you need this project—" He held his hand out farther.

"Need it?" I interrupted.

"Need the distraction."

"How will that help?"

"It will keep you sane while you work this out."

"I gave up on 'sane' about four stops back," I said.

"If not sane, then busy. In doing so, I believe you'll come up with something." Clearly having given up on my accepting his assistance, he reached down and pulled me to my feet.

"I warn you," I said. "This could be a bumpy ride."

"I have no doubt of it. You are some sort of giant mayhem magnet."

292

"Someone else called me a lodestone."

"You do seem to attract more than your share of trouble."

As we walked back toward school, I had to admit I felt slightly better. Just having one person say, "I believe in you," made a difference, even after being called a "mayhem magnet." Granted, I'd have preferred it to be Jack, would have expected it to be him, but the situation didn't afford for that. I'd just have to make do with Marik. Even if he was just another piece of space junk I'd pulled in like some huge strip of cosmic flypaper.

While walking up the front steps, I heard an engine gun. I turned around to catch the tail end of a truck — a beat-up old green thing — fishtailing around the corner.

Marik froze, folding in two with pain. "You said . . ."

I looked from Marik to the corner and back. The truck was a block away by then.

"He's gone," I said, fearing the truth of the words as they exited my mouth.

# CHAPTER FORTY-FOUR

Wednesday after school I was in Ms. Bryant's classroom using her aerosol adhesive to mount our graphics onto the trifold display board. Marik had been right. Go figure. With every other thing falling apart in my life, somehow the assignment became of paramount importance. It made about as much sense as flossing after the Last Supper, but focusing on this one thing put me to bed late and woke me up early two days in a row.

Even with the windows open, the spray glue emitted a stinging plume of toxic haze. Burrowing my mouth and nose into the crook of my elbow, I sat back on my haunches.

At home, things were in a holding pattern. Leira was still hospitalized but had stabilized enough to be taken off the ventilator. Her doctors weren't happy with her overall "failure to thrive," but the little fighter was hanging in there. Afi had been discharged and was convalescing at home. The doctors hadn't found an infection so were stumped as to the cause of the edema. Lack of oxygen didn't keep an old cuss like Afi from grumbling, which was probably a good sign. My chart-maker mom had devised a schedule so that Afi had dinner and someone to kvetch at every night of the week. My turn had been yesterday; I'd made BLTs and split-pea soup, the latter a favorite of Afi's, not mine.

Jack was the sandbag on my chest. On at least two occasions I'd thought I'd heard or seen his truck. I couldn't be sure, but both times my heart had crashed to my heels.

"Whoa," Ms. Bryant said, entering the room and fanning the air. "Maybe you should do that outside."

I took a deep breath, reexposing my airways to the vapors. I feared almost nothing at this point. "I'm done. Sorry about the fumes."

She picked up a file folder from her desk and waved it back and forth in front of her. "How's your grandfather doing today?"

"Better." I pressed my lips together, wondering how she knew he was sick. I hadn't said anything.

"And did your dad decide to go with chili or beef stew for his meal with him tonight?"

Now I added a jaw clench to my clamped lips. I had definitely not mentioned our meals-on-wheels program. Moreover, I didn't even know tonight was my dad's turn, never mind menu options. This was odd. I'd just spoken to my dad last night. It wasn't like him to keep anything from me. So if he and Ms. Bryant were conversing, he'd have told me. Unless . . .

"I'm not sure which he's going with," I said, playing along.

Ms. Bryant had taken a seat at her desk and tapped a pencil against a stack of papers. "He thinks the beef stew is probably the safer choice. He claims the chili is his specialty, but it packs a bit of heat." Ms. Bryant looked up, her eyes focused on something out the window, and her index finger trailed along her bottom lip. "If it's even half as hot as his kisses, it should only be served with a fire extinguisher handy."

"I beg your pardon," I said, lurching to a stand.

"The chili—your dad says it might be too hot for your grandfather."

I was myself a fireball of confusion. With that TMI tidbit—so unlike Ms. Bryant and so inappropriate for a teacher—she'd been running her finger over her lips, her closed lips.

"I have to go," I said, grabbing my book bag.

"Oh. OK. You and Marik are all set, then, for Friday."

"Yep. See ya."

If Ms. Bryant had added anything else to our parting comments, I didn't hear it; I was probably halfway to the parking lot by then.

I found Ofelia behind the counter at the store. She was ringing up items for an elderly customer. Hoping to speed the process, I stepped in and bagged up the few groceries. My heart flatlined for a moment when I lifted a clear plastic bag of pink apples, Snjosson Farms apples, into the brown sack. The moment the woman exited the store, I turned on Ofelia.

"I need your help," I said.

"In what way?" She moved an errant dime from the quarter compartment of the register.

"I'm not sure, but I think . . ."

Memories rushed at me like linebackers. Birta's "as if we'd want to put any more ideas in Katla's head" comment, for one. As well as the guy in Starbucks and his suggestive comments.

"Ofelia, I think I'm hearing what people are thinking."

She froze for a moment and then closed the cash-register drawer, triggering its bell.

"I have always wondered—"

"Wondered what?" I asked.

"Why I was called here."

"What? Why? I'm so confused."

"Katla, I know Hulda has told you that your gifts are special, even among our ranks. And your most recent bestowment, it shows a power beyond what Hulda probably ever imagined."

I exhaled. "Except those powers may get me disciplined."

"Yes, they may, but that does not negate their existence. And if you're tapping into people's thoughts, your gifts are continuing to grow and expand."

"I never asked for any of this." I backhanded an imaginary *this* away from me. "Especially not this new psychic nuisance. I just want . . . I just want to be normal again." With the admission, tears puddled in my eyes.

"Be careful what you wish for," Ofelia said with a twitch of her eyebrows. "As to your newest gift, I imagine it will prove useful soon, if it hasn't already."

Something Ofelia had said earlier burbled to the surface of my consciousness. "You mentioned you'd been called here. Why do you think that is?"

"I suspect that you have the ability to draw out the special among us."

Again with the whole lodestone concept.

"To have an individual gift is not unheard of," Ofelia continued. "Mine you knew of, of course. Many Storks also have the power of healing."

I thought of Hulda and Grim ministering to Jack at the portal when Wade had torched him in an attempted sacrifice. The Bleika Norn and her purported healing abilities also came to mind, as well as her Asgard counterparts: Bleik and Eyra.

"I wonder, and it's just a theory, if you haven't assembled — even if unwittingly — those you learn from, draw powers from."

Now I wasn't just a lure, I was a leech, too. My use of Jinky's talents came to mind here.

"So this mind-reading thing, can I turn it off?" I asked with a pout. "There are some things I seriously don't want to know."

"You can't turn it off, but you will eventually become inured to the distractions, the way we often don't register background noise like traffic or mowers or barking dogs."

When another customer entered, reciting his shopping list over and over in his head — eggs, milk, Kleenex, Nyquil, eggs, milk, Kleenex, Nyquil — I mentally overrode him with my own to-dos: *Spare Leira, get Jack back, save the world. Spare Leira, get Jack back, save the world.* I waved good-bye to Ofelia. At the door, I was careful to cover my hand with my sleeve so as not to get slimed by the guy's germs.

# CHAPTER FORTY-FIVE

No one was home at my house, so, after a quick snack of chocolate milk and SunChips, I headed across the street in search of Marik. Our project required a ten-minute presentation, which was the one component we had let slide.

I had never been inside the house of the elderly couple hosting Jinky and Marik. After the woman, Mrs. Cantwright, let me in, she cornered me in the foyer, asking about my mom and Stanley and describing her great joy in having "kids" in the neighborhood again.

"Is that why you take in exchange students?" I asked.

"Goodness, no, I didn't even know such a thing was possible. Someone from the international agency called me late in the summer. Well, it seemed about time we had some young ones in the house again."

I wondered at who or what was behind this arrangement. My head hurt with the exercise of it. Because random simply wasn't.

A few minutes later and an inadvertent tap into her sadness that her grandchildren lived so far away, I was directed up the stairs to the second bedroom on the right. Family portraits lined both walls of the staircase, and I took note of a black-and-white photo of a crew-shorn Mr. Cantwright, a cat-eye-bespectacled Mrs. Cantwright, and a clutch of five toothy kids. So maybe a house would seem a little empty after a big brood like that.

At the top of the stairs I passed the first doorway, which was ajar and revealed Jinky sitting at a large oak desk. At the sound of my footsteps, she looked up and waved me in.

Scattered across the desktop was an array of antique-looking items: a small scale, a glass cork-stoppered bottle, a bundle of dried herbs, and a box containing even more instruments that looked like they came out of an old-fashioned drugstore.

"What's all this?" I asked.

"Display items for Friday."

I was still shocked that Jinky had managed to hijack their project. Nor did I rule out some kind of coercive charm or potion. I wasn't even sure if Penny fully comprehended the metaphysical nature of their merchandise and services. She still described it as a kind of gift shop selling candles, jewelry, and aromatherapy products.

"They look old. Where did you get them?" I lifted the bottle. Whatever it had once contained was now a dark film at the bottom.

"From Mrs. Cantwright. When I described the idea of our shop to her, she said she had some apothecary items in her basement." Jinky, I noticed, kept her thoughts to the point, much like her eyeliner. It was interesting, anyway, to catch that she thought I looked tired and pale and wondered if she shouldn't reread my runes. I was grateful for the warning. Maybe this mind-reading thing would come in handy, after all.

Marik appeared at the open door. "Ah, I thought I heard Katla's voice."

"I was hoping to go over our presentation," I said, setting the bottle down. "It's worth twenty percent of our grade."

Marik bit back a smile; he was obviously vindicated by my recent preoccupation with our project.

"Sure, let's practice." He stepped aside for me to lead the way out of the room.

I felt funny in Marik's room and made a point of leaving the door wide open. Whereas Jinky's scattered belongings—her leather coat and boots, a basket of makeup, and her surprisingly numerous photos—lent personality to the space, Marik's room was bare bone-colored walls and military clean. Even the bed looked hard and sharp. I sat in a straight-backed chair while Marik sat on the edge of the tightly tucked mattress.

I had typed up a script but found on our three run-throughs that Marik had a tendency to ad-lib, playing the charm card with the audience, even when the crowd was imaginary. At the end of the last of these shows, he grabbed his side.

"Is it getting worse?" I asked.

He nodded yes.

"Is that a bad sign?"

His affirmation was, again, a bob of the head.

"Can you think of nothing that would help? Some kind of medicine or therapy that would exist on both Midgard and Vatnheim?" I thought of the herbs and instruments at Jinky's disposal.

"Medicine cannot make me human. Not in the important ways, anyway," he said, wincing with the effort of it. "I'm quite resigned to my lot. I only hope that yours and Leira's are different."

His *lot?* It sounded so fatalistic. All at once, what Hulda had told me about fate and karma came to mind. She had claimed them similar except that karma was "our will as we swim in the river of our past and present." She'd gone on to clarify that "we cannot change the course of the river, but the strokes of our swim influence our destination."

"Maybe we have more influence in our destiny than we give ourselves credit for," I said.

"Were it only true." He nodded with pouted lips. "I do not share your optimism, but I think it's a lovely thing to behold."

He gave me one of those molten looks, the kind that had Penny and the entire female population of Norse Falls High beset with a heaving bosom. Mine may not have had much in the volume department but it was billowing like a sail. I could feel the blush creeping up my chin and cheeks, and I ducked my head to keep my composure.

"Time to go," I said, gathering up my index cards.

"So soon?"

"If I want to see Leira tonight, I have to get there before visiting hours are over."

For the third time that day, as I had with Ms. Bryant and Ofelia, I left someone in my rearview with a hasty and awkward retreat as subtle as tire marks.

Mrs. Cantwright caught me with my hand on the door. "It was nice to meet you, dear," she said. "And it's lovely to see the house looking in the pink again." She giggled as she said it, obviously enjoying her pun.

The way she said "pink" with affection made me

think of a possible connection. "Did you by any chance know its former occupant?"

"Yes. She was already an old woman when we first moved in, but so kindly and helpful."

"Helpful?"

"Well, you know, she had a way with people." Ms. Cantwright brought her hand to her cheek. "She was well known for her green thumb and her healing touch. My oldest, Ruth, had the worst asthma as a child. I don't know what we would have done without her help."

The collection of items up in Jinky's room suddenly made more sense. "Were those her things that Jinky's using for her project?"

"Yes, as a matter of fact, they were. I was so surprised when she left them to me."

"What exactly did she use them for?"

Lost in thought, she pinched her chin. "It was such a long time ago. I know she made a poultice of honey, ginger, onion, and mustard oil. Caraway seeds, apple seeds, and turmeric were ground and mixed with lemon and hot water and taken as a drink. Well, there were any number of remedies for any number of ailments."

"It's nice of you to lend them to Jinky."

"I enjoy seeing them in the hands of someone who values them and takes an interest in their original purpose. She puts up a tough front, but deep down she has a natural empathy for others. She'd make a good nurse."

Personally I couldn't imagine Jinky in one of those cotton smocks or white-soled shoes, but it was fun to picture it.

Later that night, watching Leira's tiny chest labor up and down, but finally of her own accord, I was struck by the vagaries of life. She could be taken from us at any time; Marik claimed a prophecy foretold as much. Afi, too, was vulnerable. The "break" with Jack already felt like a death to me. It was torture knowing that I had hurt him. Too painful, in fact, to dwell on. And I felt low imagining Marik's demise. His exuberance and excitement at every little thing gave him a childlike quality. It seemed so unfair that it would be cut short. On the other hand, as a mercreature, he'd already had a long life, but one that was soulless. Did it count? Did it compare? Was it anything close to a fair trade-off?

With every puff of life Leira fought for, I, too, was filled with purpose. And in between, in the valleys where her ribs collapsed and she had to begin again, I raged against the fear that had kept me from what had to be done.

"Honey, you look so tired," my mom said, pulling me from the undertow of my thoughts. "Why don't you go? Leira's holding her own. I'm going to stay until she settles, but you look exhausted; you should head home."

"I will," I said, "in a minute."

I watched my mom cooing and rubbing Leira's twig-thin arm. Leira's eyes followed my mom's every movement and she visibly settled with every loving stroke. For my mom's part, her words, both spoken and unspoken, were encouragement. I felt the power of her positive energy and sensed that meditative support — faith, hope, and the like — had far more benefit than was given credit. Soon, the familiar lullaby filled the room. I sat for a moment in the bedside chair, allowing myself to drift along with the cadence of the sound. At the last course, I snapped to. *"That the swan's snowy span is but a wish away. May this comfort you as you wake to this day full of love, full of hope, full of glory."* The swan, of course! With that, another piece of my plan clicked into place.

"Good night, Mom. Good night, Leira." I blew them both a kiss from the doorway. My mom, her tender focus still on Leira, waved distractedly.

At home, and in the privacy of my room, I paced the length of the space, sequencing all that I knew.

Brigid couldn't break through, not alone, anyway.

I'd vowed to renege on Safira, but, without a disruption to the *essentials* of the agreement, the pact held.

Marik, whose animus was one of those essentials, had offered to help me.

Furthermore, to survive here, Marik needed a soul. I delivered souls.

Birta—not knowing I could hear her—had mentioned an "autonomous bestowment." Somewhere, somehow, the process had been achieved without Stork council approval.

If Marik got his soul, this would alter one of the essentials. If, by doing so and in going full-on renegade, I were temporarily suspended, this would also be a sabotage of the spell. There was Jaelle, too. Why not help her out in the process?

The plan wasn't without its flaws. Leira's compromised lungs and long-term prognosis were a concern. But I was making progress.

I face-planted onto my bed. My great master plan had more variables than a calculus textbook. It was all too much. I didn't change into PJs, brush my teeth, or even turn out my light. I simply allowed the tug of sleep and my abilities to take over.

# CHAPTER FORTY-SIX

"Get up!" I yell at the zombified Jaelle, who, just as I last found her, sits on a log. Nothing. I shake her shoulder. Still nothing. Her eyes are open, and she stares ahead.

I take in the scenery. We're at the shore. Waves crash over a sandy beach.

With quick glances left and right, I check on the boy and girl. They're still there, but both appear agitated now. The baby girl sucks on her fist with her twitching mouth just one gasp away from a wail. The boy rocks back and forth with his knees folded into his chest and his eyes wide with fear.

Again the sand shifts under my feet, and I comprehend the precariousness of the situation. Unless I do something now, it will all slip away.

Spying a giant clamshell the size of a sink, I struggle through the collapsing terrain. The shell is massively heavy, and I lug it to the water's edge on legs now cramping with each torturous step. A breaker slams a wall of cold water into me, but it also fills the shell.

The return trek is even more difficult. My outstretched arms grow weary with the weight of the makeshift basin, and it's difficult not to spill.

Finally, I reach the still-catatonic Jaelle, and, with a heave-ho that almost bowls me over, too, I dump the seawater over her. She splutters, mumbling expletives; never am I so happy to be cussed out.

As Jaelle grumbles and pulls at her drenched nightgown, I gather the baby girl to my chest. She squirms, screaming with fear. I press her into Jaelle's arms, and they both gasp and hush. A sob draws my eyes to the boy. He stands, wiping tears from his dirty cheeks and looks ready to run off. I hurry to him, grasping his warm, dry hand in mine.

A boom fills my ears as a giant roller crashes onto the beach. Water is rushing toward us. I scoop the boy up. Jaelle stands and the water reaches her knees. High ground is only a short jog away; Jaelle's eyes are already focused there. I shift the boy onto my hip, readying for the climb, when I spot something floating in the water. I unclasp the boy's hands from around my neck and thrust him—roughly, I regret—onto Jaelle's back. "Run," I yell, pushing her away from the still surging surf.

I don't have time to contemplate what I've done, because it's a body that's borne by the current. I wade through the now-receding tide to find Marik facedown. I roll him over and can't tell by his closed lids if he's sleeping or unconscious or dead.

As I reach out to check for signs of life, a bird flits into view. A gull. It darts in and out just above my head so that I have to lift my eyes to swat at it. With the expanded view, I notice the beach is dotted with dozens of giant clamshells, all closed except for three that are hinged open and contain infants, gurgling and babbling.

I am momentarily filled with joy until the sound of an approaching wave roars in my ears. I watch as the shells close while another swell floods the area. I lift Marik under his arms, keeping his head above this newest deluge. When it recedes, the three shells not only remain closed but have been scattered and are indistinguishable from the others, now numbering in the hundreds.

The gull continues to hover and pester me. I bat at it until it wings away to a nearby shell, upon which it lands and begins cawing.

A sign? I rush over, the bird flies off, and I wrench the massive shell open. It's empty. I fall back on my butt into the wet sand and survey a beach littered with closed shells. It's a shell game, an impossible shell game. I scream in frustration.

# CHAPTER FORTY-SEVEN

Waking, I sat forward with a gasp. I had physically joined Jaelle with two children. In the dream state, I had never before bodily united the potential mother with the hovering soul before. Was it an autonomous bestowment?

And what about Marik? He'd been lifeless. Equally distressing was the fact that I hadn't accomplished anything on his behalf. As if aware of this setback, he appeared particularly run-down, and even a little withdrawn, that day.

After school a whole crew of us headed over to Pinewood to set up the gymnasium for Friday night's show. I drove Penny, Jinky, and Marik.

From the backseat, Penny moaned. "I can't believe we're even cooperating with them on this Design Show. Why isn't it in our gym?"

Theirs was bigger and had a built-in PA system, ample electrical outlets, and an adequate supply of folding tables, but I kept my mouth shut and punched at the radio dial.

If the balance of power with the setup crew was any indication of how things would be after the proposed merge, Norse Falls was going to be serfs to Pinewood's landed gentry. Mr. Derry, Ms. Bryant's counterpart from Pinewood, made a brief appearance to warn us against scratching the shiny new floors, dinging their mascot-painted walls, or grubbing up the foyer with our Norse Falls foulness. OK, so that last part was a fabrication, but, sheesh, the guy was one nitpicking old noodge. Ms. Bryant had explained that he was counting down to his pension party, but that didn't explain why the students weren't pitching in. Meanwhile our gang, chaperones included, hauled tables, set out the display boards, hung signs, and mapped out the room plan according to Ms. Bryant's schematic.

It was a bear of a job, one for which Marik's (albeit diminished) brawn, Ms. Bryant's brain, and my dad's brand of humor came in handy. He was pretty good at impersonations, and Mr. Derry did have an Elmer Fuddish quality to his voice. With everyone helping out, we had the room looking show-worthy in just under two hours. The teams were then allowed to store their boards and display materials under their assigned table.

"Ooh. Ooh. Ooh," my dad had said when he saw a box full of our items. "Playtime."

Ms. Bryant laughed like he was joking, but I happened to know that he had a bizarre fondness for any and all toys. A little odd for any forty-something man. It wouldn't have mattered; I was pretty sure Ms. Bryant was at that bedazzled stage when the other person can do no wrong. Not that I was tapping into her thoughts. I was getting much better at drowning her out when my dad was around. I slipped once, though, right after his comment about toys. Ms. Bryant mused how fun and high-energy he was but odd that such a young soul would father an old one. Hearing that, I just about blew a lung. I knew she could guess people's ages, but young souls and old souls? The latter a category she filed me under. Was I? And was my dad a new model? How could that be? And, more importantly, how could she know it? Such thoughts were interrupted by my dad continuing to thumb through our box of items. He pulled out a fireman's helmet and plopped it on his head.

"Let me guess," he said to Marik, "Kat has dedicated a section of the store to dress-up."

I opened my mouth to protest his teasing tone, but what was there to say? I had planned for a costume corner, because what little boy doesn't want to strap on a holster or little girl want to wrap a faux mink stole around her shoulders, or vice versa?

"No discussing the project," I said in mock irritation. "We haven't been graded yet."

"Party pooper." My dad removed the hat, replaced it in the box, and tucked the box flaps one over another.

I didn't have time to defend myself or to further contemplate Ms. Bryant's interesting thoughts because my head started to itch, indicating I had a date with council.

Figuring a meeting summons meant disciplinary action was upon me, I had to get out of that gym for a bracer of fresh air. I told the others to wrap up and meet me out front, where I'd pull up.

Walking to my car, I was so lost in dread that I didn't notice the figure leaning against my driver's-side door until I was just a few steps away.

"Jack. What are you doing here?" I looked left, right, and behind me. The last thing I needed was Marik coming out now.

Jack's eyes chased mine. I could see the hurt and anger spark in them.

"I don't buy it for a minute, you know." His hands were dug so deep into his pockets that his pants rode low. A ribbon of taut tummy was visible between his jeans and his T-shirt.

"Buy what?"

"Any of it. Something's up. Something's wrong. And you don't want a break any more than I do."

"Well, you're wrong. And I do," I said with all the steel I could cut into my voice. "Now, can you move away from my car?" Fearing the others wouldn't wait at the front doors, I shot a look over my shoulder.

"Is that really what you want?"

"Yes."

"Then I'll go, but I want you to know one thing."

"What?"

"I still got your back."

I turned away from him, squeezing my eyes shut. "Just go, Jack."

Behind me I heard footsteps. And then nothing.

# CHAPTER FORTY-EIGHT

That evening, my heart wouldn't stay put. It yo-yoed from my throat to my bowels with wrenching lurches. I took my seat at the council meeting and immediately noticed a somber mood. Hulda was the last to arrive. She trod wearily from the door to her first chair, stopping to brace herself on the backs of several of the seats en route. I sucked in a big stash of air.

Even roll call had a melancholy tone to it. I wasn't the only one picking up on some heavy vibes.

"Our first order of business will be to discuss the findings of the World Tribunal as pertains to the impasse involving Sister Katla's recent bestowment. There have been, I am informed, developments which necessitate a new course of action."

Developments? I could only guess.

"It seems," Hulda continued, "that the two hovering souls have found placement."

True to form, the old gals reacted with a cacophony of squawks and honks of alarm.

"Your attention, please." Hulda pounded her fist on the table. With that single gesture, I knew what was to follow.

"Sister Katla, did you have anything to do with this turn of events?"

"Yes."

Hulda's entire frame deflated with my reply. Even her eyes seemed to shrink into the crinkled folds of her lids. "And did you place the essences with a vessel of your own choosing without council approval?"

"Yes."

I heard more than one of my counterparts utter shocked reactions: "Beyond her abilities." "Such powers are unheard of."

Hulda stood and motioned for me to do the same. My heavy chair scraped across the slab floor. She then unrolled a tube of brown paper, one I recognized from Fru Dorit's fall from grace.

"Katla Gudrun Leblanc, you are under investigation for the abuse of Stork privileges."

At the ensuing gasps, I hung my head.

"The Tribunal's decision," Hulda continued, "is an

immediate suspension of Stork affiliation and privileges pending trial. While you will continue to possess your magical abilities during this interim, you will be powerless to access them. Is this understood?"

"Yes, Fru Hulda."

I should have been happy. I had, after all, achieved my goal: one of the three essentials to the pact was altered. The spell was broken. The bonus of which was that Jaelle would soon have news to share. But I wasn't. I was deeply ashamed. And disappointed to have failed on another score. Even with my eyes on the toes of my shoes, I could sense their shocked faces and disapproving glares.

"Katla, we must ask you to leave now," Hulda said.

With this, the mass in my throat expanded, constricting air and bringing tears to my eyes. I ran from the room without uttering a word in my defense or even glancing back. If all went according to plan, they'd know my motives soon enough. And it wouldn't matter.

# CHAPTER FORTY-NINE

On Friday, it was cruddy out and unseasonably cold, which matched my overall mood. I kept reminding myself that the suspension was temporary, and of my own doing, but it didn't help. My body attended school that day; my mind however was in another dimension, one I'm sure will eventually prove the existence of zombies.

In Design, Marik and I made our presentation. Much to my surprise, he stuck to the script and nailed it. The way he articulated both our name and slogan—"The Toy Box, because today's games are the building blocks of tomorrow's discoveries,"—had even Ms. Bryant nodding appreciatively. I, on the other hand, sucked. I couldn't concentrate and probably now have the record

for most "umms" uttered in a five-minute span. *Go me.*
It hadn't helped that we followed Penny and Jinky, who
were superb. I saw the way Marik looked at Penny as she
breezed her way through a flawless delivery.

Afterward, in the hallway, I saw him double over
in pain. The effort of our speech had cost him. It was
another indication that we were game-on.

Once school let out, I found myself slumped over
my steering wheel with inertia buckling my backbone.
A light rain pinged upon the roof, and the sky was the
color of ash. I was expected at Pinewood; we were allot-
ted a half hour to move our display items onto the tables,
after which the show was open and the appointed judges
would be circulating with their first-, second-, and third-
place ribbons. Though I tried not to, I thought of Jack. I
missed him so much. Funny thing about the word *miss*
is that it would seem to indicate a sensation that something was lacking, the way your head feels lighter after
a haircut. Missing Jack was instead this heavy thing that
lodged in my throat, making breathing difficult, and
slowed my reactions, making operating a vehicle a dangerous prospect.

On the drive over to Pinewood, the horizon seemed
squatter than usual, as if the clouds hung lower and the
band of space between the earth and the sky were com-
pacted. I attributed it to my shriveled mood and the
gloomy wet weather.

Having put the finishing touches on our project setup, a somewhat recovered Marik and I waited silently by our table.

"Do you think we got the blue ribbon?" Marik asked.

"I do." And I did. With its primary colors and sample toys, our project was visually stimulating. And to highlight our slogan, we had an array of block-themed toys. My favorite—something I'd taken to calling Andi, given its androgynous nature—was a stack of four blocks in a vertical case that assembled a human figure in four parts: head, upper body, lower torso, and legs. By flipping the six-sided cube, one was able to alter the image radically. I tended to favor the head of the girl with pigtails, a bikini top, tutu, and Dutch clogs with knee socks. Marik, to my annoyance and with some fairly deft hand movements, went for the guy with a 'fro, jacket and tie, swim trunks, and army boots.

"I do, too." Marik rubbed his hands together in anticipation.

"Though it wouldn't hurt for you to use some of that magic charm of yours on the judges." I couldn't believe I was suggesting he influence the outcome. It was testament to how badly I needed just one thing to go right.

"My magic what?" Marik asked.

"You know, charm, hocus-pocus. What you've used since you got here to turn the girls to mush and even had someone like Mean Dean playing nice."

"I don't know what you're talking about."

"Come on," I said.

He stared at me.

"You mean to tell me," I continued, "all that was genuine?"

He continued to eye me blankly.

"And people just . . . like you?"

"Why wouldn't they?" Marik said. "I like them. I like everything. No magic necessary."

I sat contemplating this news. It was rather startling. And while amazingly simple in theory, still incredible all the same.

A judge walked toward us. Marik sucked in his breath but let it go with a big sputter when we were passed by. Instead, the official affixed the blue ribbon to Jinky and Penny's project.

"I guess that proves it," Marik said with a wink. "No hocus-pocus involved."

I watched Penny and Jinky hug in celebration of their win. Their project was good, darn them. The floor plan called for an aromatherapy corner, an herbal-remedy section, a book nook, and a metaphysical wares area. Even with all its voodoo gimmicks, it was tastefully done and deliberately treated in soothing pastels, soft lines, and nature-inspired images, the handiwork of Jinky and her artistic eye.

"Reporting for chaperone duty," my out-of-breath dad said.

I thought he may as well just term it a date with Ms. Bryant but held my tongue.

He tapped one of our sample items, one that Marik had found somewhere. It was a can labeled MIXED SALTED NUTS. When you opened it up, a toy snake sprang up and even made a rattling sound. It wasn't my favorite item, mostly because Marik still liked to brag about how he "got me" that first time. "Oldest trick in the book," my dad said, "but a classic. You kids are looking good."

"Thanks," I said, "but we didn't place."

"What?" my dad said. "You guys got robbed." He began fiddling with Andi. He put cowboy boots where the head should go, a poodle skirt where the shoulders belonged, the head of a freckled boy below that, and a football jersey as the base. "This project is top drawer. And, come on, a toy store. What could be better than that?"

"Penny and Jinky's wiccan wares. It took first."

"Wiccan?" my dad asked. "Really?"

"No, not really, but New Age with a focus on healing and the metaphysical."

"That sounds very unique," my dad said. He had moved on to our magnetized Lincoln-Logs, but the way he had left Andi bothered me. I found the misplaced body parts grotesque and a little unsettling. My dad watched me replace the pieces into their anatomically correct locations and flip a few to the girly selections. When I was done, he gave me a must-you lift of his brow.

"What?" I asked, ready to defend the natural order of things. "It bugged me."

"For someone who I've personally witnessed pair an army jacket with ballet shoes, it doesn't make sense."

"Not the accessory mash-up. That doesn't bother me. But the mutations. Ick."

"Sometimes you gotta think outside the box," my dad said. "Take a fresh look at things. Besides, it's a game; you gotta play the whole board."

*Box. A fresh look. Play the whole board.* Holy Hasbro. My dad was a freakin' genius.

"I think I see the lovely Ms. Bryant," my dad said. "I think I'll offer her some nuts." He took off with the gag gift and a goofy grin on his face.

OK, so maybe not a genius in the strictest sense, but a master gamer and fun-loving, which had its applications.

How had I never thought to confer with my dad on the anagram in my dream, even surreptitiously? He was the scramble king, after all. The blocks and his mention of "box" made me think of "parcel." I had taken "parcel" as is, but on my vision quest, the girl—Idunn— had thrown all the letters up in the air to scatter them, "parcel" included. The phrase was never intended to remain as "parcel dinky pal." *All* the letters were meant to be reworked. "Dinky pal" to "pink lady." And "parcel" to . . . I grabbed a pen and paper from my backpack and scribbled furiously. Carpel. Holy crap, "parcel" scrambled to "carpel." And "pink lady" wasn't a house, wasn't the cameo, and wasn't the Bleika Norn; it was a type of apple. Pretty much anyone had heard of that variety, but only a girl with an apple-farmer boyfriend would know that carpels were the seed compartments inside apples. Naturally, I was *that* girl. *Break* or no *break*.

All of a sudden, something didn't feel right. Like at the Asking Fire, I sensed a low, humming vibration. One look at the water bottle on our table confirmed this. It was rippling ever so slightly.

"Marik, we need to go."

"Go now?" He clutched at his side as if fatigued by the mere idea.

"Do you think you can make it?"

"If you think it's important."

"I suspect Leira's life depends on it. And if I can change Leira's fate—"

"Let's go," he said through gritted teeth. He looked pale as bleached bones, and there was a fine sheen of perspiration across his forehead. As sidekicks went, he was the short-of-breath straw, but better, I supposed, than going it alone.

# CHAPTER FIFTY

Overwhelmed with urgency and not wanting to attract the attention of my dad, Ms. Bryant, or Penny, I directed us to the closest exit, double doors leading from Pinewood's gym to the back of the school. It appeared to be a staff parking lot and bus pickup and drop-off area. Beyond it was an open field horseshoed by woods.

The moment the door closed behind us, I sensed a changed world. The horizon that had earlier seemed oddly lower was now visibly compressed into a thick purple wedge of churning clouds and darkening sky.

At once, the blare of sirens filled the air, and I brought my hands to my ears. Below my feet, the swell of vibration grew until my calves thrummed with pain.

Marik was also suffering from the sensory assaults and looked around wild-eyed. "What is that noise?"

"A tornado warning."

A shriek of wind joined the cacophony of sirens, and its accompanying gust lifted my hair and shirttails.

"What does it mean?" Marik asked.

"Take cover. Underground."

Marik looked at his feet as if expecting some sort of hatch to open up. By the strain on his face, he'd have taken any shortcut out of there.

"If we were smart, we'd head back to the building," I said, shouting above the wails of the alarm and the howl of the wind.

"Are we smart?" Marik asked with sincerity, his voice hoarse with the effort.

"No. I'm not, anyway."

As if to prove that point, it began to rain, an entirely inadequate word for the onslaught that pelted us. It fell as a curtain of water that instantly plastered my hair to my face and my clothes to my body. With an audible crack, the temperature plunged, and I hugged my arms to my soaking-wet sides.

"Something's not right," Marik said. "I feel sick." He staggered, and as I put an arm out to help him, he buckled to his knees.

I fell beside him, my own knees splashing in the already pooling water. From this low-to-the-ground position, the reverberation of the earth was even more pronounced. My whole body rocked with quick vibrations until the bucking ground transitioned to rolling waves of slower but greater magnitude. But I knew earthquakes, and this was no run-of-Midgard temblor.

"We have to get out of here," I said. "Can you make it to my car on the other side of the building?"

A crack of lightning split the sky, forking into white-hot branches.

"I don't know," Marik said, gasping for air. "Maybe you should go without me."

"What? No!" I shouted. As I struggled to assist him to a stand, something hit me in the shoulder. It was hard and round, and it hurt. Another, about the size of a quarter, glanced off my forehead and another off my back until the sound of them pinging the parking lot all around us joined with the roar of the wind.

"Now what is it?" Marik yelled, covering his face with his arm.

"Hail," I called back over the din of the thundering ice balls that slammed against my face, arms, and head, and were getting bigger. "We need to take cover."

Along the side of the parking lot there was a covered bus stop. The good folks of Pinewood had at least the wherewithal to factor the elements into their school design.

I yanked Marik to his feet and pulled him through

the bizarre storm. The hail hurt like hell, its source in all probability, and I knew I'd have welts and bruises. Just as we reached the small corrugated-tin-covered stop, the roar of falling missiles became deafening. We huddled to the back of the narrow three-sided structure and watched ice balls now the size of oranges grow to the size of grapefruit.

Fearing the roof would collapse, I pulled Marik down to the ground, and we cowered under the cement bench. Marik, I could see, was fading fast. His breath came in rasps, and he shook uncontrollably. In his eyes I saw pure fear.

"Safira's coming," he said, casting his head from side to side.

I had surmised as much. Counted on it, even. But the enormity of it still made my heart rattle against my ribs like something caged.

"But how?" Marik asked, contorting in fear and pain. "She must have help."

With that, the clouds turned black and angry as if the product of a violent rage. They filled the sky, expanding seemingly for miles. I noticed then a rotation forming. Above me, an edge folded in on itself and began curling downward and then up until it spun into a dizzying funnel of pure malice.

Marik emitted a final animal-like bray and then went still. With his slump, a last bang of hail hit the tin roof with a jolt. Looking up into the maw of twisting fury, I saw objects caught in the swirl of energy. A car hood, an entire tree, a section of fencing, and more spun before me as if churning in some great sky-high blender, the roar of which was like nothing I'd ever heard. Among the spiraling debris, something new began to take shape. I squinted and covered my eyes, not trusting any of my overwhelmed senses to convey intelligible information from the pandemonium surrounding me. Out of coiling sky snapped the head of a snake the size of my VW bug. I screamed full-throttle, clambering backward.

Next, and almost simultaneously, two things happened. The monstrous serpent lowered itself until just a few yards in front of me and, from atop its tapered head, Brigid and a companion—none other than Safira—swung down.

The other shocking turn of events was, from my peripheral vision, the arrival of a battered green truck. It pulled to a screeching halt.

Jack. I let out a muffled gasp. It was equal parts relief and dismay. Relief in that Jack had come for me. Even while mad, hurt, and disappointed in me, he came through. Because that was the kind of stand-up guy he was. As sidekicks went, *he* was long on everything. Dismay in that he would witness my plan and possibly try to stop me.

Scrambling out of his truck, he ducked and shielded

his face and head from the flying debris. A trash can came out of nowhere to wedge itself under his front bumper. He searched about frantically, flinching noticeably upon beholding Brigid and Safira, not to mention the monstrous snakehead. He also shuddered at the sight of Marik in a crumpled heap. When his eyes found me cowering at the back of the small shelter, his relief was so palpable I saw his Adam's apple punch up and down.

Brigid, however, didn't share Jack's devotion to me. The look she slashed me with was one of pure, arctic-blast hatred. She stood imperially with her arms crossed and away from her body and her stance wide and defiant. Her silvery gown, a new one, sparkled with a crystalline shimmer as it flapped in the wind. Beside Brigid, Safira seemed almost elfin. Whereas Brigid was tall, dark-eyed, and with long, flowing ebony hair, Safira was petite, my size or smaller, with pale skin, and her opal-white hair twisted into a tidy bun. Her sea-green dress, the one I'd only seen from the waist up and taken for sequins, I now saw as thousands of tiny, shiny fish scales, an epidural layer of her upper body but flowing to a long dress below. Its full skirt, puddling at her feet—or lack thereof—hid whatever form her lower body had taken on lowly Midgard. She remained rigid at Brigid's side with her hands on her hips, and though I couldn't quite place her fixed expression, it sure as heck wasn't a social call.

Jack sprinted to my side and gathered me in his arms.

"Are you all right?" he asked.

"Yes," I said, my voice blubbery. "And no."

With his right hand he spanned the back of my neck, drawing me toward him. "How's this possible?"

Before I could answer him, Brigid took a step toward us. "We meet again," she said, shouting over the roar of the wind. "But I don't think you'll be pleased with the outcome. This time there are two of us conspiring to thwart Midgard's excesses." She gestured to her accomplice, who stood as waxen as she had before. "There is but one solution, is there not, Queen Safira?"

Safira finally turned her head toward me, though she appeared resentful of the necessity. "Prior to our bargain, your earth, in its greed, had already upset the balance of the worlds." She, too, had to shout to be heard over the wind. "Your reparations are too little, too late and have left us no choice but to reset order. And now with our pact broken, Brigid has convinced me that Ragnarök is our only recourse."

The very word filled me with rage and, just as importantly, adrenaline. Jumping to my feet, I stood, sensing Jack do the same behind me. "You trust Brigid for advice? She doesn't care about your realm. She'd like nothing more than to freeze it over right alongside earth."

With my indictment, Brigid raised her arms above her head and held them outstretched to the funnel cloud.

"The chosen among us are prophesied to survive. From Midgard's rubble, Safira and I will rebuild our respective worlds." Brigid then began lassoing her right arm above her head. The giant serpent spun faster, his immense body writhing in and out of the twisting air mass.

"The Midgard Serpent is one of the signs," Brigid continued in her menacing voice. "It was all too eager to be awakened from a long slumber."

The snake spun closer to the ground, his enormous tail flying lower and lower until, with a sickening snap, it struck Pinewood High School. A wall of sound ensued as, upon impact, bricks and glass and wood and all that once comprised the building exploded into shards and splinters and was sucked up into the horrific twisting chaw of the serpent.

I fell backward in horror; Jack caught me, but the shock of the destruction had us both reeling with disbelief.

At the sight of the wreckage, Brigid was giddy. "Join with me, sister queen," she called to Safira, and then took and lifted Safira's arm above their heads. "Together we have the power to tumble mountains, turn the sun black, and lift the oceans to swallow it all."

She cackled with laughter so catlike and menacing that even the serpent recoiled. The reverberation of its retreat sent dozens of mini tornadoes skittering across the sky.

I felt Jack's arm encircle me from behind. I sensed it was a sign of solidarity, yet it briefly transported me to two previous occasions when, in death's clutches, I was embraced. Then Jack stepped in front of me. I watched as his body rippled with exertion, his neck elongating into ropy chords and veins bulging at his temples. In response and from somewhere primeval, he issued his own feral sound, more animal than human. In the distance and as if in reply, I heard a cry. At first, I thought it was an echo or the wind, but soon I realized it was a howl, wolfish in nature, rabid with anger, and the very sound that had sent Frigg and her maidens scattering during my vision quest.

Jack continued to writhe in agony. Within moments, a dense fog descended; it was as thick as batting and fell so suddenly I lost Jack, who stood only inches away from me. A final groan confirmed his whereabouts and the source of the mist.

Brigid screamed like a demon, no doubt a reaction to her rage at being plunged into a blinding haze.

Safira's voice was much more controlled as she called out, "Your tricks are for naught; Fenrir sets out for Odin."

I remembered that one of Ragnarök's major events is a battle to the death between Odin — husband of Frigg and ruler of Asgard — and Fenrir the giant wolf. But there was more about Safira's words that worried me. At her mention of the word "tricks," I'd heard the lark song: *tee, tee, hoo.* Idunn's calling card. *Of all times, of all places!*

Jack's thick-as-fleece fog bought us a moment, one I intended to use wisely.

"Jack," I whispered, fumbling for his hand.

"I'm here." He squeezed my fingers.

"I need you to understand." Emotions overtook me, and I had to pause to regain my composure. "Everything I've done . . . what I'm about to do . . . was to protect you, Leira, and others. Please remember that."

"Kat, you're not making any sense."

"It will, I hope—at least I hope you'll understand that there was no other choice."

"What are you talking about? You're scaring me."

The mist turned suddenly icy, so frigid, in fact, that it hurt to breathe. The cold was particulate, pricking me like thousands of pinpoints. I knew, however, that this blast wasn't Brigid's. Jack, confused and desperate to understand me, was at the mercy of his gift. I had always been his undoing. At the minimum, he'd be released of this vulnerability.

"There's something I have to do. Something only I can do."

I was so frightened, my chest felt like it was imploding. The resultant hole was black and infinite. Where would I get the courage?

So many events were happening at once, and

compounded by the blinding mist, that I didn't trust my senses to interpret them. The Midgard Serpent hissed. The air whinnied like the bay of a horse. Then I again heard the wolf Fenrir's eerie howl. He was growing closer. Though the fog still banked us in obscurity, I could hear the impact of the distant tornadoes as they touched down. As they made contact, the sound of their destruction was horrifying.

There was no time to lose. As I had on two previous occasions, I closed my eyes and focused on the thing I required, the thing I wished for most in that moment. In this case it was to take Leira's place behind the sealed portals with Brigid and Safira as travel companions. Safira required one of royal lineage. I was as much a descendant of Afi's selkie line as Leira. If Safira were appeased, if she no longer had reason to conspire with Brigid, maybe it wasn't too late. I figured whatever access they'd created on the strength of their combined powers must still be open. It was the only way, without being in spirit form, to transition.

I stood with my arms away from my body, willing a Swan Maiden—Blith or Frith, one of whom I was sure had encircled me on two previous occasions and delivered me from the threshold of death—to grant me my third and final wish. Hulda, who wasted not a single word, had first told me that a Swan Maiden had come to her on her first bestowment. When Jack and I had survived a near-drowning experience as kids, something feathery had encircled me from behind. And as the Brigid and the Frost Giants bore down on us in Niflheim, I'd again felt the downy crush of wings.

Standing there, channeling what I felt was my final chance — humanity's last hope, for that matter — I felt the mildly familiar presence of something powerful and heard a whoosh. Air blew my hair back, and I knew she was close. When I was grabbed from behind, I gave myself freely to the passage.

# CHAPTER FIFTY-ONE

I thought I had given myself, anyway. Very soon, however, I became aware that the arms around me were Jack's. Above me, though faint and receding, I heard the lark song, an impishly merry sound.

I barely had time to process these two things before I was knocked to my butt by something with one nasty kickback. Jack and I crumpled in a heap of tangled body parts. From this pileup, I watched as the blanket of fog lifted from around me. In its upward draft, it began to spin until I realized it was being sucked up into the raging storm above. With the rise of the mist, Safira and Brigid became visible. They were both fighting gale-force winds that had Brigid's hair lifting and both of their elaborate gowns wrapping around their legs. They weren't the only ones engulfed in the swirling funnel. Nyah, Frigg's messenger, atop her flying steed was flailing to remain saddled. Her satchel had blown open, and its contents, blush-colored apples, were aloft as if juggled by some invisible jester, until I noticed the mischievous Idunn swoop a deft arm in their graceful arc and extract a single golden orb and stow it in her once-empty basket. In the next instant, the four otherworldly visitors were all airborne and tumbling like clothes in a dryer. Through it all, Brigid's fit of anger, Safira's cries of surprise, and Idunn's laughter were audible in churning fragments. The force of the vacuum almost pulled Jack and me upward as well. I screamed as the roaring, whistling mass lifted around us. And then with a final pop, like a cork being pulled from a bottle, the column of spiraling air disappeared, taking Brigid, Safira, Nyah and her horse, Idunn, most of Pinewood High School, and who knew what else with it. I rolled to my side, feeling something small and hard wedge into my ribs. I expected a hailstone but instead what I found was an apple, a perfect pink apple. With hardly a thought, I dropped it into the front pocket of my jacket. I had more immediate concerns, like sorting out exactly what had just happened.

The moment the sky cleared, I knew that I was different, forever altered. At first, I attributed it to a case of near-death disorder, a condition that had become fairly chronic with me. Its symptoms were dizziness, confusion, and an overpowering urge to kiss the ground and then Jack Snjosson. Beside me, the object of my compulsion grunted.

"Are you OK?" I threw myself on top of him, probably breaking every rule in a post-impact, potential first-aid situation, the mouth-to-mouth a possible exception.

"Better now, I think." He rolled to his side. "But what the hell was all that?"

Where to begin?

"I think that was my third and final wish being granted by a Swan Maiden, but something went haywire."

Despite getting my still-here-on-earth legs back, I felt leaden and lethargic.

"Your what?" He struggled to a sitting position.

"Can I give you the short version for now?" What was it with me? I felt so slow, like some important cog in my get-up-and-go was broken or missing.

"Sure."

*Here goes,* I thought, taking a deep breath. "When Brigid took you to Niflheim, I had to get there. Queen Safira of Vatnheim tricked me into a deal, one where I promised Leira to the water realm. Afterward, Marik was sent here as a sort of collector. I was warned that to tell you or anyone else was to endanger them, so I just tried to buy time until I could figure out how to break the pact."

"So you and Marik . . . ?" Jack asked.

I shook my head. "I just needed to keep you away from him. Jack Frost and a merman are a bad combination. For the water guy, anyway."

I could tell that Jack was getting riled up by the story, that he was both angered to be so clueless and relieved by some of the information.

"Meanwhile," I continued before he could interject, "the sinkhole and dead birds were Brigid trying to break through. When Marik made it clear that he was out of time and that Leira would die soon in order to transition, I lost it and deliberately broke the pact by getting my Stork powers suspended. After that, Safira teamed up with Brigid to begin Ragnarök, the, well, end of the world. As earth knows it, anyway. They were banking on surviving, and starting from scratch without us. But I recently figured out—thanks to Hulda, as usual—that during our two near-death experiences, I made wishes. Wishes that were answered. By a Swan Maiden. I used my third and final one to offer myself instead of Leira."

"You did what?" Jack asked, alarm spiking his voice.

"Except it didn't work, because . . ."

"Because what?"

"I got tricked by Idunn, the Goddess of Youth, someone I suspect has a lineage as blue-blooded as Leira's and mine, maybe even more so. She's mischievous and a game player and has either earned her way back into the goddess Frigg's good graces or has pulled off the ultimate grift. I honestly don't know what just happened."

From the looks of it, Jack was having a hard time processing it all. I still didn't feel right, either. The light-headedness I was experiencing wasn't exactly dizziness; it was more of an emptiness. Jack didn't look so hot himself. Except, from what I could tell . . .

"Jack, are you shaking?"

He brought both arms to his chest, drawing himself in tight. "A little."

"It couldn't be —"

"What?" he asked, huddling.

"Are you cold?"

"No. Of course not."

"So what is it, then?"

"I don't know. The chills of some sort."

My mind had more gears spinning than the Tour de France. "If you've never been cold, how would you even know?"

"Because I don't get cold. You know that."

*Could it be?* She was a trickster, sure, but a thief, too? I felt fundamentally altered; Jack was beset by unknown-to-him chills.

"We've been had," I said. "Or rescued. I hardly know what to think, but you reached out to me at the precise moment that . . . Holy crap! We've always said that we're stronger with our powers combined. But could it be?"

"What?"

Before I could explain further, I heard a grunt.

"Marik!" I shouted.

With everything happening faster than I could track, I'd almost forgotten his presence. I ran to him as he shifted and groaned.

"Are you all right?" I kneeled beside him, not daring to touch him. He looked pale and weak and—balled as he was—smaller than I remembered.

Jack, at my side, helped Marik to a sitting position.

"What happened? Where is she? I don't feel her," Marik said, scanning the area with a haunted look in his eyes.

"Safira and Brigid have gone," I said, kneading my left knuckles with my right thumb. "Forever, if I'm not mistaken. Which means . . ."

What was—without exaggeration—a rescue from the brink of destruction for all of earth was the kiss of death to Marik. If, as I suspected, the portals had been resealed with Marik on this side, there was nothing to be done for him.

"I know what it means," Marik said, closing his eyes and leaning back against a leg of the bench.

"Am I missing something?" Jack asked.

"Marik will not survive here. He's . . ."

"Not human," Marik finished for me, his lids weighted with the effort of reopening. "Never meant to survive long-term on earth."

Sirens approaching expanded our sphere of attention. Before us, what was once Pinewood High School was a jagged patch of bricks and twisted metal, and it slammed me back to reality. Everyone — my dad, Penny, Ms. Bryant, Jinky, and dozens of others — had been in that building. The entire structure was no longer there; it had been sucked up like some kind of house of cards by a malevolent magician.

"We have to check on the others," I said, panic straining my voice. "They were in the school."

Jack looked across the parking lot to the shorn plot of broken walls. The muscles in his neck and shoulders were corded and tight.

"Go," Marik rasped. "I'll be fine." He stretched and climbed weakly up onto the bench. It wasn't very reassuring, but I knew there was nothing we could do for him.

With more sirens now rushing to the scene, Jack and I took off across the parking lot. Given what remained of the building, I had very little hope. From this vantage point, the back side, the structure had been all but leveled. The gym, however, was on the other side.

With my heart pounding on every jarring lunge of my all-out dash, we raced to the front of the school. A cry caught in my throat and then released like a trapped animal as I surveyed a scene of equal, if not greater, devastation. I barely recognized the place. How could, in mere minutes, an entire building be sucked up and away? A building not one hundred feet from where I had been on the same property. A building that contained my father, friends, and favorite teacher.

When the first fire truck pulled to the curb alongside what had once been the front entrance, I felt sick to my stomach. What was there left to save? *Who* was there left to save?

Then a movement from around the opposite side of the school caught my eye. First a single person strolled into view. And then another. Until they were filing around the side of the building in a line. As soon as I saw my dad holding Ms. Bryant's arm, I ran to him like some kind of charging bull.

"What happened?" I shouted, sprinting to him and nearly bowling them both over. "Where were you? How did . . . ? Is everyone . . . ? Oh, my God! Oh, my God!"

It all hit me when I saw Penny and Jinky round the corner. The latter assisted the former, who had a decided limp but was fine. *Fine!* From the looks of it, they were *all* fine! I didn't even realize I was sobbing until I felt the spasm in my shoulders.

My dad hugged me to his chest. "Where did you go? I almost tore the door down to get to you, but they had us on lockdown in that shelter." He looked around, grimacing at the altered scene before him. "How did you . . . ?"

"Huddled in the bus stop," I said quickly. "Jack showed up at the last minute. If he hadn't . . ." I thought about the fog he'd created. It had bought me valuable time.

Marik hobbled into view; he didn't look good, but the sight of him sent Penny from Jinky's side and hurrying to him. She really cared about him, and, judging by the expression on his face, the feeling was mutual. He appeared sallow, greenish almost. Not everyone had escaped unscathed.

I could see the firefighters and now a few paramedics working their way toward us, sorting the crowd into triage areas. There were injuries; most looked like cuts and scrapes or the occasional twisted ankle. Mr. Derry, who, from the looks of it, was suffering with chest pains, appeared to be the worst of the group.

"Your dad's a real hero," Ms. Bryant said. "He organized the teachers and chaperones into groups and found two kids during his final sweep of the gym. They only had moments to spare. If he hadn't gone back up for a last search . . ."

Ms. Bryant gazed at my dad with admiration as she said this. I couldn't help thinking that his self-sacrifice, his bravery, had something to do with the youth of his soul. His heedless actions could easily be considered rash, reckless even, but I'd wager he never doubted his chances.

Pulling away from my dad, I said, "I'm going to see how Penny is."

She and Marik had formed a quiet pocket among the still-rattled throngs. They seemed to be holding each other up as Jack and I approached.

"The paramedics are checking everyone, making sure those in need of medical attention are seen to," I said.

Marik's eyes lifted to mine. I read alarm in them.

"I don't want help," he said, scanning left and right.

"But you don't seem well," Penny said. "I think I'll have my knee looked at. When I fell on it, I swear something popped."

"I'll walk you over to their staging area," I said, offering her my arm.

"You should come, too," Penny said, looking at Marik with an earnest appeal.

"I just want to go home," Marik said. "I had quite the scare, but that's it. And I find all this commotion a little too much right now."

"I'll drive him," Jack said. "My truck escaped damage."

"I'll stay with Penny and my dad," I said.

Before Penny could protest further, I steered her in the direction of the ambulances. Below her skirt, I could see her knee had swollen to twice its size.

After what we'd been through, nothing should have shocked me, but watching Jack and Marik ramble off—Jack even lending Marik an arm for support—was quite the scene.

I got Penny settled onto the curb, where a paramedic began taking her vitals, when I saw a woman from the local news station sound-checking with her cameraman not six feet from where we were. With a nod of his head, he gave her a silent countdown: three fingers, two fingers, one finger.

"This is Deborah Manning reporting from Pinewood, Minnesota, where what is believed to be an F4 tornado has recently torn through this small northern community. The weather event began with a freak storm producing hailstones over six inches in diameter and was followed by a flash fog reducing visibility to almost zero, all of which limited meteorologists' abilities to predict the scale of what is believed to be the largest tornado ever to hit the area."

Deborah Manning, dressed in a yellow raincoat as if she just finished taping a segment for *Deadliest Catch,* walked a few steps to her right. "I'm standing in front of what was just a short while ago the high school and where some quick-thinking teachers and chaperones led students—with only minutes to spare—into a lower-level shelter. Other areas of the community weren't so lucky. At least fifty homes are believed to have been lost in the original twister or one of its tributary cells that, in their own right, produced gusts of over one hundred miles an hour. Missing-person reports are accumulating as residents scramble out of shelters and venture forth to check on neighbors and loved ones. News of two highway deaths has just been reported." Deborah paused and held a finger to her headset while receiving, presumably, a live feed. "We're also just now learning of extensive damage to Pinewood Memorial Hospital."

I had been watching the reporter, mesmerized by her unfaltering delivery, until her comments regarding the hospital were like dropping off a cliff. The hospital. Leira. My mom and Stanley.

"Penny, tell my dad I went to the hospital," I said, vaulting to my feet.

"Sure, but hasn't the hospital kind of, like, come to us? Is something wrong?" she asked, giving me a head-to-toe once-over.

"Not me. Leira. The reporter just said there was damage to the hospital."

"Oh," Penny said. "Do you think your car is still here?"

As opposed to not here, as in sucked up and away and now possibly floating on the surface of Vatnheim or buried in a Niflheim snowbank? The image of my little green bug as some kind of anachronistic oddity was the mental image I tried to focus on — without

351

complete success — to stop myself from hyperventilating while running to where I'd parked. Two highway deaths already attributed to the storm. *What if my car landed belly-up in a water-realm pool like some helpless roly-poly bug?* Reports of missing persons coming in. *It could have landed atop Brigid in some entirely fitting reenactment of* The Wizard of Oz. More than fifty homes reportedly wiped out. *Brigid's legs could shrivel and disappear, leaving only her fur mukluks behind.* Extensive damage to the hospital, where Leira was already struggling.

# CHAPTER FIFTY-TWO

My car was not where I left it. Nor were there any vehicles in the spaces that had surrounded it. I searched about, tracking an almost surgical cut of destruction through the lot of cars. About five rows over, I spied a sleek black BMW and ran to it. Once inside, I only had to push the ignition button. Quoting the low crime statistics of the area and boasting of the vehicle's remote start, my dad kept the key fob in the unlocked-car's center console. I was thankful for both his carelessness and German engineering as I sped out of the parking lot.

I tried my mom and Stanley repeatedly, but there was no cell coverage. En route, I shuddered at every scene of carnage. Cars were upended, trees lay on their sides like fallen giants, an intact roof sat on the highway's shoulder, and there was debris everywhere. I recognized fencing materials, car parts, a bike, a front door, and strewn clothing scattered about as if some petulant child had tossed aside her beloved dollhouse.

At the hospital, I encountered a scene of panic. Two ambulances with their sirens blaring were pulling up to the emergency bay ahead of me. A stream of cars was already filing into the parking lot, and I could see other people arriving on foot. This would be — I determined — command central for the reporting of lost ones and the delivery of both good and bad news. I hoped to discover the former as I slammed my dad's Beemer into park. The top floors of the newer west wing, a multilevel addition, had obvious damage. As I stood surveying yet another scene of wreckage, a car pulled into the space next to mine. I watched as a frazzled mother lifted a screaming baby out of its backseat carrier and took off through the parking lot on a tear. Noticing a large gash to the baby's leg, I fell in step behind them. Two police officers had set up a security detail, and a large sign stated EMERGENCY ADMITTANCE ONLY, VISITORS' ACCESS TEMPORARILY SUSPENDED. They stood aside and let the woman race past them. I took advantage of the timing and hustled through as if a member of their party.

"The emergency room is just ahead," I shouted to the woman at the first fork in the labyrinth of hallways.

While she raced forward, I turned left for the stairs to the upper levels.

Leira was on the third-floor neonatal intensive care unit, NIC, as it was called. Arriving onto the wing, I noticed shattered glass below a window and darkness, a telltale sign that power was out or being conserved. Betty, a nurse whose name had always amused me, hurried past, pushing an empty incubator. I fell in step with her.

"Are the babies all right?" I asked. "Do you know anything about my sister, Leira?"

"Everyone's fine. This wing was spared for the most part, thankfully," the harried nurse said, "but we're operating on generators and trying to transfer all the little ones to the undamaged east wing until the building structure can be guaranteed."

That didn't sound good. I looked around as if expecting the walls to buckle or the ceiling to collapse at any moment. I followed Betty and arrived at a staging area set up near the main nurses' desk. Leira was last in a lineup of six cribs. They must have been the babies deemed stable enough to wait while the more critical of the tiny patients — those attached to machines and gizmos — were painstakingly moved one at a time.

I hurried over to where Leira tossed in her wheeled crib. Her tiny face was screwed up tight, and she bleated like a baby lamb. I had heard the nurses before stating that the ability to cry was a good sign for the lung-compromised preemies, but something about her keening and overall coloring didn't seem right to me. Though she was in a hospital with access to modern medical care, she required, I knew, the kind of reinforcements that only my sister Storks could provide.

Darting around a corner, I found a deserted room and — as I had one year ago in the clearing with Wade — reached deep into my ancestral skills to send out a distress call. Try to, anyway. As I'd feared and with a sickening resign, I felt nothing, was no longer in touch with my primitive instincts. I cursed Idunn under my breath and jogged back to the area where, watching from around the corner, I noticed another nurse on the phone, a landline, behind the desk. She barked some commands into the receiver and then hung up abruptly, hurrying back over to the helpless charges. After checking on Leira and her companions, she hurried along the dark corridor.

Crouching low as I scurried to the nurses' station, I grabbed the phone and ducked under the desk for cover. If Hulda even owned a phone, I doubted it was listed with the operator, not one without ties to some kind of Stork directory, anyway. There was only one number I knew off the top of my head that would do me any good in this situation, as much as I hated to admit it.

The phone rang two times before a ragged "Hello" sounded from the other end.

"Fru Grimilla," I said, "it's Katla. First of all, Penny

is fine. She banged up her knee, but it's not serious. All the kids who were at the school are OK."

Grim let out a muffled cry of relief. It was the most human response I'd heard escape her lips, ever.

"The reason I'm calling . . ." My voice was cracking, emotion splitting it into a desperate half sob, half croak. "It's my baby sister. She's failing, and I suspect there's nothing to be done for her here at the hospital." I stopped to catch my breath and tried, in vain, to compose myself. "But I believe there is something you and Hulda could do for her. At the Snjossons' farm, where the sinkhole occurred, I have reason to suspect it's a magical place, a vortex or whatever, and I have something that I think will help her."

Before I could continue, Grim interrupted, "Can you get there with the child?"

"Yes. I think so."

"Waste no time," she said. "Whatever forces have preyed upon us this evening, their properties are diminishing. If we're to borrow from the universe's powers, it must be done soon."

After hanging up, I stuck my head up over the desk and scanned the area. The elevator dinged and Nurse Betty stepped off, accompanied by another nurse and an orderly, who held the door open. Betty walked over to Leira and the lineup and pulled two of the wheeled cribs toward the waiting elevator. I held my breath as she went back for another two, leaving only Leira and one other remaining. The elevator, I could see, was full; a second trip would be required. Betty watched as the door closed on the other nurse, the orderly, and the first four transfers. Needing a diversion, I crept around to the side of the desk, where a rolling cafeteria cart had been abandoned with its metal-dome-capped meals stacked one atop another, and jugs of liquids and paper-capped glass tumblers. With a swift kick, I knocked it to its side. It landed with a clatter of metal, breaking glass, and spilled liquids. I heard Betty's "What now?" exclamation as she charged to investigate.

Moving like quicksilver, I snatched Leira up into my arms and made for the stairwell. I felt like a thief with stolen wares clutched to my chest. Bounding down the stairs, I could hear Leira's labored breathing. She burbled as if her breaths were struggling through liquid. I recognized the sound from Afi's fluid-filled lungs and knew it was a bad sign, a very bad sign.

Avoiding the front entrance, I turned left out of the stairwell exit and pushed through a door marked "Hospital Personnel Only." It led to a warren of administration offices, which, after some searching on my part, led to a private exit and a staff parking lot. Running around the side of the building, I discovered the main parking lot to still be a crush of people. In the scene of all-around chaos and confusion, no one gave a wild-eyed teen and the bundle pressed to her heaving breast a second glance.

For all intents and purposes, I had already stolen a car and abducted a child that evening. What difference would it make to add the theft of a car seat to my growing rap sheet? I opened the unlocked back door of the car next to my dad's and pulled out the infant carrier. So much for the low crime stats my dad loved to quote.

Leira felt like a bag of bones as I lowered her into the seat. I came so close to running her back into the hospital. What possible proof did I have that this would work? Surveillance information from Operation Vision Quest? A message from Idunn? She was hardly the most reliable of sources. I still couldn't decide if she was a thief or a hero. And who had I turned to at this most vulnerable of moments? Grim! Another whose motives toward me were as murky as a mud pit.

Should stunt drivers ever be needed in northern Minnesota, I could boast experience. No curb or lawn was off-limits in my roundabout path from the congested parking lot to the road. Leira, the trooper, wheezed in reaction but didn't cry.

As I drove from Pinewood to Norse Falls, I was only slightly relieved to notice the effects of the storm diminishing. Pinewood had clearly taken the worst of it, but Norse Falls hadn't been entirely spared. Trees were down, as were utility poles and streetlights, power was out in all the surrounding homes and businesses, and debris littered the road.

I tried my mom, Stanley, and Jack on my cell. No luck. The towers must have suffered damage, too. I pulled down the long gravel drive to Jack's farm, cutting my lights and hoping to avoid the notice of his parents. I was disappointed not to see Jack's truck out in front of their home. It meant he was probably out looking for me.

My dad's car was, again, surprisingly nimble over the rutted farm road, though I could hear Leira's pained gurgle with every pothole we navigated. When I finally pulled up alongside the sinkhole, I let out a hack of nervous relief. I quickly gathered Leira to me, noticing in the car's dome lights that her face had a bluish quality to it. She wasn't getting enough oxygen; we didn't have much time. I held her to my chest and ran.

# CHAPTER FIFTY-THREE

As I approached the rim of the sinkhole, an area still roped off with yellow tape and orange cones, something moved in the shadows off to the side. My heart skipped a beat and then leaped with joy as I recognized first Grim's tall, gaunt form followed by Hulda's short, hunched figure.

"She's not breathing." I gasped for air myself, overcome with the passage of precious moments.

"Hand me the child," Hulda said with authority.

I did so, noticing Leira's thin face was purplish now, and she wasn't moving.

Hulda removed a shawl from around her shoulders and laid it on the ground. She then gently eased Leira onto it, and both she and Grim fell to their knees.

"We need to grind the seeds, the carpel, from this apple," I said, removing it from my pocket.

A look passed between Hulda and Grim. They clearly questioned the source of the offering. Hulda then nodded to Grim, who dragged forth her medicine bag, the one she had used once upon a time to heal Jack's burns. She opened it and removed a mortar and pestle. Meanwhile, with the sleight of hand of a magician and the skill of a surgeon, Hulda sliced the apple in half with a pocketknife and lifted out the five-pointed carpel. Grim was at the ready with the pestle and pounded at the small brown specimens, no doubt envisioning it was my head she was pummeling to a pulpy mash. She had that look in her eyes; one I recognized well.

When the seeds were ground, Hulda scooped the paste onto the tip of her baby finger and, opening Leira's mouth, ran the substance along her gums and tongue. Nothing happened. I choked with fear and anger. Hulda and Grim proceeded with an eerie chant. Whatever it was, it made the funereal screech of a murder of crows sound light and snappy.

Then, sitting back on her heels and raising her arms to the sky with one final appeal to whatever or whomever she and Grim were beseeching, she bent down, took a deep breath, and blew one blasting puff into Leira's tiny blue lips.

I saw her chest rise and fall like bellows, after which

her mouth trembled and her entire body flinched as she gasped and sucked in air with two or three rattling breaths. And then she wailed with all the subtlety of nails on a chalkboard. Never had anything sounded so wonderful.

I thought of what the nurses had said about the ability to cry being a good sign, and I choked in my own attempt to take in air with everything else: disbelief, gratitude, relief, and joy.

"Praise be," Hulda said, falling forward in exhaustion.

"Too close. Much, much too close." Grim tsk-tsked and shook her head back and forth, but she dropped her arm across Hulda's shoulders in a display of camaraderie that took me by surprise.

Hulda and Grim weren't the only ones who were exhausted after the ordeal. I felt faint and weak; even my arms seemed too heavy to support and swung like thick chains at my sides. I was so out of it, in fact, I barely registered the fact that from behind, someone had thrown their arm around my waist in support. Jack. I had no idea how long he'd been there or where he'd come from, but it didn't matter. He was there and, as usual, had my back. But the ordeals of the evening hadn't been without their costs, even to him. His face was gray and tightly drawn, and he slapped at his biceps as if trying to get some circulation going.

"So it's true, then," Hulda said, shaking her head sadly. "You've both lost your powers."

My head snapped up. Although it was as I had suspected, this was confirmation. "I . . . It . . . How did you know?"

"You are altered, Katla," Hulda said.

There was such melancholy in her voice as she said this that I felt glum, too.

"And Jack," she continued, "I believe, has shared in your fate, as he was destined to do."

The mention of fate and destiny knocked the wind from my pipes. Just yesterday it had been Leira's fate to die and take her rightful place in line for Vatnheim's throne. Yet here she was before me, squirming with life. And, once upon a time, Hulda had told me a Native American legend about Sky Girl, who, by destiny, had been drawn to an apple tree as the ground split open. According to the tale, she had been saved by being borne away to Water World by swans. So many elements of that legend—a part-bird, part-female creature, deliverance by swans, a Water World, apple as the tree-of-life symbol—were significant. And Jack. He had once told me of an unshakable sense of fate since the moment he laid eyes on me.

"Is it permanent?" I asked, reaching for Jack's hand.

"Yes, I suspect it is," Hulda said. "Let this sacrifice during an act of great heroism be your consolation. I myself shall be sorry not to witness one of such potential rise in our ranks. I felt sure you were the harbinger of change our flock awaited. But your powers were meant to serve other purposes."

Leira stretched and began a fresh volley of wails.

"It is time to return this one to the hospital," Hulda said. "Suspicions will be roused already."

I hadn't thought about that. What possible excuse could I have for running off with her? The truth — healing her at a power place — wasn't going to fly.

"Let's go," I said to Jack. "I'll think of an alibi on the way." I turned and gave Hulda a wave. Something in the sad nod she returned made my eyes well with tears. Grim stood stonily at her side. After all we'd been through, with everything I was willing to risk, I'd hoped for some small sign on her part. Oh, well. I could save the world, but other things, like Grim, were beyond my control.

# CHAPTER FIFTY-FOUR

Driving back, a hundred possible excuses as to why I took off with Leira ran through my head. None of them were any good and were a distraction I really didn't need while driving. Leira had already been through one scrape with death that day, as had Jack and I. It took Jack's jerk on the wheel and the blare of a passing car's horn to jar me back to reality. I gave up on a feasible story; we'd just have to wing it, a prospect that seemed dicey now that I was no longer "bird girl."

I parked as close to my original spot as possible. Jack lifted his brows but didn't say a word when, after gently removing Leira, I chucked the infant carrier into the backseat of some random-to-him car we passed on our way into the building.

Luckily, the hospital was still teeming with people. It appeared that the newer, multilevel wing had been completely evacuated, and the security detail had been reassigned to deny admittance to the upper floors. Having hatched a pretty thin plan, I described it to Jack, found my way to a standing-room-only waiting room, located an out-of-the-way corner, and slunk down against the wall.

"Good luck," I said to Jack. "You know where to find me."

I still don't know how much time transpired between then and my mom shaking me awake. As much as I'd like to proclaim it a thorough acting job, I really had nodded off.

"Kat, wake up. What on earth are you doing?" my mom said.

"What? Huh?" I noticed Jack standing behind her.

"Where have you been?" She scooped up the also-slumbering Leira and pressed her to a wet cheek. "I was so worried. No one knew what happened to you two. Betty had seen you up on the floor, but . . . Why were you even there? If I hadn't bumped into Jack, I'd still be looking."

I rubbed at my eyes. I was having a hard time keeping track of who was aware of my double life and who wasn't. It was a lot to do when just coming to. And now I had to fabricate.

"They said there had been damage to the hospital," I said. "There was no cell coverage, either. I rushed over to check on her. They were moving everyone off the wing because of possible structural damage, but at one point she'd been left in the hallway unattended." Because I had kicked over a cafeteria cart, but it was no time for unnecessary details. "So I brought her down here," I continued. "She seemed better while I was holding her. She settled down and slept, so I just found us a safe corner."

"She does seem better," my mom said, her eyes growing big. "A lot better."

"I hope I didn't get anyone in trouble," I said. Meaning me, most of all.

"But I've walked through this waiting room at least twice." Frown lines pressed her forehead into waves. "I would have seen you."

An all-white-clad figure with a crisply starched smock over polyester floods and lace-up, mall-walker shoes appeared before us. "I see you're awake now." The stern voice first addressed me. "I've taken it upon myself to check on the two of them from time to time," Grim said, then leveled that steady gaze of hers upon my mother. She straightened her volunteer badge.

"Oh, you've been here?" my mom asked.

"All evening," Grim said with authority.

OK, so that uppity clack of hers had its advantages. And for the first time ever, I sensed we were on the same team, flock as Hulda had so recently called it. Too bad such solidarity had to come post-suspension, post-loss of powers.

Another figure, one with a clipboard, hurried up to Grim and reported to her like a new recruit to a general. "I have another three volunteers arriving who need assignments," she said to Grim.

I had to blink back my surprise. This subservient do-gooder was none other than Dorit, our expelled-for-revealing-secrets former Stork, who—last I'd heard—had left town amid a cloud of shame, distrust, and suspicions. I started to open my mouth but received such a quick flare of nostrils from Dorit that I clamped my lips, biting my cheek in the process.

"I will be right with them," Grim said. "As long as everything here is fine."

"Yes," I mumbled.

"And thank you," my mom added. "Thank you so much."

Grim nodded to my mother, nodded to me, and strode away with Dorit scurrying behind her.

A lump formed in my throat. So I hadn't been right about everything. Life, people still had the capacity to surprise me. And Grim looked good in white; it flattered her features, rendered her softer, prettier even.

"I should find Stanley and let the nurses know everything's fine." Again, my mom hugged Leira close to her.

"I just can't get over how robust she looks, though I hardly dare say it." She walked away, cooing to a pink-faced Leira.

Jack lowered himself to sit beside me on the carpeted floor. "I caught a bit of CNN while I was roaming, trying to bump into your mom."

"What's going on?"

"A lot of head-scratching over the coincidence of so many natural disasters."

"Like?"

"Earthquakes in Australia and California. Electrical storms along the eastern seaboard. An avalanche in the Andes. A wildfire in China."

"So our storm?"

"Just a blip on the world's radar."

"A blip," I repeated.

He nodded his head yes.

"I think I could get used to being a blip." I tucked my hand under his.

"Me, too," he said, cupping his own around my fingers and squeezing.

"Wanna be blips together?"

"Sure. One thing, though."

*Uh-oh.*

"What?" I asked.

"No more secrets, no more heroics, no more asinine, self-sacrificing plots."

*Asinine. Ouch.*

"How could I, anyway? Just a blip, remember?" I said.

He didn't look convinced.

I dropped my head on his shoulder. "You know I did what I thought was my only option, but I'm sorry if it . . . excluded you."

He lifted my chin with his finger. "Don't ever . . ." He had a hard time continuing.

"What?"

"Just promise you'll include me in your travel plans next time."

"I promise." I laughed and then melted into him for a kiss. It was sweet and hot and promise-worthy. I definitely intended to include him in my future travel plans, all plans, for that matter.

# CHAPTER FIFTY-FIVE

Saturday morning I headed over to Afi's to help out. Jack, I knew, was at his parents' place doing his part in their cleanup. This shared activity felt like a small connection during our day-after duties.

Upon arrival, I couldn't help exclaiming, "Whoa. This place is a—"

"Damn mess," Afi finished for me.

I surveyed the scene before me. A tree limb had crashed though the front window. Daylight streamed through its jagged edges, casting a zigzag reflection upon the merchandise-littered floor. A broom-in-hand Ofelia came around one of the aisles, sweeping as she went. Dust floated up like mist, obscuring the space between us. When it had settled, I found her giving me a puzzled look, which turned quickly to surprise, then disappointment.

"Did you hear about Leira?" I asked her, diverting attention from me.

"Doing better, I hear," Ofelia said.

"She's being discharged today. The doctors are calling it a remarkable turnaround."

"That's wonderful," Ofelia said. "Your mother and Stanley must be so happy."

"Over the moon," I said. "And back again." I pointed to the dark light fixture overhead. "Any word on power?"

"Sure," Afi said. "The word is *out*."

"What does the back room look like?" I asked, biting back a smile.

"That's the worst of it. If I'd wanted a gosh-darn skylight," Afi said, shaking his head, "I'd have put one in myself."

My eyes popped open. "That doesn't sound good."

"That's what the insurance agent said." Afi scratched his stubbly chin. "Could be the damage exceeds the value of the place."

"That sounds even worse," I said.

"If it comes to that, I'll take it as a sign. I needed this like I needed a hole in my . . . roof." He swiped at the air with his hand and turned on his heel, heading for the back.

The front door chimed; Jinky and Penny walked in. Penny's knee was bandaged, but her limp was already improved from the day before.

"Hey, guys," I said. "What's going on?"

"We came to help," Penny said. "Jinky told me she was on her way over, and I volunteered."

"That's so nice of you guys," I said. "But are you sure that's a good idea with your injury?"

"It's just banged up. Besides, it feels good to get out of the house and do something." Penny tugged a rope bracelet back into position. "Keeps me from worrying too much."

"About what?" I asked.

Penny exchanged a look with Jinky. "Marik. He's just not himself. I keep trying to get him to go to the doctor, but he won't listen. He's just so stubborn."

"It's a guy thing," Jinky said, nudging her shoulder into Penny's. "Don't worry, I'll keep an eye on him for you."

It seemed a promise Jinky couldn't keep. I wondered how much she understood of what had transpired yesterday. Not the full story, it would appear.

Marik was my biggest regret. Because the shell-game dream and my subsequent suspension were both followed so quickly by Idunn's grift, I never had the chance to snag him a soul. And I would have, dang it all.

"What's the word around here?" Penny asked. "It doesn't look so bad."

"The back took the brunt of it," Ofelia said. "A sizable chunk of the roof was blown away."

"Oh, no," Penny said.

"Unfortunately, it could be the final straw that forces him out of this place," I said. "And I can't imagine Norse Falls without the store." I covered my mouth with my hand. "Oh. I hadn't thought about how this would affect you, Ofelia. What would you do?"

She leaned on her broom. "You know, Jinky came to me for advice on that New Age shop she and Penny designed. It's not a bad idea. Something to think about for the future." She lifted her mischief-filled eyes. "And I know of a multitalented individual who would be an ideal . . . consultant, coworker, whatever she could manage."

Jinky smiled. It may have been the first time I'd ever seen her gums. They looked pink and healthy. She obviously had excellent dental hygiene. Another surprise.

"I guess the whole thing could have been worse," Penny said. "Pinewood's the one that got hammered. Besides the high school, I heard they lost their post office, a bank, a grocery store, not to mention the fatalities. . . ."

Her voice trailed off, and a silence fell over us. No one had brought up the dead all day, as if it were a jar best left sealed.

"What's the count now?" I asked, my voice small and tight.

"Five. All in Pinewood," Penny said. "For the size of the storm, they're saying that number could have been a lot higher. Just think if your dad hadn't found those last couple of kids hiding in the gym . . ."

As much as I understood just what had been saved yesterday, I still swallowed something bitter and hard with every reminder of a death toll. It should have included me. I still felt uneasy—guilty, were I to put a name to it—about surviving when others hadn't.

We divided into teams. Ofelia and I took care of the front of the store: sweeping up glass, tossing spoiled perishables from the freezer cases, and duct-taping a patchwork of flattened boxes over the hole in the front window. Penny and Jinky volunteered for back-room duty, where more sweeping up and sorting of salvageable merchandise was to be done. For his part, Afi moved between the two zones, shaking his head and carping about "damn Mother Nature" or was on the phone with the insurance agent, the window-repair company, and the power company.

Ofelia and I had been at it for a long time without word from the back when we heard a loud creaking sound and then a muffled thud; Jinky and Penny emerged looking as if they'd been blasted fifty years into the future. Their hair and skin were covered with a fine gray powder.

"What happened to you guys?" I asked.

Jinky shook her head, demonstrating the possible origins of the headbangers brand of dance style.

Penny, on the other hand, scratched at her head with both hands. "Uh, the ceiling kind of heaved and then buckled, sending a shower of dust down on us." She grimaced. "You don't think this stuff is asbestos or anything like that, do you?" She raked a hand deep into her scalp.

Afi, who had discharged of his phone call at the sight of them, said, "Shouldn't be. The building's old, but the roof is new. My guess is it's gypsum from the drywall, but I suggest you run on home and take a good, long shower." He lifted the phone back to his ear with a sigh. "I'll call my roof guy to make sure, but I wouldn't worry too much about it."

Jinky, true to her nature, accepted the situation with a mere scowl and uttered something — in the Icelandic-expletive family, I'd guess — under her breath.

Penny had the more physical of their reactions. She scraped at her head like some flea-bitten pooch and rushed Jinky out of the store without time to hear the apologies and thank-yous that Afi, Ofelia, and I voiced in their wake.

Afi declared the back room off-limits. It immediately struck me that this would impact the Storks as well. Could they still meet here? Would they have anyway, now that I was out? And if not here, where? I felt a pang of hurt that I, quite possibly, would never know.

"I suppose we should call it a day," Ofelia said. "We've done what we can up front here; the rest will depend on the insurance agent and an inspection. Besides, I for one am exhausted." She took a seat on the stool behind the register. As she lifted a bottle of water to her lips, I noticed her hand, ever so briefly, touch her hairline. Anyone else would surely have thought she was tucking a stray wisp of hair into her trademark twist. But I knew better; I knew it was a call, *the call,* rather. I couldn't help it; I stared at her.

When the phone rang and Afi answered it, I rounded on Ofelia. "Did you—"

Ofelia held up her hand to stop me, and I remembered my vow of silence. I pressed my lips closed, but my bulging eyes said it all.

She took off in a hurry, which left just me and Afi in the closed-until-further-notice store.

"Leira's probably home by now. Should we head over and welcome her back?" I asked.

Afi looked rail thin, and his pale blue eyes blinked back from behind a crush of wrinkles. "It does seem a thing that should be celebrated. And we could all stand a little good news for a change." His voice had that slurry quality, the one I'd recognized in Leira before her miraculous recovery.

When Afi flipped the lights off, shouldered the front door closed, and clicked the key in the lock, I was overcome with emotion. For the shop, I felt a small swell of nostalgia. On Afi's behalf, I just wished there was something that would see those lungs of his through a bit of retirement.

# CHAPTER FIFTY-SIX

Jack dropped a piled-high bucket of apples at my feet. "The pink ones. Your favorite," he said.

When Jack had called that morning, Sunday, to suggest a cider press, I thought he was crazy. It just didn't seem like the appropriate weekend for something so trivial. But he'd insisted, arguing we needed a break and an excuse to see each other. That point won me over.

Penny, Marik, Jinky, Shauna, and Tina came clomping up the gravel path with a crunch of gravel under their feet. Shauna was already a surprise addition, but . . .

"Tina!" I squealed, barreling into her for a hug-turned-body-slam encounter. I could tell she was flattered by the attention, once she got her wind back, anyway.

"When did you get in? What are you doing home? How's Iowa State? How's Matthew? When did you cut your hair?" I hadn't realized how much I missed Tina, who had been such an important component of my transition to Norse Falls last year. Had it not been for her and Penny, I'd have been new-girl roadkill.

Tina held her thumb up. "I got in yesterday." She brought her index finger to join it. "I wanted to check on my family after all the reports of damage." Her middle finger was next to join the lineup. "Good, but tough." She added the ringman. "Still my guy." With her "about two weeks ago" comment, she brought the whole hand to her hair for a fluff of the new do.

"Is everything all right with your family?" I asked, biting back my top lip.

"Yes. They're fine, thank goodness. We lost a couple of trees and an old shed out back, but nothing major. There was a mountain of crap to clean up, but it could have been a lot worse."

We were all quiet for a moment. I thought again of those who weren't so lucky. An apology formed in my throat, but I managed to swallow it.

"I, for one, think we've all earned a little breather today." Penny stepped between Tina and me. "I can't tell you what a great idea this is. Anything to divert attention from . . ." She nervously adjusted the crochet cap from under which dropped two thick russet braids. ". . . All the hard work we've been doing."

"Check it out," Jack said, calling the group's attention to a contraption that, by all appearances, was predated only by the wheel. "It's an old-fashioned barrel press."

"That thing is sick," Shauna said. I thought it was a compliment, but I wasn't entirely sure.

Jack demonstrated the workings of the contraption for everyone. It looked like nothing more than an old washtub on a stand with a top funnel device, some kind of crank handle, and a spigot at the bottom. It was as simple and crude-looking as anything I'd ever seen. Jack dumped the apples—skin, stems, and all—into the top opening. As he cranked on the noisy wheel, the apples were smashed into their subatomic particles, and a slush of cloudy cider poured into a bucket positioned below the tap. It wasn't the most sophisticated or pristine of operations, but, then again, my own *afi* had a meat grinder on his kitchen counter. Yuck.

"It smells wonderful," Marik said. Up until then he'd been so uncharacteristically quiet that I'd failed to really notice him. His skin was so pale it was translucent, and he had the stoop of an old man. Of course, he was an old man, a very old man. The problem being that he wasn't an old soul, or any kind of soul, for that matter. Yet even in this deteriorating state, he was enjoying himself.

The cider was poured into an old metal jug, from

which speckled tin cups were filled. Once again, I was struck by the way Jack's family farm was like a wormhole to the past. No wonder the Álaga Blettur, a power place, had gone undetected here. The entire property was a wonderful little bubble of magic and history. Though I was sure that, with the post-storm rebuilding, Norse Falls and Pinewood were in for changes, I sensed that this place would resist.

When Marik eased himself onto a battered picnic bench, I noticed Shauna eyeing him.

"Are you OK there?" she asked. "You don't look so hot."

"On top of everything else, there's a virus going around. A bad one," Penny said, talking fast, even for her. "My grandmother volunteered at the hospital Friday night and said they had an above-average caseload of severe flu symptoms."

Shauna took a step back. "If you're contagious, shouldn't you be holed up at home?"

Marik ran a hand over his glistening forehead. "I should have listened to Penny earlier. Maybe she's right. To be on the safe side—"

"I'll drive you," Penny interrupted, "if it won't leave anyone stranded."

"I can take the others home," Tina offered. By the look on Shauna's face, she was more than happy to avoid the walking contagion that was Marik.

As they strode away, I witnessed a crushingly tender moment between Penny and Marik, who appeared to be arm in arm but with him listing toward her on every third or fourth step. I couldn't help feeling gutted by the sight of them. It was going to end badly — very badly — for both. I felt my whole body shrivel with the thought of it.

The entire party seemed to fade a little with their absence. We ate cinnamon-and-sugar-dusted donuts, homemade by Jack's mom. Jack and Jinky pitched horse-shoes at a pin, while Shauna, Tina, and I sat atop the picnic table, dusting crumbs from our lap. I asked Tina more about Iowa State and her course load. She claimed to like the school but made no mention of their unfortunate mascot.

"Any news from Pedro?" I asked finally.

"Liking Minnesota State," she said. "Matthew keeps in touch with him."

Pedro, Penny's boyfriend last year, had been a little harsh during their breakup, but, overall, he was a good guy, and I was glad to hear he was doing well.

"Well, I'm driving back tonight," Tina said, standing and stretching. "Are you two ready?" she asked Jinky and Shauna.

Once the others were gone, Jack grabbed his back-pack from under the picnic table and removed a small, clear water bottle with an inch or so of brown sludge at the bottom.

"A gift," he said.

I looked at it. It didn't appear to be much more than a swallow and, well, nasty-looking.

"You shouldn't have," I said, not taking it.

He shook it at me expectantly.

"No, really," I said.

He forced it into my unwilling hands. "You're as stubborn as your *afi,* who, by the way, this is for."

"For Afi?" I asked, confused.

"When I got there Friday night, you, Hulda, and Penny's grandmother were so busy you didn't even notice me. Hulda had dropped the other half of the apple she sliced into. I picked it up for her and brushed it off, and next thing I knew Leira was crying, and the crisis seemed to be over. And you know how I believe in an apple a day. Even if this was just a half, it seemed special. And your *afi* could stand a little boost, could he not? So I kept it and pressed it, figuring what the heck?"

"Thank you. Thank you," I said, throwing my arms around Jack's neck while holding the bottle aloft like something precious and fragile. So it wouldn't be administered at a vortex while the universe's powers were in flux, but it couldn't hurt. And if anyone could cheat death out of an extra hand or two, it was Afi. Stubborn old coot!

# CHAPTER FIFTY-SEVEN

School felt like a changed place come Monday morning. It felt a little disingenuous walking the pre-first-bell halls when Pinewood didn't have any. Besides local damage, all anyone could talk about was the leveling of their building. An emergency session of the school board — make that combined school boards, for both communities — had been called for that evening. Speculations were rampant that Norse Falls High would accommodate the displaced students from Pinewood.

Even as all this was, almost spookily, sorting itself out, another mystery was in the making. Both Penny and Marik were no-shows for first period. I texted Penny twice but got no reply. With respect to Marik, this had

potentially tragic implications. Penny I didn't get, however. Especially with so much news to cover.

"Where's Marik?" I whispered to Jinky as the bell
rang to second-period Design and there was still no sign
of them.

She pumped her shoulders, the universal *dunno*
signal.

"And Penny?" I asked.

She gave me the same response with a slight widening of her eyes. It seemed to indicate concern. Looking
around, there were more than a few unoccupied seats.
Word was that counselors were available to everyone
who had been huddled down in Pinewood's shelter. Or
anyone else who had PTSD. Ironic that it had been a
term Marik had to learn for that first school-board meeting. Maybe Penny was having a harder time dealing
with Friday's events than she'd let on. It couldn't be easy
for her to be so close to all the weirdness I'd brought to
Norse Falls, except without my, Jack's, Marik's, or even
Jinky's, for that matter, unique perspective on it all. It
had to be like living next to a graveyard and wondering
at so many passersby in period attire.

Ms. Bryant took the first half of class to discuss the
events of Friday. A lot of kids wanted to talk about the
experience, and others had questions about the rumors of
an accelerated merger. As always, Ms. Bryant was cool
and collected. Though not at all like my earthy mom,

she, nonetheless, had a maturity that complemented my dad's personality. His heroics during the crisis showed a side of him that I had always known was there, but it was nice to think that others — Ms. Bryant and my mom, even — would see a depth in him, too, now. Perhaps not an old soul, but one who was growing. No doubt he'd always be the first to run for the ice-cream truck, but he'd save you a place in line, and probably buy.

Just as Ms. Bryant segued to the topic of our top-notch projects at Friday's show, there was a commotion at the door, through which entered none other than Penny and Marik, looking rosy, robust, and almost obscenely goo-goo eyed. I nearly smacked my chin on the desk, my mouth fell open so quickly.

Ms. Bryant seemed to be unsettled, too. As Marik — looking as he had the first day of school with his easy-going smile, burly frame, and vitality — passed by her desk, she covered her mouth in an attempt to hide her surprise. She undoubtedly picked up on what I was sensing as well. Marik was better. Marik was different.

For the rest of the period, I had a hard time concentrating. Luckily, Ms. Bryant's similarly distracted state kept her from delving into anything that was testworthy material.

The moment the bell rang, I was on Penny like a bug on a windshield. I blocked her path to the door.

"What's up?" Penny asked, cocking her head to the side, cool and coy as a da Vinci girl.

My suspicions, for one. And my heart rate, for another. I perched on a nearby desktop, saying, "Oh, you know, a bird, a plane, Superman."

With the last of my "up" items, I gestured with my head to Marik, who had come to stand beside Penny. His recovery was miraculous; his eyes were bright and fiery, his cheeks plump, and even his shaggy hair had spring to it.

"You're looking better, Marik," I said. "Was it the flu, after all?"

After the ceiling incident in Afi's back room, Penny's head had been an itchy mess, but Jinky had been fine. Shortly thereafter, Ofelia got the call.

"A mild case," Penny answered for him.

Penny had worn a hat to Jack's yesterday. She never wore hats. I was the hat girl, particularly if it was the day after a meeting-signaling scalp rash. I remembered how nasty the affliction was those first few times. *But Penny? Could she really be . . . ?* But what other explanation was there? *Penny, a Stork!* Why hadn't I seen it coming? How had she even known that Marik needed a soul? And how had she accomplished so much in so little time? It indicated a power exceeding my own, one that surely confirmed her rightful inheritance of the Bleika Norn's cameo. I also thought of Jinky's rune reading. Penny had chosen Othala, the stone of ancestral property, which could represent both a physical and a spiritual inheritance. No surprise that it was right on both scores. And once again, Hulda's words—that they awaited a harbinger of change—proved prophetic. Why wouldn't Penny be a Stork? *That* Stork, moreover. Her birthright was as legitimate as mine. *Birds of a feather* . . . , I couldn't help thinking.

"Glad to hear you're feeling better, Marik," I said, starting for the exit with drunken steps. By then, Jinky had joined us.

"Penelopa came over with an herbal remedy," Marik said, following me through the doorway.

His use of Penny's full name did not elude me. Penelopa scrambled to *one apple,* which I had known all along but had never interpreted as Penny's rightful role in it all, her connection to the Pink Lady cameo, her ties to the life-giving symbol, and her magical destiny.

"It was something my *amma* mixed up for him, some kind of herbal infusion," Penny said. "Like I told you, she's good with home remedies. Maybe some of them learned from the Bleika Norn."

So this was how it would have to be. An understanding between us that would be danced around and batted back and forth but would never be put into words. The four of us walked as a group toward our bank of lockers.

"That's cool," I said.

"Maybe the whole concept of a metaphysical shop here in Norse Falls isn't such a bad idea, after all," Penny said.

"Finally she admits it." Jinky lifted her chin in a small display of pride.

"It's better than a hat store, anyway," I said.

"I don't know," Penny said. "I think you single-handedly brought them back into style, around here, anyway. I'm thinking of getting a beret."

"What color?" I asked.

"Something in the gray family," Penny said, "not dark, more of a —"

"Dove gray?"

"Yes." Penny's eyes sparked.

Naturally, she'd be the bird of peace. And I got it in one guess. My father's daughter or what?

# CHAPTER FIFTY-EIGHT

Having left my grams, my dad, and Sage — the term of
address I now called my dad's steady girlfriend — back
at Gram's condo slaving over the holiday meal, Jack
and I slipped out for a little alone time. We stood in the
sand gaping at the vast Pacific. It was oddly comforting
to feel insignificant in the face of such power. We were
just two kids on vacation at the beach. Never mind that
Jack, due to his Winter People ancestry, had never been
to the ocean. Never mind that I had Stork and selkie lineage. Never mind that we both knew firsthand of a few
of life's marvels and mysteries.

"So what do you think?" I asked.

"It's incredible."

I grabbed his hand. "And are you ready for a swim?"

"As I'll ever be."

"Not scared?"

"No." He shook his head. "In keeping with the occasion, I'm thankful."

*Thankful,* indeed an appropriate theme for Thanksgiving Day. This year I felt the spirit of the holiday intensely. I was humbled by the wonder and precariousness of life and just plain old grateful to be alive. I knew that I hadn't, in any way, single-handedly prevented Ragnarök. Everything and everyone in my circle of love—corny as that sounded—had played a role. The now-pregnant-with-twins Jaelle and her hopes for a child. My mom and Stanley's new relationship, which led to Leira. The ancestry I inherited from Afi and Amma. Hulda's invaluable wisdom and guidance. Jinky's shaman skills. Marik's zest for life. Penny's friendship and transformation. Old Grim and even Dorit coming around. The influence Sage had on my hero dad's young soul. And Jack, of course. No longer my superpower sidekick, no longer connected with me on a telekinetically charged level, but we had each other's back. We had each other, period.

"Do you think you could get used to it—you know, live here?"

He rolled his shoulders forward. "I don't know."

It was noncommittal *and* the correct answer. I still

dreamed of a career in fashion. New York and LA were the two U.S. epicenters of the industry, but I also knew that Jack's spirit thrived when surrounded by nature. Anyway, those kinds of decisions seemed far off and trivial in the face of land, sky, and sea melding before us.

"Come on," I yelled, yanking on his arm.

We ran full out and barreled straight into the frigid ocean. When the water was thigh-high, I jumped on Jack's bare back and wrapped my arms around his neck and my legs around his waist. A breaker crashed over us with the force of a semi, sending us spiraling. With the wave's retreat, I found myself on my hands and knees, with sand in my eyes and mouth, my hair plastered to my face, and gasping for air. I looked over to where Jack lay just a few feet away on his back. I crawled over to him, shaking his shoulder.

"Are you OK?" I asked.

One of his eyes opened slowly. The other soon joined it, and then a smile parted his lips. "Oh, yeah."

I looked up to see another wave headed our way, a big one. When, moments later, we were still hanging on to each other, and laughing, even, I took it as an omen: stronger together with or without our powers. Stronger. Together.